# The Glass Harpoon

Robert Horne

# The Glass Harpoon

*The Glass Harpoon*
ISBN 978 1 76109 040 0
Copyright © text Robert Horne 2020
Cover image: *The Trespassers*, William Cawthorne, 1845

First published 2020 by
**GINNINDERRA PRESS**
PO Box 3461 Port Adelaide 5015
www.ginninderrapress.com.au

# Contents

# 1

# The North – October 1843

He closes the book of Keats and crumples up the gum leaf that had marked the page, then shoves it in the linen sack with his other books: Shelley, Blake and *Mansfield Park*. He bunches fresh leaves over them all, then fixes the string and rests his head once more upon them.

That is better. When he came from England, they said he was young for his twenty-two years: 'the look of a barely bearded youth,' Cawthorne had said when they first met. His face is creased with sun and knowledge now, but he knows that knowledge is not the truth. He remembered the lines of Keats about beauty and truth and that is all ye need to know. Whatever had defined the beauty of Keats was opaque and foreign to him now, and the new truth of this bush land was still not clear to him.

Not yet.

He can feel the branches above him bending in the gully breeze and the sunset carolling of the magpies comes down to him. At least they would warble a *kind* of song, but here the parrots screeched like a ptero-dactyl might have in another age. Once he would have scratched out some lines 'On the pterodactyl and the lorikeet,' and juxtaposed the nightingale or the lark, but not now. Still he tries to recall a line of Keats, something about oblivion, something easeful.

Easeful death.

There comes the crack of his brother James's boot heel on dried kin-dling wood, then the chunk of their axe on a fallen log they had dragged up from the creek. He pokes a finger through a crack in the bark of their hut and looks out. The low brown hills on the west of the valley were spilling tree shadows over the bare slopes that were ragged like some wild and frizzled bushranger's beard. At the shaggy edges of the beard the late sun burnt the lowlands into a roseate carpet – the wild range lay beyond.

This would be James's place when the stone house was finished and all the boundaries were fenced and the question of the natives was re-solved, titled half to James and half to Matthew when he reached the age of twenty five. But it was James's in fact, in spirit – his betrothed coming from England soon, Adela. Matthew would stay just long enough to do his duty to the family, James would pay him out a modest sum, then to his own adventures in the colony, or further, New South Wales perhaps – the lure of freedom. Matthew could love and hate this place in turns, James could not.

'Come on, you, back on deck.' So came James's cheer-making voice, the one he used to greet neighbours, to make deals in the smoking par-lours of the town – the only voice he had left now, after a year or more in the colony.

Matthew drew his knees up to his chest and quickly rolled his weight up right onto his shoulders and then back onto his feet and he stood, then pushed through their hessian door and stepped outside. A pannikin of water had been fetched ready for the sweet tea they drank by the gallon every morning and night. James was stuffing a plug of baccy into a small pipe which he lit with a flaming twig of dried euca-lyptus. He nodded at the fire as if to say, You make the tea.

James leaned back onto a rounded stone, puffed at his pipe and stared out over the valley.

The sun's last rays were soon strangled in the trees and the bushranger's beard grew and swallowed them. Matthew drew his coat around him and collected his brother's from the nail they had ham-mered into a wooden upright and threw it out to him. They hurried up the fire: the day had been hot, the work difficult; now the evening would be cold, the damper had to be mixed, chops of hogget cooked –

no woman out here, not yet by any means. A painter with his easel could have returned every night for a month and Matthew and James would be captured there, hunched around the campfire, like cockatoos in a grand cage, each with its place at either end of a common perch. By eight o'clock, there would be nothing to do but sleep. By five, they would be awake; the space around Matthew in his bed would be frozen. But now there was a fire. He thought of the bottle of sherry in his bag.

'This waiting is the devil's work,' James said, sitting back upright with his tin mug of tea on a sawn-off log in front of him. 'Tomorrow is Sunday. I say we take a leg of lamb to the Jenks place and roast it in their oven. They will have potatoes,' he raised an eyebrow towards Matthew, 'and claret.'

The Larkin brothers had no potatoes of their own, nor claret.

'Correction, I say take two legs off the beast,' James went on, 'and cook them both – one for them and one for me.'

'And I a third. But we must be here ready for the new flock.' Matthew would be happier spending the day in the town of Clare, in the pub with the characters – the artisans of the town and shepherds on their weekly spree. Jenks was conceited and contrived. 'They could arrive in a day or two, those sheep.'

'More likely three. I fear for them. It is a long way from Gundagai to Clare and the natives on the Murray are treacherous fellows. Even those around here refuse to learn the laws of property, and we have been kind to them beyond what is necessary. But they sneak in and spear some meat and take it away as if it will not be noticed. And they laugh at us.' James's voice rose.

'They do not laugh, James. They have shared with us. We bring the meat to their land and they take their tithe. Their bellies are full with hogget once a week and they are not unhappy with that. There are fewer kangaroos now than there were six months ago. Even the opossum is scarce.'

'I know you have an eye for it.'

'In the town, with Cawthorne, I learnt a little about the natives. I wish all colonists had the same experience. It is only from education and improvement that we become better people. The life unexamined, brother, is not worth living. I think Socrates said it first.'

James grunted. 'We are not in the position to examine – that is the prerogative of the secure and well fed. Out here we must act to survive. And the natural law is the same on land as it is at sea: when patience fails, then the lash.'

Their father, Admiral Larkin, had risen through the ranks at sea; his experience had taught him that the maintenance of order was achieved in direct proportion to his men's fear of the lash.

'Yes, brother. Forgive my mistake. Of course, yes indeed, we should show them the civilisation of the lash.'

James raised an eyebrow and mocked a glare at his younger brother. Their arguments had lost their venom and were now like a lesson learned by heart, a game of quoits played to pass the time on board ship – the rhetoric going up and back in its predictable path, like players changing ends in a game in which the outcome was of little consequence.

But the arguments sustained Matthew. Once the inevitable child-hood admiration of his father and three older brothers had evaporated, and he was to be sent off to school, the question of who he was and what he would do came inevitably into focus. The Larkin family may have been technically gentle but its real money was only two or three generations old. His grandfather had shared in the profits from the transportation of slaves from Africa to the West Indies; the emptied ships returned to England filled with sugar for the table and molasses for rum.

Thus the family had been made respectable and the admiral's career had been enabled by it too. Then his own sons: the first managing their property in Sussex; the second following his father onto the sea and rising to lieutenant already. Business had been decided for the third, James, and when the colony of South Australia was announced, it seemed to beg for exploitation. But the question of Matthew had been left open. It was thought that he might be some consolation to his mother in her state of decline into nervous disorders, and could remain in England and work at something. But professions were not the admiral's suit and the making of a decision had not been an urgent matter.

When Matthew was eleven years old, he was stricken with a severe cough and cold. The admiral, at home during a two-month respite from the sea, had declared that the boy should learn to ride out such things and that the doctor should be kept away. But after a week, the matter had not improved, and the boy had run to a fever – a high temperature accompanied by mental disorientation.

The doctor asked the boy to stick out his tongue. The enlarged red papillae prickling through a white coating he called 'white strawberry' on account of its appearance as a huge strawberry with the colours reversed. Scarlet fever was pronounced, no doubt of it, and Mrs Larkin went into a spin. The doctor advised that a spin was the last thing the boy needed, and that rest and serenity formed the proper foundations of a cure.

The fever reached its zenith after five more days and from then abated tortuously for six weeks. During the third week, once the boy was out of immediate danger but still in a state of discomfort, he began to complain of boredom. The only remedy to this condition that Mrs Larkin could prescribe was to read. She had books brought up from the family library – *Ivanhoe*, *The Tales of the Crusaders* and other such dashing yarns of which the admiral would approve.

Matthew devoured all that was put before him; the life of the imaginative mind had been stimulated. Even after his rehabilitation was complete, he began to prefer this way of being to that of games and sports. He was, after all, going to places no Larkin had been before and was carving an identity out of the damp clay of his hitherto unremarkable life. He particularly loved the snippets of a weirdly glamorous Eastern life which inhabited pockets of the tales of conquest and exploration. His interests began to snake out into the fields of exotic literature.

At the age of thirteen, he turned over the first pages of *Tales of the*

*Arabian Nights* and discovered the story of Scheherazade. A sultan discovered that his wife was disloyal to him and had consequently decreed that a different young bride be brought to him each night, that she may lie with him one time and be executed in the morning. Scheherazade could have avoided this fate – she was the daughter of the vizier, after all – but instead she volunteered. In the morning after lying with the sultan, she began to tell him a tantalising story, but one that required her survival until the next day for it to be finished. And then on the next morning another story, and another and another for years until the sultan had learnt the lessons of forgiveness she had buried in her tales, and proclaimed his love for her. After a thousand nights, his decree was lifted. Confident of her genius, Scheherazade risked her life to save the girls of the city; she was a healer and she had altered her world for good.

With his excitement piqued, Matthew searched through bookshops for more of the exotic, the Eastern, the unusual; by the time he was seventeen, many rebellious and politically aberrant volumes had passed under his gaze. On the admiral's return from sea one time, an acquaintance at the club whispered to him that his boy had been seen in Regent Street sporting a Phrygian cap – *un bonnet rouge*! – in the manner of William Blake.

The admiral returned immediately to the family home and marched straight up the stairs to inspect his boy's room. Here he found that, where there had once been a ship constructed within a bottle and next to it a stuffed lion's head, the place was now full of well-thumbed books. The first volume he picked up was *Wolfstein* by Percy Shelley – a notorious piece, an outrage against nature and common sense! They were calling it 'Gothic horror' now in some feeble attempt to legitimise it, but there was no doubt regarding the degeneracy of its purpose and execution. Then Keats and Byron and Blake. Yes, there was Blake, a known madman and bully, who had been charged with sedition and with using words insulting to the military! *The Marriage of Heaven and*

*Hell*, no less. Then more Shelley, everywhere Shelley – the man should have been horsewhipped!

The admiral sat on the side of the boy's bed and gazed about him in anguish. His fourth son had already caused him more headaches than the first three put together. The mother had taken him over as if he was her property, and he had remained in her keep for seven years since his fever. He blamed himself in part, did the admiral – away too long, now at the height of his career. He consoled himself that his absence was all for the good of the empire, for England; but what good was empire and civilisation when there was degeneracy at home.

The admiral had risen through his ability to make sound and speedy decisions, but his son was not a matter to be addressed in the same manner as a French frigate – he knew that much. He thought the matter over for a full minute. She can have him, was his decision; he can stay here with her. He was a hard man, but not unreasonable. With three sons organised, he conceded that the fourth could stay with Mrs Larkin. But he simply could not give in completely. He decided then and there that if the boy wanted his books so much, he could go up to Oxford and study some more useful ones – a don in the family! The admiral's thoughts turned always to ambition. Matthew could write the history of the empire – the cherry on top of the Larkin cake. But then he grimaced sourly to himself as he had a further thought – religion! Better still. There was some irony in that. Ha! The disciplined application to orders would surely cure Matthew of his Romantics and his Gothics.

The admiral shoved his hat upon his head and marched back downstairs to announce his decision to the boy's mother and proceed to make the necessary arrangements.

But, in the years after that, he had never been completely at ease with the idea of his son a parson. So when Matthew came down from Oxford during his second year and pronounced the wish to follow his brother James to the new colony, the admiral was speechless for a moment, then his heart soared, on two accounts. Not only had his son finally shown some buccaneering Larkin spirit, but it was as if his own plan of attack had brought long-term fruit. The boy might have stuck at history, but not religion. He had cornered his son in the skirts of the priesthood, and forced him out into the open.

Matthew swore that he would never force or cajole or manipulate; he would never threaten or use the lash. He would find his Scheherazade somewhere.

'So, James, what do you think should be the law of taking over the land on which these Aborigines have roamed for so many centuries?'

James was the most rational and thoughtful of his brothers, the only one who would tolerate being baited. 'I know, Matthew. This was debated in the town.'

'Indeed, brother, it was.'

'And the law was made that we need make no compensation. We improve them and encourage them to learn, the ones that are capable of it.'

'But Westminster has the South Australian native as British subjects and fully in protection of the law – a fine thought that was.'

'Westminster,' said James with distaste. 'The law was made by the Whigs! And now that we have Peel as prime minister it could be changed, but there is no will to do so.'

'You held the Whigs in less distaste when they were voted in. You supported them yourself, if I recall.'

'Aye, so it was. But we were in England then. We hold a different view once here.'

They both knew the blacks out here were wilder by nature than those of the southern plains near the town. They were harder to talk to and more difficult to influence. And there was more space out here, fewer white men.

Far fewer.

They both stared out to fields of native grass that stretched away to their little stream and a stand of pale gums whose trunks turned from white to yellow then pink and purple in five minutes before their eyes. The whole valley turned to a mellow peace; the magpies were quiet at last.

'Indeed, brother,' said Matthew eventually, steering the Larkin family ship to calm waters, ''tis harder than we thought. This life, eh?'

They would talk about sheep, and fields, and shepherds, and timber and the types of stone they had found on their property and their virtues for building the big house, the foundations of which already stood on higher ground one hundred yards away.

'We could spend two days working on the house, before the flock arrives. There are stones to be brought in and put in place.'

'It would be a welcome change from fencing, James. And Adela must have her palace, when she comes.'

'With space for you and Lucy Bray too, if you want it.'

Matthew sipped his tea.

'You would have the approval of the admiral, I have no doubt.'

'Ha!' Matthew laughed. 'I'm sure he would be astounded to see me do so well. But she is young, brother.'

'Seventeen is old enough, Matthew.'

The very thought of marriage. He had been in the colony less than one year.

'Ah, yes, brother, it would be good for the family. But life would be simpler for you if I slipped away. You are made for this place but I fear I am not.'

James hurled the dregs in his tin cup over his shoulder into the bush. 'Where do you think you would be, young brother, without your family?'

'I have thought about that many times – pushing a barrow in Covent Garden, perhaps. There's a life.'

'If you were lucky. There's much worse. There are those who spend their lives ankle deep in freezing mud in a field somewhere in a northern winter pulling turnips.'

'But where would anyone be, if things were different, eh? The accidents of birth and life do not bear thinking about. We must do what we can with what we have.' For that moment, he wanted no more than to fade into the ghostly gums and join the world of the spirits of the forest. 'Ah,' he exclaimed, '"that I might drink, and leave the world un-seen, And with thee fade away into the forest dim."' He had the line now – away with all this work and grind!

'I doubt your Mr Keats would have prospered in these climes, Matthew,' said James, 'with his shirtsleeves up, sinking fence posts in the midday sun.'

Matthew joined James in mirth for he knew it was best to share in the humour of men, when there was no harm in it, and when it was the only corrective to idle bitter thoughts and the long cold night.

But as the night began to close around them, a faint and distant thrumming of hooves came to their ears. The two brothers stood and leaned forward in the direction of the sound, then went to the edge of their clearing – someone out this late, in near darkness! After a minute of waiting, the rider wheeled around the low hill a hundred yards from the little rise on which their camp was built. It was the shape of their neighbour Phillips which emerged.

Matthew fetched water for the horse as Phillips dismounted.

James poured the last of their strong tea. 'Phillips, sit down.'

He took his tea and nodded thanks. He sat and gave his news with-out ceremony. 'A rider has come, to Balgowlie. He has a bandaged wound from a native spear in his thigh.'

'An attack?' James was all ears.

'Not here. My wife is tending to the man now. He had to be helped from his horse and given water before he could speak. My boy has gone to Clare for Tibbs, but we are much afraid that he will not survive the night.'

'Do we know this man?'

'This is his second day in South Australia and probably his last. He has come, or so he said, from the River Murray, where he was one mem-ber of a party overlanding three thousand sheep from Gundagai.'

James jumped to his feet. 'What do you say?'

'Over land!' cried Matthew, returning to the campfire.

'Your sheep, James,' said Phillips, ignoring Matthew, 'bound for this place. There was an attack by the native. Two men were murdered, an ox was speared to death. Almost all of the sheep were driven off. The man who rode was put upon a horse and bid to come and tell the news. His wound was of the flesh only, but infection has set in and a fever is upon him.'

Phillips and Matthew both looked at James.

'His ride has killed him,' said James.

'I fear it,' Phillips replied. 'That makes *three men dead.*'

Phillips had emphasised three dead and Matthew knew that in the accepted terms of the other men of the valley this meant reprisals – a kind of war that may last a couple of days, or a week, or two weeks if the spirit was high and there was little to do on the farms. Phillips was known to be strongly in favour of quick and ruthless reprisals.

The calm autumn of James and Matthew's arrival in the north had quickly turned into a hard winter of riding and clearing, cutting timber for posts. Few men in the town had been this far north and there had been no one to warn them of the gelid winds and blighting frost. They had wanted to make peace with the Aborigines, who walked in bare foot through all weathers, but there had been resistance from both the natives and the settlers. By August, Matthew had turned inward with frustration and confusion at the purpose of their undertaking. The romance of the bush had turned into heat and boredom and the endless repetition of simple tasks.

And now this news: three thousand Spanish merino crossed with South Downs stock from Hampshire – the finest breed in the colonies, developed and adapted over forty years in New South Wales. Nearly half their capital had gone into that flock. The action was deeper in the bush than they had ever been before. Matthew was at one time elated over the adventure so suddenly before him, but dismayed by the prospect of shooting at the Aborigines – blood brothers of his friends in the south.

'We must go to the river,' said James.

'Of course we must go,' said Phillips, 'with every man and gun of quality we can muster.'

'We must recover our property and secure the capture and imprisonment of any of the scoundrels involved.' James repeated the word of the governor's law.

Phillips spat into the dust. 'If I go with you, I can tell you now that I will not be capturing any natives.' Phillips's eye glinted at James. 'And you will need me there.'

James was fully aware that an experienced man like Phillips was exactly what he did need.

'The law is that natives of South Australia are British subjects and entitled to the protection of the law and the presumption of innocence.'

Thousands of stars had begun their presidency over the unspoiled sky. The three men were silent at their campfire. James looked into the heart of Phillips; Phillips regarded the fire; Matthew glanced from Phillips to his brother and back again.

Phillips looked up. 'The protector of Aborigines is in Adelaide three and a half days ride from the river. And our good fortune is that we are here,' he gestured to the valley and the confining hills, 'in the midst of nature.' Phillips grinned at them, his face dropping on one side into a leer. 'And we have brought our civilisation with us.'

The brothers knew that Phillips was not only talking about their ploughs and hoes and agriculture, their horses and carriages and clothing and all the other things that showed the white man to be superior; he nodded to the pistol sitting on the stump of tree beside James.

'You will remain with us the night,' said James, his cheering voice coming to his assistance. 'We will breakfast even before first light.'

'All?' said Phillips, his head inclined towards Matthew.

'All,' said James. 'It is my brother's flock as much as mine.'

'You will not need someone left behind to keep control of your stock here?'

'We will bring the shepherds and the flocks in to the near hold. That will do for a week.'

Phillips looked sourly at his tea and tossed its lees into the fire. 'All then,' he managed, finally. 'You will take care of where you are pointing your weapons if you are to be in the same campaign as I,' said Phillips, looking at Matthew directly for the first time since he had arrived and then back to the flames of the fire.

Matthew burned with shame. Phillips spoke of a time three weeks before when they had gone out in fruitless search of blacks who had hit and run with two sheep. Matthew's handgun had discharged by accident as his horse crossed a little stream. The shot had startled Phillips's horse, so that Phillips had to work to control the beast. Matthew was in no doubt that Phillips thought him callow and unworldly, that he was too much excited by the events of the chase and would be best left behind with his book of Keats.

'My brother is in control of his weapons, Mr Phillips. Rest assured.'

'And of himself?'

'What do you mean, Phillips?'

'We must know where we stand in God's order of things, Mr Larkin. I believe Matthew is not certain of his own place in the world, nor of the place of the white man in it.' Phillips looked from one to the other of the two Larkins, as if daring a reply. The first law of the valley was that all men must act as one, in accordance with an unspoken but well-understood doctrine.

In his childhood, Matthew had been encouraged by his mother to tell the truth. But, as he grew, he had learnt that there are conventions in truth and that so much became truthful by the omission of potentially contradictory information. He had also been taught that it was impolite to confront people with some truths that were of even the most obvious nature. His nature leant towards disputation, and in order to avoid obvious conflict he had taken to the art of turning a negation into a question. He had once used this technique in the town and his friend Cawthorne had congratulated him on his use of 'Socratic irony'.

'Have you noticed, Mr Phillips, how the countryside here is in clumps of trees and then there are open places where the grass is best and where the sheep and kangaroos alike are wont to graze?'

'I've noticed.' Phillips could not help a defensive note in his voice.

'It has made the work easier for all of us, has it not, to have a place to put our first flocks without taking out so much as a tree? Our selection when we first arrived did resemble in parts not so much a wild place as the heath at Hampstead, did it not, brother?'

James remained silent but half nodded and pursed his lips in acknowledgement.

'All are wont to notice this, but not to remark upon it with such fervour.' Phillips's tone now was savage and weary all at once. 'They say the strikes of lightning burn the trees away and the grass grows back. It is a fortunate thing.'

'Yet have we not also seen places where lightning fires have burnt and shoots smile up at us within a fortnight? After six months, saplings can be seen from a mile off and trees are back within a year.'

'Aye, there may be craft in it. Native craft, I know you will say.'

'Some say they burn it deliberately every year or two or three, else the arbour would grow back, the grass would be defeated and the animals would not come and graze to be speared down.'

Silence reigned over the campfire for a minute, except for the gentle breeze and the crackling of twigs in the blaze. Diffused with irony or not, Matthew had challenged Phillips, a man twenty-five years his senior.

'I saw action in South Africa as well as India,' said Phillips, staring into the fire. 'I was at Peshawar under Pollock and we went against the Afghans. All the way to Kabul we beat those heathens back.'

'The Army of Retribution,' said James, attempting to introduce a note of restrained admiration.

'You take the boot away from the Afghan's throat and they will be back at you within a minute. It was a worthy life, spreading civilisation and order to the world. But sergeant is as far as a man like me can go.' It was not the first time they had heard Phillips tell his story.

'You were captain of police in Adelaide, Phillips.' Matthew tried his own tepid conciliation with their neighbour.

'Aye, they needed someone who could bring order to a rabble. I did what I could do, just as you have done copying dispatches at Government House, Matthew. We all have our abilities. But it was land that I came here for, to this colony, with my family – for land.' And he tossed his head back in the direction he had come, back to Balgowlie – to his acres, his wife and his two sons. 'It is an incomparable opportunity, for me.' There was resentment in his voice, but at the same time triumph – his family, an estate, some power. He had risen through his personal power and was now a man who would expect to be appeased.

James leaned behind him and opened the box of provisions. He extracted the bottle of superior sherry, a rare thing outside of Adelaide and reserved for occasions of note. He passed the bottle of wine across the fire. 'Come, Phillips,' he said, 'have one drink, for the cold, and for fellowship. We toast the success of our undertaking tomorrow.'

'Aye,' said Phillips, and as he accepted the bottle and looked at Matthew with what may have been a wink. 'If we are to ride together, here is to your health, lad,' and he upended the bottle and took a solid swig. He had seen young men make a mistake and then learn from it. 'One swallow, for companionship, and for the cold, and there's an end to it for the night.'

He passed the bottle to Matthew, who followed him with a good swig of the strong liquor. James nodded to him, in a way that was barely perceptible, that the dictate of Phillips should be agreed to.

'Of course, Phillips, clear heads on the morrow,' Matthew said as he passed the bottle back to James.

'Clear heads,' said James and took his swallow.

They had all drunk from the same bottle and the ceremony was complete.

They built up their fire to a blaze that crackled hard, using more boughs than normal economy would allow. The fire became a thing of itself, in which men could seek answers to mysteries of which they themselves were barely aware. As the flames rose and fell and flickered, the face of Phillips across from Matthew fell into darkness and then back into light, then into the dark again, and Matthew could not read the thoughts of the man. Perhaps in their minds they were all rehearsing their part in the action that was before them.

Soon they rose from the blaze and stuffed their saddlebags with rations of tea and flour and sugar. They swept up leaves to make a bed for Phillips at the fire. Then there was nothing else to do but sit through the night till dawn, dreaming of the new day; none slept more fitfully than Matthew, whose anticipation was heightened and excited.

At the first peep of dawn, they were all awake and at breakfast.

Matthew stirred up the fire then mixed some flour and water into dough and cooked it in a skillet along with two hogget chops for each of them. Phillips ate with relish, James less so, and Matthew mimicked heartiness as his teeth tore at the damper; he chewed and chewed but swallowed with difficulty. They would not find the place the overland expedition had been intercepted until the next day or one after that, but the altercation would come.

Phillips motioned with his fork, Eat up, and Matthew forced three mouthfuls down. He had filled this same skillet with dough for Cawthorne and his friends Kadlitpinna and Willa Willa on the plains of Adelaide. He remembered the natives eating the white man's food with amused relish, and would never forget their rapture over the metal contraption in which it was cooked. They had turned the skillet over and knocked it with their knuckles to hear the sounds it made, then chuckled heartily at its dull plangent novelty. Now Matthew shoved his bread in a pocket and winked at Phillips. For the trip, was his meaning, and Phillips grunted.

Soon they were on their horses and away. James carried the shotgun and one handgun, and Matthew a handgun and a smaller rifle designed for bringing down animals; with Phillips carrying his own holstered handgun, they were a tight and well-armed posse as they trotted to Phillips's section.

Phillips's elder son Peter increased their party to four; another son George must have been but fifteen years and was itching to join them, but did not dare to challenge his father when he was told to stay with the house. One policeman from Clare came out to investigate the matter of the wounded rider and he resolved to join in their good work. George Phillips had ridden out at dawn to spread the word and, as they were stacking their bags with bread from Mrs Phillips's oven, Jones the Welshman and three more good men rode up to do what they could. They were jovial about the shoot and quietly glad too to be creating a store of favours for a neighbour which would be sure to be repaid in kind one day. For the Larkins, the matter was less sporting. The policeman from Clare kept a serious face, not allowing his own avidity for the adventure to show.

Mrs Phillips waved a handkerchief from the porch and George, between a boy and a man, stood silently beside her. As they bore inland, the countryside became brown and flat as they moved into the rainshadow of the hills, and after a long and uneventful ride they camped one night in a stand of gums near a waterhole. If there were natives about, they kept well clear.

At night, the cockiness drained from the men and they kept a nervous pair rotating watch – in strange territory at night, listening for a dried twig breaking under foot. Matthew slept and was awoken at one in the morning, and stood the freezing sentry time until three. He alone knew there would be no attack, not at night, unprovoked; passing through a strange land, they were travellers vouched safe. They had done nothing to inflame the inhabitants, not yet. When his sentry post was over, he slept heavily, gratefully; there was still a full day of riding and perhaps another morning before engagement.

In the morning, they arose, still groggy from broken sleep. As they approached the river, they were entranced by the prolific gum trees teeming with birdlife. Much comment was made upon it, perhaps to overlay the fears that swam in their hearts but to which they could not give voice. Not one of them had seen the river before and it was a sight, winding its way before them between high cliffs that gave way from time to time to little landings perfect for setting out a canoe. Swarms of crested pigeon were so profuse that they formed a shadow overhead as they passed. One burst of shot would bring down three or four and they ate a great many roasted at their second camp.

They rode along the river cliff the next morning and soon came upon the hut of a pair of sectioners who directed them further northwards. They rode for another twenty silent minutes, listening through the trees for whispers but hearing only the silent gums, searching the spaces for moving shadows but seeing only waving boughs. Just a few feet away from the bullock tracks, the bush began and the rules changed, for there was the kingdom of the native.

Presently they came to the place, a bend in the track, and there, a scene of devastation over which a morbid stillness still hung. At their approach, half a dozen fat crows squarked indignantly and took to the air, the pollution of human carrion dripping from their beaks, to be distributed by them over the countryside. The victual trunk of Field the Overlander had been prised open and its contents were strewn about: tea, flour, sugar, even tobacco, which they would have thought prized by the native. Two bullocks lay slaughtered nearby with spearholes in their necks, one with a hindquarter hacked pitilessly off, no doubt with the overlanders' own tomahawk. Then the body of a man, worm-riddled and putrefied, exposed as it was in the midday sun. He lay back with his arms flung outwards as if he had been turned over by his assailants. His eyes were pecked and there were sightless, soulless caverns where a man may once have been; he was the most hideous and galvanising sight that any of these men had seen in all their days. The natives had proclaimed their prevalence over this place and in five days no white man had dared come near.

The sight of ravaged and unburied Christians was a provocation to the leaders of the expedition. Phillips and the constable exchanged glances and they began at once to search among the bushes for signs of exit.

'We must find those sheep,' said James.

'Aye,' said Phillips, 'and we must avenge this now.'

The men looked towards the policeman from Clare, whose report would find its way to his sergeant's desk soon enough, thence in the fullness of time as far south as the Protector.

He nodded quickly and tersely said, 'Yes, now.'

'This is no time for digging,' said Matthew, knowing that the decision had been made already, with or without his consent. 'We must do it now.' His voice was as firm as he could make it and Phillips inclined his head an inch in support. 'We will return soon enough to dignify this man,' Matthew added sagely, nodding to the corpse of Field, and murmurs of Aye aye rose from the men around him.

# 2

# The Town – September 1842

Lucy Bray folded over a linen handkerchief and wiped the condensation from her first-floor parlour window, then looked out into the spring-time morning. 'It is fine today, Mary,' she cried. 'The sun is out.'

'But still with icicles drippin' off the rafters, miss. I'll stir up the fire.'

'Oh yes, Mary. I wouldn't bring anyone into this room with it so chilly.' Lucy had to be open for visitors, even in the mornings.

Lucy had been with Mary since she was a girl, long before her parents passed away. No voyage to the colony could have been thought of without her. And in the two years since the death of her mother, they had come even closer. Mary had decided that it was her duty to broaden Lucy's education with some stories of her youth, just enough to allow Lucy to see what some girls were allowed to do and for her to be able to have a more informed understanding of what she saw around her in London – a second education outside of the textbook.

Thirty yards away stood another of the few stone houses of the colony. Across the road from that, some 'temporary' huts of bark and twine had been set around branches shoved into the earth, with rushes and yakka flax for roofs; some more permanent places boasted sawn and planed uprights set in concrete, some with planking for the sides and thatch on top. The unsealed roadway between them was potted with holes still filled with a tan slurry from the rains of the afternoon before. A dray came past, its driver picking his way carefully to the stores of Hindley Street, horses breathing billows of steam that drifted into vaporous clouds and disappeared into the morning.

'Oh look, miss, do you see?'

Lucy Bray peeped through her defrosted window to the three-foot jacaranda tree that they had planted the day of their arrival in the colony three months before. A walk around the stores of the Cape of Good Hope had found it, and the idea of a tree seemed so perfect that Mary had straightaway called a marine to bundle it on board. And it had sat below their first-floor window, quiet and aloof through the winter.

But now, Lucy saw what Mary pointed out, its first blue flower peeping into the morning sun, full of breaking vitality. 'Ah,' she gasped, 'it will be like our lilac tree in Kilburn.'

'More blue perhaps, miss.'

'Of course you are right, but I suspect a strong blue purple is somehow more apt for this place.' Lucy was an optimist; she would make judgements on instinct and her loyalties then were unbreakable. She brooked no opposition to plans she would make.

When her mother had been alive, their garden in London had been Lucy's cradle. The lilac tree played sheltering host to a spring and summer pageant: crocus with delicate saffron stamens, the yolk-yellow centres of creamy jonquils, and daffodils and snowdrops sweeping down to the shady lawn where she would sit and read and think.

When her father was killed, she'd had two years to sit and read and think. She had taught herself the culture of ancient Athens, and learnt about their wars with the Spartans. She knew that in Athens men exercised naked and in Sparta women ran farms and rode horses and carried whips. She had read the democratic philosophy of Thomas Paine and the poems of the Romantics.

The news of her father's death had been delivered to her just two weeks after her uncle had set out on a two-year run to Southern Africa, India and even Australia. A man came from the ministry and said that her father had been unlucky – a stray shot above the eye at Grahamstown. He wished her well – a fifteen-year-old girl just finished schooling, her mother gone three years before. Her uncle Alfred was now her legal parent.

Two years later, her uncle's visit had been much forewarned and Lucy presented herself in the hallway to greet him. She could barely remember his face, for she had taken no particular notice of him when he'd last been there. But now he was a man of towering importance to her and in the three days since the announcement of his coming visit, she had interrogated her memory for resemblance to the dark and delicate features of her own father. But she had come up with little.

An air of decision and fatefulness hung over the house. Sheets were washed and aired, cutlery polished. Servants rehearsed their greeting positions in the hall – finally a horse and carriage, then footsteps. Her aunt went to the door and the man came through. His features were stronger, his set of body thicker. At seventeen years, Lucy was no fool when it came to humans, and buried in her uncle's eyes she could also see the onus of responsibility, the care of a man accustomed to making hard resolutions and decisions that must stick – the strength to see them through. His first glance looked into her and through her.

She greeted him in the hallway with a curtsy.

'For heaven's sake,' her uncle waved his hand in dismissal, 'none of that. Come here.' And he held out his arms and gave her a hug and a wet kiss on one cheek. 'My poor, dear Lucy,' he said, beholding her, hands out at arm's length and examining her eyes again. 'You must understand,' he said, 'I am not a great one for mincing manners.'

At dinner, he asked her about her life with the great aunt who cared for her, about her cousin, the nature of her schooling, and about her poor Mama's garden, which he could see she kept in excellent order. He assessed her responses. The girl was as lively and clever as he remembered. Balancing this, there was a sharp edge to her prettiness, an obsidian flint of determination that made her almost unsettling to look at. Her eyes assessed and sorted, seemed to be giving marks and categorising; she was a restless creature. She will lose that, he thought. In no way was she turned in upon herself or taken to the morbid or the gloomy. At least not in that part of her that she presented to him and, he guessed, to the world at large. That was good. Whatever lay within was for every man or woman, or girl for that matter, to work out for themselves and was not to be his concern.

Lucy had been fitted for gowns a month before and was being readied for presentation into the social world.

'Your first ball is in the offing, eh,' he chewed at her.

'Yes, sir,' she replied.

'Is it a matter of life and death for you?'

The question was a complete surprise to her and Lucy returned him a quizzical look. The way it had been put implied that there would be an importance attached to its answering, that she was to be judged on what she said. She guessed also that too coquettish an attention to the matter of balls and gowns would see her marked down in her uncle's eyes, and she was a girl who sought nothing but high scores.

'Why,' she said, with a shrug of nonchalance, 'it is what is expected.' And then, raising her chin in a parody of high aristocracy, she finished, 'One must do one's duty, after all.'

'Hah,' her uncle threw his head back and chortled. 'Hah, you are a one, that is for sure.'

Lucy was uncertain as to what a 'one' particularly was, but was sure it was something good. She could see too that her uncle was a man who would be happy for her to speak her mind, or at least he would tolerate it. She decided that she liked him and, further, that she could influence him, manage him even.

'Lucy,' he said, pulling the napkin from his collar and leaning his elbows on the table, 'I am to be governor of South Australia.'

Lucy put her hand to her mouth.

'As you know, I am not married. As I embark in seven days, I have no time to find a suitable unmarried woman and to perform the necessary rituals.'

For once in her life, Lucy was stunned into silence, as if waiting for the pronouncement of her fate.

'I have assessed your intelligence and maturity to be thoroughly satisfactory. You will come with me to South Australia and assist me with the management of the gentler section of the community. I need a woman.'

'But I am just a girl,' said Lucy. She did not think at all that she was just a girl, but mock self-depreciation was the first thing she could think to say that had any stamp of intelligence on it.

'Hmmph, you are woman enough,' her uncle raised an eyebrow across the table, 'and will become more so. You will attend to official and social functions. Some have said that I am abrupt and dour. You will balance me. I am sorry you will have to leave your house and your balls and your mother's garden retreat and all the rest of it, but,' he paused a moment and raised a finger for satirical emphasis, 'one must do one's duty, after all.'

Lucy raised her eyebrow back across the table and was privately astounded at the way one's life could be altered forever in a matter of seconds.

During her almost two years of waiting for the visit of her uncle, Lucy's social education had continued in the parlour of her great-aunt Eliza. The women would come and go during an at-home afternoon, sometimes with young men attached: matrons bringing their nephews to see and learn.

The gold standard of politesse was that unannounced guests must stay a minimum of fifteen minutes or offence would be caused; intimates might stay half an hour or even more. So, if the intention was to cause a mild but indefinable affront, the regime was to stay fifteen minutes *and no longer*. Visitors would keep track of time and think of some agreeable things to say, then depart on the stroke of fifteen minutes. It was a way of saying, There, we've made our visit, duty done, but we have no real interest in you. No specific offence was made, but matters of rank and station were being settled.

When she arrived in the colony, what wives there were would come calling, as they must. Some would observe and inspect her, assessing her for marriage as well as for her apparent vice-regal fitness and capacity. A governor had to be respected, as should his consort, whether it be a wife or a young relative. But how long would a governor stay? Two years, three? The position of the girl was negotiable: she could be ignored, or tolerated, or embraced. One woman peered at her through opera glasses, then wrote notes in a small book which she produced from her bag.

She was asked if she could play.

'Oh yes, in England I did practise every morning at eight. When father passed away, there was no money for a tutor, so I taught myself.' She saw no reason to gild her origins; her family had risen from yeoman class, but so had most of the colonists. 'I do love the piano, and dancing, but one cannot play all day, or dance, it would seem.'

'Indeed not.'

'The servants would be driven mad.'

'One does not think of servants.'

The lady had left on the stroke of fifteen minutes.

One morning, she received a call from Mrs Newsome, the wife of the protector of Aborigines. Here was a section of society in which she and her uncle were welcome. In the debates around the town regarding what to do with the Aborigines, the forces for rough treatment had been growing more vocal. The governor had been put in place by Whitehall partly because of his sympathy with the native, to place a curb on the ambitions of would-be landowners. But after an outline of the arguments in favour of assimilating and educating the Kaurna people, Lucy found that Mrs Newsome was of a mind to talk frankly about the young men of the colony.

Sensing that Lucy was distancing herself from all the marriageable prospects she had met so far, Mrs Newsome ventured further. 'There is a new Larkin in the colony. The young brother of James has followed him out. It seems he likes to treat all the men as equals, as the modern way seems to be, listens to their stories and takes heed of their views. For myself, I'd say that I'm all for it. This is not Parliament Square, after all.'

Lucy tittered.

'And,' Mrs Newsome went on, 'quite a looker he is, if one might say it. I was told he was as pretty as Rabbie Burns and I didn't believe it,' and she dropped her voice an octave to a suggestive tone of confidence, 'until I saw.' Mrs Newsome winked at her as she rose to leave. She had stayed for thirty five minutes.

Matthew Larkin sat back in his chair and gazed over his desk in the wattle hut they called Government House. A small wooden cradle, just larger than the sheets of report paper it was designed to accommodate, sat on his right side in the corner of the desk next to the door through which the senior clerk would come from time to time to collect Matthew's copied reports. Before him were three or four sheets of surveyors' observations from last week's trip to the Inman Valley, full of calculations that he didn't particularly understand but must reproduce in exact detail. Beneath that was something a little more interesting, a report by the senior clerk on the last month's visit of inspection to the German settlement at Klemzig, and then something had come in from the inspector of customs at the port which detailed tariffs collected for the import of barrels of pickles. Matthew would begin one such dispatch, then become bored and in his frustration he would turn to another, then another, and another. Eventually, he would return to one of the first and finish it off in a burst of activity, then slide it triumphantly into his Out cradle and heave a sigh.

Colonisation was such a serious business.

He pushed the chair back in his desk and walked over to the rude window that gave out to the west where the River Torrens wrapped itself around the plateau hill of North Adelaide before heading to the sea. Beyond the bend, not half a mile away, he knew would be the camp of the Aborigines.

'I shall go out for my walk now, Thompson,' said Matthew, 'it is terribly close in here.'

Thompson looked up from the report he was copying. His fingers were splayed to keep both documents steady – the original and his scrupulous facsimile – though little breeze disturbed them. He would copy his original all the way through without faltering. 'It is not so bad,' he said. Then as he dipped his pen into the well of ink that sat in a pre-cut aperture in his desk, he glanced up again. 'There will be much worse in three months' time,' he said, with a warning eyebrow.

'When the new building is complete, we shall have a place on the first floor. The breezes will cool us.'

'Hmmm,' said Thompson, without conviction. 'But if the air will do you good,' he went on, looking up, 'then you may as well go off on your tootle.'

Thompson, by the measure of his employment having endured two months longer than his colleague's three weeks, was Matthew's senior. However, he was wary of the newcomer whose father bore some naval kinship to the governor. Excellent outcomes at work were one thing, but connection was another. Scrutiny was made of their output and the fewer reports Larkin completed, the more solid was his own position, and the closer he was to senior clerk himself. Still, there was a greater urgency on this day and he was primarily responsible for deadlines.

'The *Bomanjee* sails tomorrow,' he said, with a motion of his hand to the batch of reports which lay on the common table from which they took their tasks. 'There is much to do.'

'Half an hour perhaps. I will work the better after a little air.'

'Of course,' said Thompson. 'Oh, and, Larkin, the governor has just announced an austerity regime.' His head inclined towards two screwed-up pages on the floor by Larkin's desk. 'Do take care.'

Matthew walked easily enough along the track that followed the stream until it arched to the north and away from civilisation, then he picked his way through light scrub and wattle until he came around the bend and in sight of the blacks' camp. Above him and away to the left and west, a stern little gaol was being raised and he could hear the faint ring of hammer on nail and could imagine the workmen bending their backs in the early afternoon sun. The extremities of colonial society were purveyed by the builders' efforts: a new Government House at one end of town and a gaol at the other. He plunged forward, away from thoughts of what grew out of the dissatisfaction of those who could not afford the price of land in the new colony. Through a stand of bushes was the rough path he had found two weeks before, where the grasses seemed beaten down by a foot that had passed through many times.

Matthew looked about him and listened. The trees were still; across the river, further on, a wisp of campfire smoke. Down by the river was a tree which had fallen, through the cause of lightning, he guessed. The trunk and branches had long since been carted away by native or white man for firewood or building but, curiously, the higher shards of the burnt remains of the stump had been cut though by a saw and made into a rude stool by a hand unknown. Here it was that Matthew became accustomed to observing the natives, whose camp lay opposite one of the best and deepest of the waterholes.

The women remained often at the camp, weaving baskets that they wore slung over the shoulder: some for the babies that they carried with them everywhere; others for herbs and fruits they collected; others were deep and narrow, designed for the toting of clubs which the men would take out hunting or into battle. Some of the women held trays of nut-grass bulbs which they pounded into a pulp. Others set off back upstream to the clear river, wearing a halter with a basket on either side, in each of them a huge shell like a conch which they would use to transport water. A man sauntered up with three or four water fowl which the women quickly plucked and tossed on the slow-cooking fire, gizzards and all; the children gathered around with looks of delight on their faces. As soon as the cooking was right and the signal came from the oldest woman, the children wrestled each other playfully for the birds and tore them limb from limb. Delighting in the sweet meat and making a game out of the eating of it, they would dab at the juice with the back of their hands and lick that away, laughing at each other all the while.

Occasionally the men came in with a kangaroo, which would be tossed down away from the fire. One of the men would cut the hide in the bottom of the leg and a quick incision was made upwards from there. Then the sinew of the leg was pulled through at some considerable effort by the butcher, the left hand pulling while the right hand guided and cut away the flesh with a tomahawk. When this had been done, the off-white tangle was thrown to the women who, with great care, would split the sinews into thin ropes for the making of a net which they used for catching fish and birds.

One time, he saw a boy, no more than twelve years of age, plunge his hand down the hollow knot of a tree and emerge with a possum, whose head he then casually knocked against the trunk of the tree.

Mathew closed his eyes and thought of himself at twelve or thirteen. He had ridden in the hunt or, rather, trailed along behind it: twenty-five horses and fifteen dogs in the pursuit of one small beast. The cacophony of the ritual was something he could barely conceive of now. He could almost hear the bugles and the dogs and the thumping of hooves as they made ground after fences; he could feel the fright of the fox, though he had never seen one alive, only the mess of one torn by the pack of dogs that had chased it down.

Matthew had been watching the scene for half an hour when a movement on the edge of the waterhole took his notice. One of the natives emerged from the water, breaking the surface with the gentleness of a caress. His two hands were together in the shape of a prayer and his head followed, dripping; his torso was fit and muscular and his arms extended into a shepherding gesture which was directed at a little pen of black swans before him. The effect was to break away from the group one large swan which he seemed to be pushing down the stream in the direction of the camp. At the same time, he ushered the mother and her brood of cygnets away towards the town.

Then from among the rushes that snuggle into the bend in the river emerged two shadows of figures. Ever so slowly, they stretched up to their height and as they did so their right arms were raised and in each right hand there was a spear of more than two yards in length. The sight of them fair put a juddering sensation of shock through Matthew. Their left legs barely broke the surface of the water as they leaned forward in perfect balance to prepare their spears for flight. The silence which hung over the river was a thing of itself, so perfectly still that Matthew could hear a bird cheeping in an old gum tree on the hill one hundred yards to the north, impertinently unaware of the silent drama being played out here.

The arms of the spear-throwers loomed back and then silently forward and the spears, which had seemed until a moment before to be a fully attached part of the hand and arm, were now in flight. With a barely audible whoosh, they both struck the swan, one in its breast beneath the neck and the other deep in its abdomen. Both spearheads protruded clean through to the other side. The first sign of death or injury was the deep red blood that then oozed into the stream, and as the heavy, handled end of the spears sank slowly into the water, the two barbed and sharpened heads rose like totems and the sun seemed to salute them and to bounce its rays off their crystal heads in triumph.

Matthew was frozen to his place. He closed his eyes and opened them again as if to confirm that it had not been a dream. But what spell had seemed to be cast over the river was suddenly broken by the cheery hand-clapping and jabbering of the natives, who strode forward to collect their prey; they evinced the contented smiles of those who have well performed a task at which they should not fail but which, when done well enough, still is all the credit to them. One hit would have been enough, but that both had made their mark was a cause for happiness. The sudden change from wraithlike to joyous could scarcely be believed. The third man, the shepherd, had meantime been gently moving the mother and its three babes away toward the rest of the pen, to safety.

Matthew had never seen such elegance attending the act of killing, nor such gentle deference to the mother and her cygnets. In England, a hunter would have killed them both and thrown the little ones to the dogs.

The throwers pulled their spears all the way through the carcass, for there was no pulling them back by the way they had entered. Then one of the natives slung the swan by its neck over his own shoulder, and what a splendid sight it made – the jet-black swan, a trickle of red at its throat, against the dark brown body of the native, off now to throw the dead bird at the feet of the women for plucking and gutting.

Matthew remained transfixed for several minutes after they had gone, in awe at the style and efficacy of the spear-throwers. Eventually, reminders of his mundane tasks came to him and he rose and dusted the seat of his pants, then turned to make his way back up the river towards the settlement. A sadness stole over him, as deep a melancholy as he had ever experienced; that he should be low about returning to Government House was not unusual, but this was depression of a sudden and sweeping magnitude. Everything he faced now seemed false and insubstantial; the friendly civility for which the colony was famed seemed self-serving and hypocritical.

He had taken just four or five steps, and looked up to gain his bearings on the path, when he stopped suddenly. There was a man, standing near river's edge, facing the action he had just witnessed, except that, unlike Matthew, he appeared to have been watching with hands in pockets, not startled or surprised by what had happened. His face was turned towards Matthew now, although his feet and whole body still faced the river, as if he had not wanted to turn himself and risk the making of a sound. His dark eyes sat in haunted, pained sockets, and their gaze was concentrated with assessment. Matthew stopped in his very tracks in shock. As he stood there, the man took his hands out of his pockets, pulled a pipe from his coat and, with a conscious nonchalance, began to stuff it in preparation to lighting.

Matthew walked carefully up the small slope towards him.

'A pretty little show,' was all the man said.

'I thought they were marvellous,' Matthew replied with sudden enthusiasm.

The man merely lit his pipe and nodded twice as if contented with his answer. 'Come, to my cottage. I will show you some of their weapons.' His very abrupt way of speaking and the directness of his manner betrayed a man not cultured in the ways of society. His trousers and shirt were sound, befitting some form of shopkeeper or civil servant, but old, perhaps five years past their best.

All of this did not shock but rather pleased Matthew, for he had until that time been kept with only his brother James and such company as was deemed suitable by him on behalf of their father, the admiral.

'There is nothing that would delight me more, sir, but I must return to my employment, copying the governor's dispatches to England.'

'A pretty little job, some might think. You must be high connected to have obtained a sinecure of that dimension, and you not one month in the colony.'

Matthew told him that he detested copying dispatches but that twice already he had accompanied the governor on rides to the bush to visit outlying settlements and to oversee surveyors mapping new lands, and how this delighted him so much more and that he hoped to observe some more of these fine blackfellows.

'You will come to me tomorrow then, at ten o'clock. I will show you my collection of native spears and other things.'

'I would be delighted, sir.'

'Oh,' he said, as if remembering something, 'I am Cawthorne, William.'

'And I am Larkin, Matthew.'

'There is something else,' Cawthorne said, after a thoughtful moment.

'What is that?'

'There is to be an affray.'


Alfred Bray had visited South Australia for three weeks in 1841 to recuperate from a difficult and ill-equipped assignment he led exploring in the north of Western Australia. He had spent three months trekking back and forth across the Kimberley, but had collapsed of nervous exhaustion and had to be sent south. By no means was he blamed for the failure. The expedition had been poorly planned and ill-equipped. In fact, Bray was reputed to have performed heroically against the odds; Whitehall was now in his debt and the ten-day voyage around the coast had given him time to reflect, at the age of fifty one, on the type of employment that would be most suited to his declining years.

While in South Australia, he had kept his eyes wide open. He was much taken with the delightful aspect of the town and its rolling treed plains, the little river that wound through it, the hills that fringed it and the sandy beaches that gave unto its peaceful and protected sea. One Adelaide matron noted in her diary that he 'went everywhere and saw everything.' His informal report to the Foreign Office on returning home had not mentioned the colony's governor by name, but it was in effect a catalogue of wastage and excessive expenditure on capital works. In Bray's view, the works were borne on blind optimism and had grown to serve the immediate interests of the steady stream of new arrivals. Indeed, the colony truly was on the brink of bankruptcy and in London investors in the South Australian Company were nervous. Bray's report kept pointing to excess at the highest level of government. There were no outright lies, just half-truths, omissions and small exaggerations.

Enough important heads at home had been impressed by Bray's own head for expenditures and by his propitiatory attitude to the natives; a fiscal lesson was to be learnt and a shining example set for the roughhouse colonies of the East on the issue of native relations. Houghton was recalled – Bray was installed.

So, although frugality had become the catchword to restoring the finances of the colony, Alfred Bray decided on the reverse course of action where the works on the new stone Government House were concerned. The large drawing room was completed with all speed and a spring ball was proclaimed as a celebration of all that had been achieved in five years of the colony. It would boost morale in a time when some of the former governor's old friends had not yet been won over to the

Bray camp, and would serve as a kind of official debut for the governor's niece, Miss Lucy Bray.

A piano had been brought from England in '39 and was to be the centrepiece of accompaniment to dancing; debate raged for weeks over the appropriateness of the different styles to be adopted. Quadrille was widely accepted, with the ladies proceeding decorously at arm's length from the men. But arguments ensued over other modes – the fashions of the day in England – which would set important standards for the future of the colony. The waltz was considered by many to be of peasant origin and too sensuous, that the spinning of a partner in the arms of another had led too often to licentious consequences (others countered that this had occurred principally on the continent) and that the practice should not be encouraged. But a strong assertion was that the playful exuberance of the polka and mazurka was another thing altogether and that the quality of wholesome joy was the very stuff of the colony. The cause of the polka had been championed by Matthew Larkin, the newly arrived clerk at Government House. While the governor's immediate impression of the younger Larkin had not been favourable on account of his raffish mustard-coloured shirts and his need to go awalking to engage with nature, his voice on the questions of dance evinced such authority and enthusiasm that the governor was inclined to agree with him.

The matter was put to the pianist, Mrs Hooper, but she declined to play anything in 2/4, so a fiddler and a squeeze box player from the German settlement at Klemzig, four miles away towards the hills, had been brought in to provide a robust finale to the evening. The governor was delighted to procure them, and happy to include these upright religious refugees into the stream of colonial society. It was an unexpected decision that put his personal stamp on the evening.

On the night, the women and girls jumped into the dancing with relish, all for the absence of any apparent rules. Matthew Larkin took Lucy Bray by the arm and modelled a well-turned mazurka. Still, refinements were lost on most of the crowd, especially as the night went on and the bowls of punch and cartons of English ale were consumed.

'What zeal the young ladies display,' said Matthew on returning with Lucy to their seats, 'to be able to leap about in such an unrestrained manner at Government House.'

'There are so few ladies, Mr Larkin, each must do the work of ten. And half of the men, it seems, must take to the corners and talk of business.' Lucy rolled her eyes in the direction of an adjacent group of men, where Matthew's brother James was engaged in earnest consultation.

'Ah, yes, business. Matters of deep moment,' said Matthew with mock gravity. 'Even the dancing must stop for business.'

'Particularly the dancing, I'm afraid, Mr Larkin. But how does your own employment suit you, sir? There is steady business at Government House, I'm sure.' Lucy had heard enough to know that Matthew's duties were not much to his taste.

'Sadly, my own employment is even less compelling than business,' Matthew began seriously. Noticing Lucy's parodic pout, he returned fire with his own form of hyperbole. 'I feel like some cloistered monk of medieval times who may but gaze on the birds and the trees through his foot-square window.' Matthew raised his eyes to a distant, imaginary cloud. 'The sky is blue and the fields are alive, but before him lies the record of harvest, and he is to copy it five times: one for the emperor, one for the taxman, one for the sheriff, one for…'

'Poor Mr Larkin,' Lucy's bottom lip protruded. 'The endless talk of men – business and barometers, wethers and weather, and of course timber.'

Matthew noted Lucy's avid conversational sally. He could not help but complete it. 'The timbre of his beloved's sweet voice…' He glanced into Lucy's attentive eyes, then continued in a low voice. 'Fortune has it that my brother attends to all of the mundane matters.'

'Fortunate indeed,' Lucy tittered. In her three months in the colony, here was the first person who had been able to engage her in verbal jousting.

'James must be responsible. Duty has borne him hither and he has no option but to attend to details. He was sent at quite short notice and

I'm not quite sure whether he counts it a blessing or not. I, however, chose to come and they will not let me close to anything of consequence. Is that not what they call an irony? It was hoped that by now James would have secured our holding, but these things drag on, it seems.'

'Ah, the speculation over prices.'

'So much land close to the town was bought up early and now the holders are seeking a grand profit and the newcomers are holding out. And I am wearing my fingertips down to nothing copying reports.'

'A terrible business indeed.' Lucy teased him again but this time Matthew turned to a more serious tone.

'I am sure it is a strain on poor James. And then there is Adela. Engaged to be married in England, then told she should shift to the end of the world – not the life she had envisaged, I'm sure.'

'Is there news?'

'With every letter that arrives, my brother's temper alters.' Matthew found it easy to say things to this girl that he would to no other; there had quickly developed between them some unspoken assumption that confidences would be kept. It was an alliance. 'Sometimes he soars, sometimes he is down. It seems to be the parents' unwillingness to part with their jewel – a death in the family, a wedding of importance, mother ill – that sort of thing.' Matthew's glance played over to his brother's resolute bunch not three yards away. 'He is not much closer to them by nature than I, and my perceptions are that my arrival in this place may have caused him as much difficulty as pleasure. He may carry situations better without my pesky loitering in the wings.'

'There are few unmarried women in the colony, sir, but I am sure your brother would experience little difficulty arranging a bride should Adela fail him. He is well cut and, as you suggest, more refined than many.' Could she inspire the emotion of jealousy in Matthew – stir something in him?

'I fear that, for James, his attachment to Adela is something which could not be easily be replaced. From the moment they met at the age of seventeen, there has been no other for either of them. To be sent here against his choosing, and then to lose his love on account of it, would be a disaster of a magnitude.'

Looking at Matthew now, Lucy could see that he was not cocky as some had said. His concern for his brother was not counterfeit – lines had formed above the bridge of his nose when he spoke of James's discomfort – rather, he was firm in his resolve to remain himself, but in doing this he was expecting disapproval every time he turned round. To refrain from being drawn in to the majority required a kind of alien strength. More than that, her flirtation had not even been noticed by him, so Lucy took another tack. 'You may yourself inspire emotions in others, sir.' She leant towards him and all but fluttered her eyes and touched him on the arm.

Matthew was amused, not by the compliment, but by the brazen style of the girl. 'Miss Lucy, I believe your nature depends on provocation as much as mine. You do take risks, which I must say is an unusual property in a woman, and one which I do admire. But you put me in mind of what my mother once said to me, that I was the brightest and least productive of the admiral's sons. It may be that James is the second brightest and second least productive of the admiral's sons. The first two have done what they must, one in competition with the other, it would seem, which brings to mind the real question: does one have to be dull to be productive.'

Lucy looked around at the room full of sun-burned farmers and wily shopkeepers. 'You have the demeanour of a poet, sir. James…' and here she faltered, seeking the right word, 'that of an architect, or a publisher. Or a man who would manage a theatre.'

Matthew listened to the fancies of Miss Lucy tumbling from her lips, but those fancies, he gave ample credit, were full of insight, had their grounding in good sense.

'He is a man of finer thoughts, but his feet are on the ground as well.'

'It is as you say, and I compliment you on your discernment. James can bide his tongue with these fellows for hours, but with me there sometimes comes a time in conversation that I cannot restrain myself from goading them.'

'Some of them could do with it.' It may have seemed that Lucy was putting her hand directly into the glove of Matthew Larkin, but her comment did reflect her own impatience with them.

'Aye, but most of them will simply push you to the ground if you are in their way. I really should stop it and remain dull-headed.'

'So what is the reason that you are here all of your own accord?'

'I had been bound for something bookish and sent to university for it.' He glanced at Lucy, 'Religion, in fact.'

Lucy returned to him a look of complete surprise.

'My father was punishing me. He decided that if I insisted on read-ing all my days – just to annoy him, you see, that in his view was the only reason I should do such a thing – then I should be taught a lesson in the most perverse way in order to show me my error.'

'Aaaahhh.' Lucy surmised what she could. 'I see.'

'After two years at Oxford, I wrote to him of my profound discovery – that books were indeed excellent meat for the days but that the nights offered more compelling diversions. He may have been amused by my impertinence. Then when James was sent here, I began to ponder the opportunity. I went down to intercept Father while he was ashore and told him of my wish. He straightened in his chair and looked me in the face for the first time in eleven years. To be honest, I was quite frightened. I felt like some seaman on the *Bounty* presenting to Captain Bligh asking for increased rations, a near-certain flogging to ensue.'

'Poor Mr Larkin.' This time there was no playfulness in Lucy's voice. She thought of her own father, who would dandle her on his knee; and then Uncle Alfred, whose stern appearance was mostly sham. She had been treated with kindness all of her life, but a father who lived and breathed a Spartan disposition each second of the day… Lucy took pause to think of it.

'When he showed me to the door, he shook my hand. It was a cu-rious experience, to be shaking hands with one's own father. In any case,

I have always felt one should be judged on what one does, rather than on the way one grips, which can always be faked.'

Lucy had often wondered about the backslapping bonhomie of the world of men – the handshake and the significance attached to it. But the world of women was not short of its falsities either.

'His final words were that he hoped I would make him proud, or some such thing. That I would add to the family fame and fortune. I do not remember now. As the door closed behind me, I could barely believe that it was true – that I was really coming. It had been an idea. Sometimes now, I think I had really been simply in love with the idea of being bold enough to come down and confront him. But within five minutes all was agreed. It was fate.'

'Your mother?'

'Ah, dear mother…was prone to lengthy periods of melancholy. She is possessed of a peculiar temperament. She will read and stay in her room for months and store thoughts up, then go forth and release them in wild bouts of excessive energy. It was thought that the country would be more serene for her than London,' he looked at Lucy, 'and less visible to the public gaze, no doubt.'

'Your father resolved two problems at one stroke.'

Matthew peered at Lucy again, for the quickness of her insight. 'So it would seem. The London house is let and when he is not at sea he will stay in Sussex or at his club – the latter, most likely.'

Servants replaced spent candles even though it was past midnight. The group of men standing by them raised their schooners of sherry in one final toast to the colony, James along with them.

'And will Adela come?' said Lucy. 'I wish it for James and for me.'

Matthew's gaze returned to her. 'Surely she must come, whatever the anguish at home. She has been promised good and proper.'

'What kind of scandal, if she did not?'

'Ah, if James were in England, it would be quite distasteful. But from this distance, I think the matter would be allowed to pass without comment. And he knows it.'

'I do see that marriage can be quite an awkward thing.' In South Australia, Lucy had received three proposals in the first two months and the flow of such representations had only been stemmed by recounts of the peremptory vigour with which she had denounced them. She had been all but poked and prodded and had her teeth examined. They would have her as a farmer's wife too soon. But this Larkin was a more subtle beast altogether – removed in nature, always in his thoughts, never obvious. In his features, there was something of her lost, unfortunate father.

Lucy took a sip from her dry sherry – fino, it was called – and placed her glass firmly on the low wooden table that skirted the wall behind them.

'Good evening, Miss Bray.' It was Matthew's brother James who spoke, turning to them from his group of men.

'Good evening, Mr Larkin. I trust you have had an enjoyable evening.'

'It has been more than passingly pleasant, Miss Lucy.' His glance strayed on the dancers, still in the stages of collapsing through fatigue. 'There has been spectacle and excitements aplenty, but still a pleasing moderation about it all.'

Matthew winced inside himself. The word 'moderation' had been thrust upon him in the way that marriage had been on Lucy.

'Such is the nature of life in the colony, brother,' Matthew put in. 'The combination of work and frivolity. I was just explaining to Miss Lucy that my work at Government House did stimulate me so.'

Lucy hesitated but half a moment, 'Indeed. Your brother was only just now saying how much very useful information is to be gained from the reading of surveyors' reports. The matters learnt of there could hold a man in good stead for years to come.'

She was quick, Matthew observed – almost too quick.

'Hmm. Yes, I see,' said James, looking dubiously from one to the other. 'He is doing well…' He knew that his reply lacked in any fitting degree of wit but he had ridden twenty miles to the north that morning to see a property, then ridden back again, entered a protracted negotiation over property near Port Wakefield with a Mr Simmons that afternoon, then visited the bank and then eaten before coming up to the governor's ball. His thoughts were of bed and peace. He turned his hat over in his hands three times.

'But what news of your bride, Mr Larkin?' Lucy sought to cover the small silence.

James faltered only momentarily. 'A letter. She is to arrive, in due course. She could be on a ship now, and I would not know it. Anyway, I bid you good evening.' James raised his hat to a shoulder high salute by way of farewell and left without another word.

Lucy could see the unease that her question had caused in James and she immediately regretted asking it. She had no wish to be seen as impertinent.

'Oh dear,' she said, turning to Matthew, 'I never thought to offend him.'

'I am sure you did not. But everyone talks about everyone, and everyone who talks will talk about James. And me too, I expect, but for different reasons no doubt.'

'But I was hoping only to show James that on a matter like this I could be a trusted friend.'

Matthew regarded afresh this young Lucy, who was indeed sharp but possessed also sensitivities that looked outward as well, an empathy of feeling for others. And she sought him out as the one with whom she could say her mind. She might help to sustain him in this place. Even so, when he spoke to her, he was reminded of the time he had sat at tea with his mother and she had reminisced of how charming and attentive the admiral had been during their courtship. The memory gave him the sense of time passing to no substantial end, the words of amour disappearing into vapour.

'I am sure he understands it and you should not fear his opinion, but it has been a long night for him…' and Matthew threw his glance towards the group of men which was now breaking up for the night.

'Yes, I am sure it has. Wethers and weather. Timber and…'

'The timbre of his beloved's voice indeed. Poor James.'

He raised his glass to her, and she to him; they clinked and sipped. Fortunate that I do not have to concern myself with matters of marriage, thought Matthew Larkin.

Matthew Larkin knocked and stepped back from the tiny front door of the house of William Cawthorne. The place was as quaint as a doll's house, with two storeys that were bordered on one side by a grocer's storehouse and on the other by nothing but open land as yet unbuilt. The windows of the lower floor were frilled with white curtains showing a touch of domesticity, while those upstairs remained bare.

Presently the door opened and out came Cawthorne. He was dressed as he had been on the river two afternoons previous and on his face was a look that could have been concern and could have been annoyance.

'Ah, Mr Cawthorne,' said Matthew, not able to restrain himself from looking in as the door closed, but seeing nothing but a bare hallway without so much as a hook or a coat hanging there.

'You have an interest in my little schoolroom, Mr Larkin.' Cawthorne directed his glance to the open upstairs window. Clearly his friend had been waiting for him, and watching.

'Schoolroom?'

'Aye, sir. That is what keeps the two of us alive.'

'Ah, you have a wife, sir,' said Matthew, not able to keep all of the surprise out of his voice.

'A mother. She is unwell today, and I shall not bring you inside. Let us away. The natives will not postpone their little business for us.'

'I say, I am all aquiver,' said Matthew as they set off.

A cracking pace was established.

'An affray, between tribes, you say.'

'That is what we call them.'

'On this day.'

'We shall see what happens. There has been talking between parties the last two days. The men from the river have come and the Adelaide men want them not.'

'Will there be a crowd?'

'Ha!' Cawthorne threw his head back in sardonic amusement. 'There will be a crowd. Indeed, there will be a crowd.' And he laughed for his own amusement. 'There will be a crowd of two today.'

'Two?'

'Aye, sir. The two of us.'

'Will no one else wish to see such a sight?'

'The natives tell me what will happen, but no one else will know,' he said, stopping for a moment and turning to Matthew, as if to tell him something important. 'They visit my house. I teach them to speak in the English language.'

'Are they adept learners?'

'Their own language has more conjugations than Latin. Simple English is well within their grasp. The men and women both will learn.'

'The women too?'

'The women too. They walk alongside the men in all things. *Kumangka* – that is their term for it. In return for education, they allow me to paint their images on canvas, which is something they had never seen before the white man came, and which amuses them immensely. They give me gifts of spears and shields. I visit their camp.' He looked closely at Matthew and his voice lifted and strengthened. 'My person is vouched safe throughout their community.'

'And you alone in the colony are allowed to see their ceremonies and, and their affrays?'

'And now you,' Cawthorne said and quickened his pace again.

Matthew thought for a moment of the privilege that had been extended to him, to be only the second European to see these things. He was excited by the fortune which had befallen him and felt he was being rewarded for the venturesome spirit that was within him and which had made him walk off from his tedious copying at Government House, to see the natives in their home. His whole being was lifted; he nearly sang as they strode along.

To meet the place appointed for the affray, they walked away from

Adelaide along the rough and winding road to the Bay, upon which Matthew had made his arrival less than four weeks before. After two miles, they turned to the south on to an even meaner track, which was so rocky and uneven that it was quicker to traverse on foot than in a cart. A horse would have been useful but they had none and anyway a beast might disturb the natives and derange the purity of the affray that was before them.

The track presently meandered into nothing and they turned into an open field with acacia scrub, among which stood dark grey peppermint box trees, rough of bark and as high as a cricket pitch is long. There were Mallee box as well and everywhere grass trees which were called yakkas and which were best avoided because of their hard protruding flower spikes which could put out a man's eye if he was not careful. Black and white magpies warbled from their places in the branches and overhead flocks of Cape Barren geese passed in profusion and then, rushing in little gangs from tree to tree, were magnificently coloured parrots in red and green and blue and yellow which, when sighted on the wing and in a bunch, made the most pleasing sight, as did the pink and grey galahs which flew fearlessly across their track.

'You seem well pleased with the natives,' said Cawthorne. There was an upward inflection in his voice at the end of his sentence which made it more into a question that invited a response.

'Oh, indeed, sir. They are most extraordinary. I wish to learn so much more about them. I have watched them fashion weapons from wood, with their hands and what are seemingly the most ancient of tools.'

'Stone tools, sir, which they have used since time began and now detest.'

'Detest, sir?'

'It could be that I speak too strongly. They may seem untouched to you, these natives, but much has changed in the four or so years since the arrival of our good colonists.'

'Indeed?'

'You wish to learn of the natives?'

'Indeed.'

'You can accompany me on some of my forays and you will learn a great many things, if you've a mind.'

Matthew's whole being stood to attention at the word 'forays'. He had seen the blacks' camp from his tree stool, he had gone out on horse-back with the governor, but these adventures had been at a distance from the natives. With Cawthorne, any such sally would be different altogether. He was suddenly beset by the fear that had to come with true excitement, for to propose action that did not induce fear could never lead to real experience. And he was determined to plunge in to fear and to emerge on the other side.

'I would indeed like to learn and experience whatever there is to know,' he said, as cool as he could be.

'What age are you?' said Cawthorne, with what Matthew now saw as his accustomed bluntness.

'Three and twenty…almost.'

'You have the look of a barely bearded boy.' His comment was hard, just short of insulting.

Here was a man, Matthew thought, who certainly was not brought up learning the niceties of parlour conversation. 'And you, sir?' he replied, allowing himself to nibble at colonial directness.

'Ha,' cried Cawthorne, as if the question was a cause of some amuse-ment to him. 'I am six years your senior.'

He said this as if he knew something about himself, about the way in which others would see him, judge him. Matthew had gauged him approaching forty, he had hanging upon his youth such a weary and defeated air, as if experience and knowledge had forced themselves into his own unguarded heart without the payment of admittance fare.

'And what was it that caused you to come to this fair colony?' Matthew ventured further, seeing that Cawthorne had been plunged into thought by his first question; but he spoke with some wariness, for he knew now that the cause of Cawthorne's appearance in South Aus-tralia was neither of the two most likely – to own land or to work upon it.

'Ha!' he cried again, and the exclamation hung upon the air like an odour and seemed to echo as it drifted away with the warm breeze. Indeed, it seemed as if he were to give no answer to Matthew's question, so long did he delay in doing so. But then he said abruptly, as if on impulse, 'I was brought.' The three words were compressed together so they seemed as one, and his rasping of them was almost a thing of violence.

'I must confess, I came here of my own accord. To join my brother.'

Cawthorne stopped and addressed Larkin to his face. 'There is a brother? Of course, there would be a brother.'

'James, he is three years older than me.'

'He will have eased his way into the society of the colony without rent or seam, no doubt, without fuss or notice.' They began on their way again. 'Still, with a new ship in the bay each week with a dozen men of the superior class, it's little wonder we don't notice them all. Why, perhaps I took him for a non-conformist German with his prayer book in his pocket and a hankering for the hills!'

'I shall go forth to the German town this week, with the governor.'

'You will? A fair day's trot in the springtime sun. I wish you well. However, I shall remain in my attic hot box.'

He thought again for a moment and Matthew waited for him to go on, already noting that Cawthorne was of a disposition to take a minute to think his answers through, but that when he spoke, what he said would stick forever. But he remained deep in his thoughts.

After ten more minutes of walking, the trees thickened into the black forest of the plains, and Cawthorne's pace slowed and he began to talk, as if the forest held its own secrets and was therefore a safer place to open himself, away from the town.

'When the British peoples arrived in this place, dear Larkin, there was a fear and commotion among all about the natives. They were astounded to see the hills all alight with flames and smoke. It was as if the holocaust were to be rained upon them. It was nothing more than the native burning off to suppress the growth of trees and to create more grassland for their wildlife. But the goodly colonist saw this as a presage of evil. They had heard of the Indians of the Americas and knew that smoke signals meant a preparation for war.' He winked in a spirit of satirical correction. 'A stockpile of weapons was created and all were braced for attack, but of course the native was in the hills simply because that was part of their seasonal migratory pattern. They were only doing what they do *comme d'habitude*, as the French would say.'

'I say, do you speak French?'

'I can do many things, Matthew, but it is not the doing of things that forges one's way in the world, not even in the world of the colony.' He paused for a moment before he went on. 'I have heard that the world of the old country is far harsher when it comes to matters of class and privilege.'

'You say you have heard. If you were brought to this colony and have not knowledge of the old country, where have you been before?'

He hesitated once more before answering thoughtfully. 'I spent many years of my life in Africa, Matthew. I learnt the ways of the natives there, for my father was much away and I was left to my own course. When mother brought me to this country in search of my father, fear of the blacks did not exist for me. They are simply men, like others. They wish no harm if their bellies are full and they are not provoked.'

'But they are so different too.'

'I feel I shall be learning about them for the rest of my life.'

'And I,' said Matthew and from the corner of his eye he saw Cawthorne smile, a smile that was knowing, and genuine, somehow affectionate. His heart glowed to see it for, besides the needy remonstrations of Lucy Bray, this was the first smile or physical demonstration he had seen since arriving in the colony that was not of the hail fellow and well met type of ingratiation.

'So in that first year of the colony, the natives were in the hills, where they ought to be. And when the season turned, so I am told, they appeared one day, in their normal camp by the river, where you have seen them for yourself. When the time was right for moving, they simply walked down and set to collecting wood for their fires.'

Matthew looked to his right from a hillock they were surmounting and there was a lagoon of fresh water several feet deep and on it a flock of wild ducks and some black swans too, with their tails up and beaks probing beneath the surface for greenery. Pelicans sailed by in their never ending quest for small fish.

'And made access of all this,' Cawthorne waved to the lagoon, one of many that trickled down through reedbeds to the Patawalonga Creek near the Bay. 'Aye, and there is less of it now than there was even three years ago.'

'There is not game for all, white man and native alike?'

'Ha!' Cawthorne exclaimed again, then stopped and spat into some bushes on the side of the track. 'Sorry if I offend your breeding, sir, but I am the son of a sea captain and was brought to believe it better out than in.' He spat again, once more. 'You do not smoke a pipe, sir.'

'I have not yet commenced.'

'You may be better off to leave it aside.' Then he returned to the topic of his upbringing. 'If I was brought up at all, for to say that I had been would be to twist things into a nicety they did not deserve.'

'Your father a seaman, sir, just as mine.'

Cawthorne gave him a querulous look; above it was one arched eyebrow. 'Not just as yours, sir. By the time we arrived in this place, Father had deserted us again, for what clime we know not – could be Calcutta, or Shanghai, or any other port between. I feel within my bones that I shall not see him again.'

Matthew thought of the mother, imagined her sitting in the tiny parlour of that little house off Hindley Street, in the protection and care of her only son.

'He was a drunkard and a rogue, sir.' Cawthorne said these last few words as if they had been long ago learnt by him, and oft repeated. 'I am venturing, sir, that such a description would not aptly fit your own father.'

'Indeed, no. My father is a man of probity, almost excessively so. And most moderate in his ways. His grandfather was a Calvinist minister and a strain of moralism runs through the family.'

'Indeed! Well, if your father is in friendly acquaintanceship with Governor Bray, he would be well ranked in the British navy, I expect.'

'My father is an admiral, sir.'

'Huh!' and Cawthorne threw his head back in an exclamation that was more complex than the hilarity it pretended to be, and which then curled back inside a shell of bitterness and disdain.

'And I am the bookish wastrel of the family, with aberrant tastes in exotic things.'

Cawthorne regarded him now with added interest. 'You possess a decent turn of phrase, sir. I take my hat off to you. But I am sure Governor Bray will provide for you most handsomely.'

'I endure a position which is most tedious.'

'Yes, and from which position you will be closely watched, I am sure. But look, we are near.'

James Larkin came in from his day in the town and sank into the softest chair in the house. He had walked a mile around town to the bank and the office of the solicitor representing a Mr Rose, whose acreage near Strathalbyn was said to be for sale. Rose had summed him up and ummed and aahed and filibustered and brought his price down such a tiny amount that it was no more than a way of testing James's character and resolve.

He had to keep the cheerful voice in spite of what he felt. He was tired from his long and fruitless ride to inspect sandy and salty ground that was priced up to be premium, as if waiting for a newcomer to the colony to buy sight unseen. He had learnt that it was necessary to check every detail of every deal for the little deceptions and confidence tricks they might contain. It was a war of nerves and James had little taste for it. They were all watching to see how much these Larkins really had to spend, comparing notes at the end of the day, most likely. A ship had arrived at the Bay the day before and he had been to the post first thing to see if there was a letter for him but he was too early and the oxcart from the Bay had not arrived, and then on his return he was so absorbed with the hidden meanings in every word and inflection of Mr Rose that he had forgotten to go back. He cursed and rapped his knuckles on the side of the chair in frustration.

He reached for his pipe and lit up the half-filled half-burnt remnants of his morning smoke, then drifted into a daydream. In his reverie, Adela was there with him at the end of his day, her gentleness absorbing strain from him like blotting paper. After ten minutes, he noticed that his pipe had gone out again and he was about to make another curse when there was a quiet knock at the door and the maid came in.

'I looked in at the post this afternoon, Mr Larkin.' She held out a letter, sealed in Adela's red wax.

'Oh, Annie, you are a marvel.' James sat up sharply and took the letter from Annie and sliced through the seal as she quietly withdrew.

To My Dear James,

I do hope this letter finds you well and that your affairs in South Australia have reached a satisfactory conclusion. It is so desperately difficult to be here and you locked away there on the other side of the world and me with the knowledge that I shall never see you again unless I come.

The summer here is high and the streets are full of men and sweat and horses and of putrid, decayed smells of dung and rotted vegetables. The weather hangs hot and steamy over the city, so much so that the smells seem to be enclosed, as if all London is in a jar and the cloud bank that contains it seals the place as good as glass. Respectable women now consider their outings, lest it be to Hyde Park and to the open freshness that proximity to the lakes might bring. Only then would a walk through the streets be bearable. So strange to think that you are cool, cold even? and reaching for your coat and scarf. Somehow I feel there is a divorce of culture between us now and sometimes I fear I may never be cut out for colonial life, that you will be forever disappointed in me.

You write of summer temperatures of one hundred degrees. Others who have returned tell us of even higher. My dear James, it is eighty three here today and I am never detached from my fan. And out there women are chopping wood and cooking for their families through lack of servants, and digging pits for waste. Whatever else must women do in the colonies?

I will find it such a wrench to leave all here. You know who I mean, but my love for you remains strong, my dear. I must come to you soon. Papa's difficulties are almost managed here and the road seems clear ahead, but it is so difficult not knowing and, being a woman, not able to influence the course of things.

And so I leave you now,

Your loving wife to be,

Adela

It was the shortest letter James had ever received from Adela. He closed it over then twitched anxiously in his chair and unfolded it again. Her notices had on other occasions been gilded with her expressions of longing; always muted and refined, but unfailingly persistent and insistent. There had been no doubt of her intentions or at least of her desires. But now 'I will find it such a wrench to leave it all here.' Of course it would be a wrench for her. Taken literally, it was simply true; he had to see it that way. But why write that now when she had not made the point of saying it before? He tried to tell himself that this was simply a case of Adela revealing more of her inner thoughts and insecurities to him than she would normally – written on a day when the mood cut deeper, when the sultry cloud dome of London had driven her further. Her previous writing had him edged, but now this. He went over the words 'unless I come', as if there was now a doubt. He read again, 'I fear I may never be cut out for colonial life' and even 'divorce of culture'. Divorce? Then once again his eyes rested on 'I will find it such a wrench.'

James folded the letter and placed it in his desk drawer. He had read it five times over in half an hour and his mind had raced to the worst conclusions – enough! He must make even more strenuous efforts to conclude his business and then to send word of it. He must find land somewhere. Then there was Matthew and his interest in the native and their camp along the river. He knew that gossip was reported back to England with every ship, and he was responsible for Matthew for two years at least. The admiral would undoubtedly seek reports on the progress of the fourth Larkin. But he could not be doing what he had to do and be watching his brother every hour of the day.

Neither could he be left standing at the altar. He must compose a letter back at once to put Adela's mind at rest; he would tell her of the cooling breezes coming off the sea, the summer house he would build. He would tell of the near conclusion of his business, and of the shiploads of fine English lasses (mostly Irish but he would not say that) landing every week and pressing for positions in service. To hell with Rose and those who were holding out. He would buy fresh country, further out.

Adela could have boarded ship a week after that letter and be only a week away from him, or two, or three, depending on the winds. Or she might be in England still. And he must drink punch with the gentlemen, discuss timber and mining and property and troublesome blacks. He must bow to the ladies and, above all, he must report on the arrival of his fiancée, each question delivered with a raised and carping eyebrow.

Before them at two hundred yards there emerged a clearing so out of character with the forest around that it was a matter of amazement to Matthew. It was as large as the best cricket ground and surrounded on every side by trees, and covered with clumps of grass that would be a grazing animal's delight. On the edge of this space, a group of sixty or more native men were standing together and talking vehemently to each other. They were armed with shields and spears and their voices seemed to be rising in pitch; the clamour increased even in the two minutes or so it took Larkin and Cawthorne to walk up. More men were arriving, emerging from the forest, and their faces were so serious and full of intent that they made Matthew shiver for a moment.

Cawthorne held his hand up for them to slow their pace, then stopped to think for a moment. 'Through here,' he said, and quickly plunged back into the trees to skirt around to the other end of the clearing.

The going was not difficult as the trees were never close together and they needed only to avoid low-hanging branches as there was little undergrowth that could snag their boots. The sun came through the light foliage in a pleasing way and their walk was not unpleasant.

Soon, the clearing became apparent once more and there was another group of men sitting together calmly with their shields and spears. Some of them Matthew recognised as men he had seen at the river camp. Cawthorne approached them at once, with Matthew a few steps behind.

And then something happened which took Matthew by complete surprise and which helped to galvanise him in the course that he would take in life. Cawthorne began to engage the Kaurna men in conversation in their native tongue. This feat astounded Matthew, so little had he expected it. He had heard the natives speak a few words of simple English, but here was Cawthorne conversing on the most serious of subjects! Matthew was filled with admiration of his skill. Here was a man who had indeed grasped the challenge of the colony, who was a natural learning person not self-satisfied with his own rudimentary culture, talking to the natives in the black forest on the plains of Adelaide in their own language! The prospect had not occurred to Matthew before, but if Cawthorne could do it, then surely he might learn as well.

When he returned, Cawthorne was excited. 'Let's be taking the shelter of that tree,' he said, and directed them straightaway to a stout gum which made for an easy climb.

No sooner were they settled in their place than the group of shouting blacks they had avoided on their arrival drew together in a kind of broken, irregular line about one hundred yards away and facing the group of sitting men. They began to advance, making warlike motions of throwing and clubbing as they moved, and contriving truculent faces as if a full-scale battle were already in progress and real assailants were before them.

At this time, the group of sitting men stood up to face them. Then all at once the shouting men ran forward, their spears were elevated and their shields clattered together and then they halted in a bunch before the other group and began to make the wildest antics. They crouched, then jumped into the air, they growled and screeched, they shook their weapons, their eyes bulging, their tongues hanging out. Then of a sudden their spears were elevated together and they grouped themselves in a sort of phalanx of the kind Matthew had read about in Spartan or Roman history. The shields were then all raised above their heads in a tortoiseshell effect and then they crouched together and a deathly silence fell upon the whole clearing of the most eerie kind as there was close to one hundred men and not a sound to be heard. Then this break of silence was followed as if from nowhere by a sound not unlike the explosion of a small military shell, but they had no military shell: the sound was the collected wind of each of sixty warriors drawn in and expelled together. They did this six or seven times, then at the last explosion they all dispersed.

Mathew was astounded to see them gather up their shields and spears and turn their backs on the watching group then return to the place from which they had come. At no moment had the standing group, whose men he had recognised, made a move to their spears and shields.

'And that,' said Cawthorne quietly, 'is our little show for today.'

The whole thing had taken only fifteen minutes to conclude, but was transfixing throughout. Every second, Matthew had expected a volley of spears to be hurled from the advancing group upon the other, with screams and bloodshed ensuing. But the affray, if that is what it was to be called, had ended with an astonishing abruptness and he was climbing down from the tree with an incomplete feeling, as if he had been cheated of some elemental experience. He felt as one did when tossed upon the seas in a small ship; a realisation that powers above were at play, and that human interest was nothing. But here the calm that comes after the storm was curiously unwelcome.

'But why did they stop? What caused them to regale themselves so fierce and then to turn away? I have never seen the like.'

'They had made their point.'

Matthew waited for him to go on.

'The river men had staked a claim by their performance, signalled their intent to remain.'

'River men?'

'From the country at the back of the ranges that goes down to the river and the lakes. They have come down here for a very special purpose, and that is to initiate their boys on this land, the land of the plains people – my friends, your friends – those they call the Kaurna.'

'The experience did not appear to have provoked enjoyment among the plainsmen.'

'It did not. They are very displeased. To come armed and unwelcomed into the territory of another tribe is very serious. It is, in fact, unheard of.'

'Why do they not do it near the river, on their own territory?'

'Ah, can you not guess why they are here. Matthew?'

He remained silent.

'It is because of you.'

'Me?'

'You and your like. Our like. Did you not see two days ago that pair of Kaurna men, fashioning out of wood their curved throwing stick.'

'I did, and speedy work they made of it too.'

'Aye, sir, with a metal hatchet that fairly glinted in the sun if I do properly recall the words you used to describe it to me.'

He recalled it well.

'A white man's tomahawk gained in exchange for services rendered: carrying goods, chopping wood and whatever it is that the white man wants. Anything made of metal or of glass is the highest prize to them. What would the natives not do to obtain a metal axe? Can you imagine the hours of labour entailed in cutting a boomerang with an axe of stone. Or the infinite hours of grinding stone on stone to fashion the axe itself. No, the white man's axes and tomahawks are very superior to their own. Do you think these river men do not want them? Why, to cut an opossum from a hollowed tree with a metal tomahawk is the work of a moment, sir.' He threw his hands up in excitement.

'I should say so. But glass?'

'Indeed, sir, to be cut into spear tips. I would not want one of those stuck in my leg, I can tell you now. And tobacco. They love to make mimicry of the white man and all his ways, with pipe and smoke no less, poor devils.'

'And if they have it, the river men want it.'

'And if the river men initiate their boys on this patch of land, that gives those men and possibly their close relations the right to hunt on this patch of land. And to hunt means to gather too, and to gather means to trade for goods with the white man, and if that means to be of service to the white man, then so be it.'

'They are fighting over us!'

'Matthew, sir,' and Cawthorne laid his hand gently on Matthew's shoulder as they walked, 'they are fighting over us.'


'Some of these expenditure savings may seem meagre, Thompson, but it is important that I am seen to be steeling my own administration the same as the rest of the colony.'

Thompson was silent, his head poised over a column of ledger entries. The morning had been chilly and they were working in overcoats and scarves, but now a light breeze zephyred its way through the window with the ten o'clock sun, and they eased their garments and were moved to optimism. From eighty yards away came the chinking chiselling of masons working on stone, then a muffled cry of satisfaction from a group of workmen as a block was lifted into the structure of the new wing of Government House. Both men stopped for a moment to listen, gauging even from this distance the pleasure that the achievement was producing in the common men who worked for them.

'We are not here to replicate the old society, Thompson…'

'No, sir.'

'…but to encourage one of independent individuals whose actions are based on rational principles.'

'Indeed, sir.'

'We are here to model consistency in our dealings with the blacks. They are citizens under British law. We must not allow the roughhouse treatment that has been seen in the other colonies. But there is wildness in the air, Thompson. I can feel it – discontent about the place.'

Thompson remained silent.

'Too many men waiting to get out onto their properties, and their labourers lagging about in the town becoming soft and taking to drink. And within this atmosphere we must make economies to restore the colony's finances and create some sense of discipline. We need to make a place where people, like you and me, can rise through their own brains and effort, eh.'

Thompson inclined his head but remained silent through modesty.

'However, a fine new Government House will give confidence to the whole colony. It will be a symbol of order. And the prestige of our offices…' Here the governor faltered for a moment.

'Is already increased, sir.' Thompson found the new building a safer vehicle for the expression of his acquiescence than the question of the blacks. 'A stone Government House will be a great boon for the summer, sir. There comes a heat unlike that of the old country.'

'But not unlike Lisbon or Rio, or any number of places up the east coast of Africa. Still, yes, the stone house will be welcome, but we must pay for it. So…' and he motioned a hand towards Thompson's ledger, 'how has the news of savings been greeted, Thompson?'

'Ah, well, sir.' Thompson fumbled for words. He had been charged with reporting back on the reception of the governor's austerity measures, but was still uncertain what the governor wanted to hear. For his part the governor was a realist; he wanted to hear the truth.

'Out with it, man. I am hardly expecting unbridled joy.'

'Yes, sir.'

The governor watched Thompson as he arranged his papers – a steady man, even sanguine, and careful, understated; but he was unaccustomed to making this kind of report, which included judgements on the character of individual colonists. Larkin, on the other hand, thought the governor, would have produced casually acerbic insights, which would probably have been brilliantly accurate, but his figures would likely have been in a muddle. If only he could smash their two heads together, he might come up with one truly useful officer. Governor material even, he now thought wryly.

'Something amuses you, sir?' Thompson had noticed the smile that played upon the governor's lips.

'Nothing, Thompson. A private thought. Proceed with your report.'

Thompson took a deep breath. 'Wilkins the surveyor is unhappy, sir. He claims that the rate of work should be increased rather than reduced, as should his rate of pay and allowances.'

'You made it clear that these were temporary measures?'

'I did. I also pointed to the backlog of reports already here for copying.'

'His response?'

'Ah, it would be fair to say that he grunted, sir.'

'I will take that as assent. Jeffers?'

'Surprisingly, he took it quietly.'

'Humph. I spoke to him myself.'

'Ah! There is some grumbling in the office, sir.' Thompson took another deep breath and ploughed on. 'To disallow two shillings and sixpence for a pane of glass in an office window, eightpence to an office boy for spilt ink, and to ban the provision of mustard with corned beef sandwiches was, well, surprising to some.'

'The example must be set at the most mundane level.'

'But there is great approval of your masterstroke with the police force. Even some amusement, sir, I might say.'

Bray had borrowed troops from Sydney on a pretext, promising to send men back in any future time of rebellion or other pressing need; this done, he postponed an increase to his own police force and made a significant saving.

'The soldiers themselves seem to have enjoyed their change of scene and have happily returned the vast majority of their wages into the local economy.'

'Ah, yes. I hear Mr Farrell's Chop House does well.'

'Indeed, sir. The last point I would make is that, ah, some are pointing to the wages of…of Mr Larkin.'

'Tell the surveyors and grumblers that Mr Larkin is gainfully employed to reduce the backlog of reports which have been incurred by the previous over expenditure on their own labours. Mr Larkin will be discharged in due time.'

'When the family property is secured?' Larkin was said to be moving out on to the land, but he spoke little about it. Thompson could not restrain himself from hinting for information.

'Exactly.' The governor gave little in return; Thompson would be rid of Larkin before long.

'Ah,' said Thompson as he nodded, trying not to be obvious about his own interest in Mr Larkin's departure.

For his part, Governor Bray could not but note the man's ambition; the more he tried to conceal it, the more it was obvious.

And so the stories of the reductions in expenditure in the governor's own office, with the exception of the wages of Mr Larkin, were spread about and it was agreed that at least what was good for the goose was good for the gander too and that Bray had set a stern example for others to follow. Bray suspended work on some of Adelaide's public buildings, but completion of the new stone Government House was to go on as previously planned, and the colony was as one behind this project. The honour and prestige of Her Majesty's representative was of high importance; and if the Duke of Kent or some other member of the royal family were to visit, what then? Could they really be welcomed into a timber and mud hut?

But the final problem now was with the labourers. The bush needed to be populated, so once a few of the best workers had been retained for the Government House job, he reduced the poor relief. Some had left the town already but some stayed behind to grumble that there was not enough work in the farms to furnish themselves with an excuse for staying put. But the issue of land price remained.

'If I could set the price of land so the early buyers got a fair profit and a fair profit only, we would have the men out felling trees and running sheep and the town's layabouts would follow them into shepherding jobs. There would be money made, there would be receipts to the colony's coffers, the world would begin turning again.'

There had always been arguments between colonists. What an uncertain business it was to join a colony. The debates before his arrival had been endless: whether to set out to prospect for minerals; whether to bring sheep on ship from Van Diemen's Land or to run them overland from New South Wales; whether to cut down certain timbers as an export crop.

Some of the settlers were for the protection of the Aborigines; many were against it. Alfred Bray had explored the north-west coast of Australia; he had contacted the natives there, and had even composed a dictionary of their language. He had sympathy for the native. The government in England had not allowed the colony to go ahead unless the natives were made citizens, and a protector had to be appointed. Colonel Torrens and the settlers had lobbied against the arrangement, but in the Colonial Office, Lord Glenelg had not budged. So the divisions continued. In the first year, there had been fights in the street, civilised men rolling up sleeves and setting to. And now the Tories had returned to power, those for extermination were walking with a spring in their step.

Thank God the Germans were no trouble. They thought it was heaven that they were able to worship as they wished without a rifle butt thrown in their faces.

'We are to visit the German town of Klemzig on Thursday, Thompson.'

'We, sir?'

Lucy had been plaguing him with requests to go to the German town with him. She could ride with the best of them and was bursting to see the colony. But what could happen in the bush was unthinkable. There were reports that bushrangers from New South Wales had moved across to escape the pursuit of police. Six months ago, a fellow called Moran had been sighted in the street and was recognised on account of his huge red beard. On being challenged, he had shrieked maniacally and leapt upon his horse, fired his pistol over the heads of the citizens and raced away for the cover of the hills where to all knowledge he remained.

Klemzig was four miles out of the town, towards the hills – indeed, the terrain did begin to rise at the beginning of their township and two miles further onwards, the ascent became more pronounced until the road gave way to fertile slopes and rocky gullies. But the visit would be safe enough and he had decided that Lucy could come.

Bray stepped over to the window and breathed in the clear air that came to him from the bay, from the sea. He stood for a moment gazing over a space that sloped down towards the river and had been cleared of trees to be the colony's first meeting place. Beyond that, ghostly gums shrouded the bend the little stream made to the north and out of view. As his eyes played over the scene, a figure emerged from the distant trees – the white breeches and light boots and the mustard-coloured shirt of Larkin. Larkin out awalking once more.

'Yes, Thompson, we. I have decided that you will accompany me to Klemzig this week.'

'Very good, sir.'

'Mr Larkin will stay behind. If any visitor comes on the day, Larkin can charm them for a few hours. That is something he can do.'

'Indeed he can, sir. In fact…'

The governor waved his hand for silence; he needed to be told nothing about Mr Larkin's strengths or shortcomings. 'I will need good notes. You will take them. And you will not quote poetry to Miss Lucy, or to me, at the blueness of the hills or over the dappled sunlight shimmering through the trees.'

'Indeed I will not, sir.'

'Excellent, then let us hope for a trouble-free trip to the German town.'

'Exactly, sir.'

*She slipped her feet out of the covers and hunched her nightdress against the cold. At the window, her eyes strained to the east for the first light from beyond the hills. There was no lock on her door; there was no sentry at the gate. The northern track went all the way there, where no woman had ever ridden alone.*

*The carrier had said…but what had he said? Both too much and not enough – repeating the talk of men in a bushland pub with nothing in their minds but beer and sherry and a storied take on the business of others. Whatever was the job ahead of her, it was not a job for a girl.*

*She took the dressmaking scissors from her drawer and hacked six inches from her hair. Three great clods of it caressed the floor. And another. She snipped roughly around her ears and at the back; then she dressed quickly in her roughest clothes. From a distance, she might seem like an enterprising lad and could be greeted along the way. She would raise her hand and give a merry shout like, say, Viola in Twelfth Night, off on an adventure.*

*She folded a dress into a saddlebag with some undergarments and then a huge chunk of bread and a thick slice of beef from the kitchen. That would do for a day. Her horse greeted her happily; she patted him and talked and pressed her face against his. She climbed up and they walked out into the yard. The first rays of dawn came through the line of gums. They turned right into King William Road; she was outside the fence now. Knee deep through the little river, then they climbed the hill to North Adelaide and she sat her horse and turned. The sun was sending out its first streams of real light and she could see all the way to Hindley Street. The baker's boy was stacking loaves into the tray of his master's cart. In places, chimneys still smoked. Some lights were being put out that had been made against the dark and cold of night.*

*She sat and watched the little town awake until there was light enough to pick her way along O'Connell Street with all its potholes that appeared each time it rained.*

*A draper with a bunch of keys opened up his store. He returned her wave with a salute that was both friendly and disinterested.*

*'Ha,' she sang out loud. Her heart exulted and she shook the reins and dug her heels and her horse responded as if waiting just for that to be her command. They cantered out to the end of O'Connell Street where the houses thinned and with the sun now bright upon her, she galloped for half a mile, just for the joy of being out, for the sun, for the day, for the adventure, and for the resolution of her doubts and fears that she would secure before two days were out.*

# 3

## The North – October 1843

Soon, they found sheep tracks and followed them; their hoof prints were plain enough and grass and small bushes were still trampled low from where the beasts had passed. After half an hour of trotting, James swept his hand out sharply to his right and the procession stopped at once. There was a waft on the air of mutton cooked upon an open fire. They could detect no sentry or lookout. They walked their horses slow and close to a place where they could see, not a hundred yards away, a dozen natives in a clearing at a campfire, feasting on new-cooked lamb. The smell of roasted leg straight off the fire enraged them all the more.

Phillips raised his arm to signal the charge, but as he did, Matthew walked his horse beside him and spoke.

'There is something awkward here. There is no sentry and they dine on meat in the middle of the day. It is unusual.'

'You would tell us not to attack?'

Matthew faltered for a moment, Phillips's furious face before him.

'We have come this far, we will not leave without a lesson being taught.'

The constable pursed his lips and nodded assent and without further discussion, Phillips cried out 'Now,' and they whipped their horses up and charged.

At the sight of the white men on horseback, the native bunch made a great noise, a general yelling and clapping of hands as made a most confusing atmosphere, and bounded into the bush; all in one direction they went with the riders in hot pursuit, drawing their pistols as they went.

They rode through a passage in the trees which was surprisingly open, there being space sufficient to drive a horse and carriage through if they had one. There was no need to duck under boughs but rough twigs from the ends of the branches scratched at Matthew's face, and he welcomed it. The prospect of some wound suffered in the cause did excite him and spurred him further – a scar to be bathed by the other men, to be worn. He dug his heels into his mount in order not to fall behind. The excitement of the chase was in him now that wiser heads had spoken and the hunt was on.

The first shot rang out and all the riders on the front horses began to fire. But as soon as they did, they came into an open place and there suddenly from out of the forest appeared a mass of natives, perhaps thirty or forty more of them, all painted up like skeletons with bold white brushstrokes upon their limbs. Phillips gave the order for all to fire and Matthew shot one of them through the head and he fell directly to the ground without ceremony. Matthew saw not only the wound in the native man's forehead above the left eye, but he believed that he could hear the noise of bullet hitting bone, and the crunching sound it made was like the hammer at slaughter yards, savagery itself. He could not tear his eyes away as the bone heaved off and a handful of brains was sloshed out and mingled with the dust as the native man crashed on the ground.

The sound of gunfire now was all around and the firing came like an endless round of cannon in his head, like nothing he had ever heard. He shot two times quite quickly but his efforts rang ineffectually into the forest around them.

Phillips drew up next to him and shouted fiercely, 'Take aim, you fool,' his face fierce and contemptuous.

A spear came from a man ten yards away and passed between them and stuck in a tree. Matthew watched the man as he made to pick up another dart off the ground. As he stood up with it, Matthew took aim and fired again. This time the shot went through his chest and the man went down, straight to earth as if he were a log sawn from a tree.

Matthew turned quickly to Phillips but he was firing steadily, his eyes looking about carefully for natives and spears.

The more experienced of them had fully expected the natives to flee when the first couple of them fell; it was perceived that the natives would throw their spears only to prove their manly temper and then would run away. But their experiences of other natives meant for little, as this lot stood their ground and set to hurling spear after spear, armed as if they had been well prepared for that affray, as if the ancestors had ordained that this was a day of reckoning for their intruder and his horses and sheep and oxen. The horses were frightened with the noise, and with the natives themselves being painted up like skeletons, they did appear the harbinger of death itself.

Among the dust and clamour, the whinnying and the explosions, Phillips's son took a spear and fell. Another spear then clattered off the helmet of the constable and fell before Matthew's horse, which reared up and whinnied for all its might. Matthew took aim and shot at another black man; the bullet passed through the bottom of his throat and Matthew saw the man stop in his action of throwing a spear and a trickle of blood ran down his chest and he fell, clutching at his wound. Matthew watched the man go down, and he was enthralled by the brief and spasmodic writhing which he enacted, before lying still with his hand to his throat and with his bug-eyes fixed on Matthew's.

In that moment of his fascination with the throes of death, Matthew presented a still target which attracted the attention of a black man who stepped forward and threw his spear. From the corner of his eye, he saw the throwing act but it was too late for him to turn and fire. The spear entered the bottom of his left shoulder above the armpit and the sharpest pain passed in a wretched spasm through him. He could not move that arm. His face was wrung in a piteous grimace and he teetered on the edge of falling. He struggled hard to ride but the weight of the handle end of the spear was such that it pulled him forwards in the saddle and threatened to dig into the ground. He would have fallen from his mount, but James rode up to him and the other men surrounded them, firing to keep the natives at bay. James leant across and snapped the spear three inches from Matthew's shoulder.

Presently the firing stopped and the smoke cleared in that fateful place and there were no more natives except for the dozen or fifteen who lay upon the ground dead or in various ways of dying. Three men were perceived howling and teetering into the bush, two of them holding an arm up in an apparent effort to staunch wounds to their chests, the third was limping heavily on his left leg and he stopped in his flight to collect from the ground a fallen branch and then to stagger three-legged into the trees. Two or three were writhing on the ground and trying to stand. They left them as they were, not wishing to waste another round on them, and gazed around the sorry sight. Many sheep had charged off into a clearing, scattered, but were there for the rounding and herding still; they would get back much of what had been lost.

Matthew could see Phillips ten yards away, crouched over the body of his son, on one knee, holding up a pannikin of water in the futile and deluded attempt to revive him.

They pulled Matthew from his horse and sat him beneath a tree. The spear was removed and the men began the job of cleaning and bandaging him as best as could be managed. The spear lay by his side half-covered in blood and gore.

'Show it to me,' he said to James.

'Steady now,' James replied and poured brandy onto the wound.

'No, I want to see.'

James wiped the spear end on a corner of his own reddened shirt, then placed it in Mathew's right palm. The constable from Clare squatted to look as well.

Matthew stared dumbly at the sharpened stick while the bandage was applied to his shoulder. 'It is made of wood, James.'

'Sharpened on a stone,' the constable interposed.

The effort required to speak was great and with his good arm Matthew slowly extracted a paper package from the fob pocket of his trousers. He passed it to the constable, who loosened the folds and drew out an object shaped like a three-barbed miniature harpoon, made not of metal or wood, but of glass. James, Matthew and the constable now were all struck by the extraordinary precision and delicacy with which the three barbs were cut. It could have been presented as a work of art, an exhibit in some gallery, it was so fine. Matthew held it up so the light could catch it in different ways and he turned it over and over to inspect it, as if the magic that poured from it could flow in his fingertips and up his arm and throughout his person to cure his wound.

'You have never shown me this,' said James. He had heard of these things around the town of Adelaide. A native spearhead made of glass, the white man's material brought from the other side of the world, salvaged by the native. To them it was like gold.

'When I was with Cawthorne…' He wanted to tell the story of the day he found the glass harpoon, but he began to feel weak; the reflected light from its barbs stunned him. The truth of death was too mad to be intelligible to humans. The harpoon: the native work, the white man's glass – the paradox of juxtaposition. Life and death were at once more simple and too complex to be understood, and what we are told is but a shadow of life, as in Plato's allegory of the cave which Cawthorne had told him: where simple people see shadows on a wall and think it is life, but the truth is that they live deluded, without the courage to turn and look into the light. And the glass harpoon now, in a way he could not yet grasp, it was the light.

In the affrays between tribes that he had witnessed with Cawthorne, the natives took the death of an enemy to be a kind of wrong, a final reluctant solution. He wanted to reconcile ideas and events, but the effort clouded his mind; all he could see was the native man's head blown away, the ooze of grey brains. He closed his eyes for a moment and laid his head on a rolled-up shirt that James placed behind him.

After ten minutes, Matthew Larkin awoke from his swoon and looked around him at the scene. The native men who had been trying to arise now lay still. Phillips's son had been removed from the pitiful tableau, and Phillips with him. James was there with water and

Matthew took a sip then waved him away. The others had gone into the bush in search of sheep. Dead natives were on the ground and the same black birds that had an hour before been attending to the gizzards of Field the Overlander now circled above and cried out their claim.

Matthew started up, as if to rise. But the effort made him dizzy. James rushed to help him back down in his place. What was death? Keats had written of it through some narcotic dream. But that was in another place – not here.

The eastern rise of the valley was mantled with boulders where the hills levelled out and resolved themselves into the alluvial matter of the fertile valley. Whenever a deputation was sent to the Larkin homestead, the native men who came would clamber down that way, jumping barefoot from one boulder to another, almost as if the point was to demonstrate their keen ability.

But the figures that came down from the hills that day did not negotiate the rocks. Instead, they made their way along the steady incline that bent around behind the stones and then led back through the valley from the north. Once on level ground, the five or six of them turned south-west again and headed in a direct line to the Larkin homestead. It was morning, early, and only three days since the Larkins had moved one hundred yards up out of their hut to the first rooms of their stone house.

The sighting of a band of natives making for the Lingalee was always a matter of high importance. The brothers were still uncertain what was in the minds of those they had pushed out into the hills. In the first week of their arrival, a group of settlers had gone out on horses and distant gunfire was heard in the southern hills. Their neighbour Phillips had told them that punitive measures had been needed over a question of persistent pilfering. He had left the Larkins with the air of a man whose mission had been to deliver a message, that the example set would be continued, and with the strong implication that they would be required to participate in future events. Since that time, some of the natives had come down in twos and threes to do odd jobs for them but had disappeared within a few days. There had been campfire parleys among the blacks and disagreements voiced. The lawman Winnaraburra was against fraternisation with the white man. And now there were figures coming from the hills.

Matthew stepped down from their veranda and out to the edge of their home paddock, the better to see. His wound was healing but he left the house only for walks, in the middle of the day. His sleep was troubled by visions of the engagement out on the river. The native man, his grey brains seeping into the red dust. And he, Matthew, like a statue, unable to take his eyes away. Phillips, cursing him. Phillips with his speared son. The cavernous sockets of the eyes of Field the Overlander, pecked by crows. The dead native man and his seeping brains again, and again, and again. When he closed his eyes at night, it was there; when he opened them three hours later, it was there, haunting his dreams.

In the mornings, he was weary and still weak. James watched him and told him not to work – best to keep away, for now. But there was little diversion in the homestead, so when a group of figures came from the hills, it was an occurrence of great moment. And now, as they came closer, he could see that the first figure among them was a woman. Her short hair had been cut away from her face as if with scissors. She wore a Western man's white shirt, much too big for her, probably traded for work with some other settler's wife. Her small breasts sat high in her shirt and she walked with a languid elegance. Flanking her and a step behind were two more, the same height but with faces flatter and broader, then three boys – two of them walking, the elder of the two about seven or eight, and a little one piggybacked on the shoulders of the second of the girls. They had seen the leading girl before; she was called Grace. Perhaps someone in the valley had given her the name because of the bearing that she had. The Larkins had not asked. She had done odd jobs around the place for two days once before; she had been shown how to wash a sheet and sweep a room. She had caught on quickly to all instructions. On the morning of the third day, Winnaraburra had come, his white hair streaming and a peg through his nose. Grace had left with him and they saw no more of her.

But now she was stepping purposefully across the valley with a band of followers behind her. She walked straight across the stream, then back up towards the homestead and made directly for the vacant hut.

'Aaaah,' the men exhaled.

Now the Larkins saw something of the girl's purpose. There was an assurance about her that made them watch her take possession of the hut.

Matthew carefully swung his arms above his head and back down by his side for ten minutes in the exercises that Dr Tibbs from Clare had told him to perform each day, and he kept an eye on the hut as he did so, then went inside to cook some bacon. After fifteen minutes, Grace emerged, having installed her family, and walked up to the house. They heard her bare feet soft on the new sawn boards of the veranda and turned to see her standing at the door.

'I work now,' she said, and the Larkin brothers looked at each other.

Matthew nodded assent to James. 'We could use her,' said Matthew. 'If it means I don't have to wash the sheets on Saturdays.'

The eldest boy could already catch small goannas and knock birds out of the trees with stones. Soon he would be going after larger game. They would be no trouble, was Matthew's advice to James, and lizard meat was a delicacy. Grace's large brown eyes went from brother to brother, one doubtful, one sympathetic.

'Hmmm,' James murmured, asking himself whether any other homestead in the valley came with a native family attached.

'Very well,' he said, if only to break the silence and the stares of the other two. 'We will give it a week.'

She did not understand all of the English words, but there was no doubting James's tone. Grace nodded her thanks to Matthew and showed a full mouth of white teeth as she smiled.

Matthew woke in the night and sat up sharply. His hand thrust out in a deranged and urgent manner for his rifle or a knife, but could find only soft and pliant things – blanket and sheet.

He had dreamed he was back at the river, in the hands of his brother, with his rifle by his side. But in his hand was the glass harpoon. He stared at its brilliant chiselled tines, sharper even than they had been in life. He closed his fingers around it until his skin was punctured and blood was drawn.

And Phillips was there again, with his boy slumped in his arms. He wanted to reach out to Phillips, to be in touch with him, to share. He had thought of Phillips's wife at home, waiting. And the son, the other one – George, waiting for his brother.

But then Phillips dropped his son to the ground and came over to him with a furious face and screamed, 'Take aim, you fool,' then stormed over to the dead native lying on the ground. 'Like this,' he cried. And Phillips picked the dead man up from the waist and shook him like a bottle of sauce but what glugged out onto the pie of dirt was grey brains making a porridge of the soil; and the dead man's eyes still open, as if still living and all-seeing. 'Like this, you see,' cried Phillips. 'Hahaha.'

The man was maniacal and it was that which made Matthew jump up in the night to grab for his rifle to shoot the eyes out of that black man in his desperate shame so that the man would never see, never ever see Matthew again.

But there was no rifle, no black man, no crazed Phillips. There was only silence and absence, cold grey sheets: no mother, no James, no Lucy Bray, just the cold clear night of perverted ideology and murderous intent. Matthew strained his ears for a sound, but there was nothing but the rustling of a breeze in the trees.

It was needed, so it was said, to clean out the rebellious ones, the thieves, those who would make war. It was no place for a woman the way it was. Not for Adela Peake, not for Lucy Bray. So the story went; and it was their story, his story, it was the story made for all of them equally, him too.

Inexorably for him too.

Three days after their arrival, the native girls sat outside the hut and waited.

The morning before, there had been a single column of fire smoke from the hills across the valley from the Larkin homestead. It was the signal of arrival and possession; the message was to wait and watch.

Grace stepped forward from the hut and bade the children go foraging with her cousins.

Fifteen minutes later, a second column of smoke had followed; it was a firm invitation to visit. It was directed at Grace, for she was in charge of the other girls and the three little boys they had taken with them.

She too had sat up suddenly in the night and strained her ears for sound. She heard the gully breeze as well, then checked her two cousins and the boys sleeping. She had known then that she would be called on the coming day. She was working for the white man and that alone was enough to trouble her and all who knew her. It could make her wake and doubt herself and the decision she had made. But she had seen the conflict that had occurred already and the boys in her charge were without fathers. The dictate of Winnaraburra was that they would be raised by all those who were left. But for how long would they be left?

In the morning, there were once more two columns of smoke in the hills, but still she stayed in her bark hut beside the white man's house. Grace had trembled within herself. Then, as the sun reached its noon place at the centre of the sky, there came a third column, thicker and darker than the other two. It was the most imperative message in the language of smoke – get here!

The afternoon passed and she did not move. The shadows lengthened and the smoke faded from the sky and still she remained at the white man's place. She slept little again the next night, waking often to listen. It would be beneath the dignity of the lawman to come for her at night, she knew this, but still there was no rest.

Then, a little time after the sun became clear in the sky above the eastern hills, two figures were seen hopping like kangaroos down the boulder-strewn hills. From nearly a mile away, the white beard of Winnaraburra was distinct against the sandy grey stone and his own dark, leathered skin. The two men made their way steadily across the valley floor and back up towards the hut, each of them holding a single spear vertical in their right hands; a five-inch peg of wood had been inserted in the cartilage under Winnaraburra's nose. String-tied loincloths covered both the men. Grace moved from the shadow of the hut out into the sun to meet them, her two cousins standing behind her, the boys in the hut as quiet as they could be.

And when they arrived, there was no courtesy from the men. The prating from Winnaraburra began as soon as he was within the distance over which he could throw his voice, and did not cease for ten minutes. His angered high-pitched hollering was so pronounced that all within the house were disturbed by it. James Larkin heard the ruckus from a far paddock and came up to the house.

Winnaraburra had been to the homestead twice before, but this was the most lengthy and forthright speech he had ever delivered. As he spoke, his arms flew up suddenly, like a starling frightened from its nest and taking urgently to flight. Twice he waved his arms toward the hills and Matthew was in no doubt as to the meaning: the girls and their children should return with him to the tribe.

After some minutes, the verbal assault ceased and Matthew could hear nothing, but could see Grace's head bowed as if gazing at the ground before Winnaraburra's feet. Grace was speaking in her low and quiet manner, but out of earshot for him. The other girls stood behind her silently and from the children there was no sound or motion in the hut; for it was really they that this conversation was about. The little boys belonged with the women, but the women should return them to the camp so their education could continue for years until their initiation.

Grace must have finished her say, for Winnaraburra began to speak again, his voice raised higher this time, angry. He shook his fist and the spear that was in it. Then he looked up to the house as if to make his point by asserting himself in the presence of this alien structure of brick and wood and by railing at it. And there he saw Matthew, standing in the doorway, leaning into the woodwork. Winnaraburra's voice rose to one last shout. Grace spoke quietly again and would not move. She had seen for herself the contest between guns and spears. It was her duty to protect the boys in her charge and also her cousins and she would not allow them to share the fate of so many of her tribe that she had seen reduced so painfully and piteously.

This was what she told old Winnaraburra the lawman, and it was a terrible affront to the dignity of his office. As he stood in the very shadows of the Lingalee, his only choice was to deal violence there and then upon the girls and to take the boys away by force, or to turn away and fight for them in another way. But for him to violate the person of Grace or the other girls in any way would have been to make another greater slur upon himself. And so, abruptly, Winnaraburra turned and walked briskly away, his apprentice close behind.

Grace looked up to the house and saw Matthew there. Their eyes met for a moment, then Grace turned into the hut to console the children, frightened as they were by the antics of the old lawman. But it was not Winnaraburra alone that they feared; consternation had already been caused by the fate of their disappearing tribe, by their precarious place in the Larkin homestead and by the fragmentation of certainty itself.

Matthew was out walking, to regain his strength.

'Rest to recover,' was what that Dr Tibbs from Clare had suggested. 'I will be back in a week. If the pain persists through that time, I may prescribe a new medicine, made of poppy seed. For the moment, I am giving it a trial on myself, for a few of my own aches and pains.' So he said seriously, then he brightened. 'But you are young and fit, not like me, ha ha. As long as things are well, in here…' and the doctor pointed to his own head and pursed his lips and narrowed his eyes.

Tibbs had seen Matthew often enough in the two taverns in the town of Clare. It was a long way for a young man to come for a drink. Some men drink to enjoy, he had thought, others drink for reasons that are more complex. He himself had found release in alcohol at a very early age, to give him confidence that he lacked and to cloud over his natural misanthropy. He had grown up with a saturnine distrust of people and, while this had sat awkwardly on the profession that he found himself in, he had turned it to a kind of profit by passing on tidbits of information about those he tended to. As a medical man, his credibility in the valley was high and his audience was generally receptive. It was a chancy hobby to practise and once or twice he had been confronted in his rooms by indignant victims, but out here his patients seemed more eager for news than any. While Matthew seemed to have no need or interest in gossip (his world view could be described as 'live and let live'), still Tibbs saw him as a kind of younger kindred spirit, with troubles that could be pushed backwards by alcohol and the company of simpler men.

Matthew did not care much for poppy seed, sprinkled on bread as it sometimes was, or stirred onto the dough of buns, so he thanked Dr Tibbs for his concern and said he hoped it would not be necessary to use the new medicine. But still he trusted in Tibbs, partly because he had no reason to do otherwise and because there was no alternative for thirty miles in any direction.

And indeed, after a week of the enforced idleness of rest, Tibbs declared Matthew out of immediate danger; his strength was to be rebuilt by walking the paddocks. Riding was forbidden for now, so he would circuit the inner fields and check the sheep, talk to the men. James told him that this work was useful, that no matter how amicable and innocuous was the tone of these contacts with the men, it kept them awake and aware of their duties. No measure made to this end would be a wasted effort. So Matthew walked, each day, in one of the four directions of the compass.

He told himself that to walk the low hills, from which their creek trickled, would test him more in his rehabilitation than would the level plains, and his steps inevitably took him there when they could. But it may also have been that something within him was seeking an answer that he did not know about consciously, nor even know enough to ask the question. Still, there lurked within him each day, out in the fields and gullies, the instinctive proclivity that he might turn over a rock and there would lay a revelation. The paths he took by instinct would always lead up the slopes, towards the tracks that would take him further to the distant camps of the blacks; but the blacks were out of sight and far away now, and when they did appear, they were not of a mind to share their time.

Six months before, such walks along the stream would have spurred Matthew to compose some raw and amateur verse, something on the beauty of nature: unshorn sheep like cotton buds; the funereal cawing and moaning of the crows; the roll of a distant hill like a woman's generous breast. But now the metaphors seemed staged and meaningless – a jarring, callow routine. It would only be with embarrassment that he would put them to a page, and then he would throw his pencil down, rip out the sheet and crunch it for the fire. The poets who wrote romantically of death had not stared it in the face. They who lived on the fruits of the empire had not murdered to make it. They had not watched a third of a man's head disappear before their eyes, and seen the grey brains spilling into the dust and had this image return to them nightly in their dreams. They had not woken in the night, alone, the voice of Phillips in their ears, 'Take aim you fool.' And he knew that he must go again, to prove himself worthy, to be a part of the undertaking that was the valley; that was what woke him in the night and it was for this purpose that he was regaining strength by these very walks.

To be in England, and to know what he knew now. He wished now too for Lucy Bray. She would understand his pain by an instinct that did not need words – a knowing child, his sister in spirit. He would write to her that afternoon. The letters that came from her and Cawthorne – they were the only two who wrote – were like oases in a flat and featureless landscape. Adela would be coming soon. They must make the place secure for her, for them, the women. They must all make the place secure; they must all shoot their way to security. All.

So Matthew would stand in his field and crook an eye towards those hills, and wonder about the men, and the women, who lived beyond them. He would wonder when the day of peace would come. And what then? What could be saved of relations between the settler and the native? To share and live in partnership, just as he, and James too, had planned.

Such thoughts of now and of the future occupied the mind of Matthew Larkin as he returned from his inspection of the eastern flock. The day was hot and he had been out all the morning. He returned along the creek in the shade of the trees there, of which he had come to know every bough and branch. A hundred yards more and he would turn to the left and pick his way along a gentle slope that led up to the homestead, where there would be tea and cold meat and bread and mustard. He crossed the creek and took three steps up its bank when there came to his ears a distant music that was not like the rustle of breeze, or the bellow of a sheep or the cawing of a crow – an alien sound that was not unearthly but was simply out of place. He stopped and listened for a moment. It came again and yet a third time.

It was the tinkle of laughter – the laughter of small children. There was the splashing of water too. His thoughts of the morning, already turning downwards, now went to melancholy memories of youth. He tried to place that sound in his own life. Had his brothers ever splashed him in a stream? James? His mother perhaps, but certainly never his father. Had such childlike kindness from another person ever been his to treasure, free of charge?

Further down its course, past the homestead and the little hut, the creek developed into a pool which bent around the roots of a huge old gum. He took a step along the creek bank in the direction of the sounds of glee. It was aching and hypnotic to him, this halcyon tinkling laughter, and he followed it. Soon the whoosh of splashing water came to his ears, in accompaniment to the higher trilling glee. He approached a bend and, through the trees, he could see brown bodies and diamond cascades of stream water flung about. Three steps further and there, on the bank, was one of Grace's cousins, her dress all wet and clinging fast to her ample shape. The three boys there, splashing about.

But there…there was Grace, her back to him, no clothes on her, knee deep in the creek water, receiving all the splashes of the little boys upon her naked body. She darted from side to side to dodge the jets of water, to the great amusement of the lads. They would flatten their hands and run them at lightning speed along the surface of the pond to shoot a jet at her and if they missed her she would laugh at them and they would go the harder at her. Then one boy looked past her shoulder at him and stopped his hands, his mouth open in amazement and sudden fear. The other two looked up and followed the gaze of the first. They too stilled their hands and ceased their merriment. And Grace turned her head to see him. The look on her face was enquiring, open, not afraid. She was afraid of nothing.

Matthew stood, up to his shins in creek water, his gaze upon the perfect nature of Grace. And then she turned her body around, to greet him openly. He saw the sinewy musculature of her broad shoulders swing in rhythm as she turned; her arms, her legs with the weight held on her right foot, she pushed to the left and turned to him – her small breasts, the dark fuzz between her legs. And she smiled.

The midday sunlight through the trees. On his face. Grace and her body. The admiral Larkin and the lash. Phillips and the Afghans. Thompson and his reports.

Scheherazade.

Matthew Larkin shook his head and laughed. It burst from him in a snapping chortle, of its own accord, like a vomit that could not be suppressed. Once, twice, three times and then he laughed out loud, not with joy, but in the appreciation of some fateful inevitability and absurd irony of which he had been only subliminally conscious until that moment. The boys saw him laugh and they jumped up and down; he would not harm them, and they could resume their game. They cared for little else, but Grace had seen something more than they, something she had already seen in Matthew. The smile she gave him before she turned back to the boys was sad and warm at once.

Without being conscious of what he was doing, Matthew sat in the stream. Now up to his waist in water, he splashed his face and cooled himself. The boys screamed with laughter and Grace turned to watch. Matthew undid the top two buttons of his shirt and slipped his left arm out, revealing his still-healing shoulder. With his right hand, he bathed his wound without knowing why. He stared in wonder at his wound for a minute, and then he stood up straight again. As he climbed the bank, Matthew took one look back at the little tableau and at that moment, by miracle or by some sixth sense, Grace too looked round again. The last thing he saw, what he remembered most, was her smile, her white teeth and her natural way of saying something to him that he did not understand, not quite yet.

*She had entered open grasslands. To her right, the northern reaches of the ranges faded into a flat and misty horizon. To her left, the sky melted into a scrub-broken flatland that obscured a sea too distant to be seen or heard. Thirty minutes ride and the town was behind her but with her too. A hawk wheeled above, out for rodents and low-flying birds. Would she take something home to her chicks?*

*She had followed a continuous track of hooves and wheel ruts since leaving the compacted streets of the town. The pistol was in her satchel. It seemed more tiny now, out here in this vast landscape, but it would have to do. If her horse shied at a snake and she was thrown? Would she have to wait three days for Watson the carrier to fetch her?*

*In the middle distance there was a puff of smoke – native or settler? Was that a chimney between the trees? She trotted her horse more quickly than was needed and presently came to a small stream and she stopped and gave the beast some water and jumped from the saddle and sat down in the shade. She could turn round and be back in the town by lunchtime. She* could say she had been to Klemzig for a ride and to visit her friends the Germans. Her uncle had learnt to pick his moments to confront her; that much he would let pass.

She could go back, now. But if she did, she would never know the truth. The north was fear; the town was ambiguity.

She walked the horse back to the track. Her left hand flicked at the rein and the horse turned north. A little further, she told herself.

Undulant grassland turned from green to flaxen yellow; they trotted for a mile and walked again for two more. A half mile off the road there was a freshly whitewashed wall incongruous among the eucalyptus trees – a house half built, a wilderness not occupied, not yet.

Her eyes turned back to the road and there – ahead! – the figure of a man upon a horse, two hundred yards away. Rough – his broad hat flapped down below his ears and even from that distance Lucy could see that it was stained with grease, had lost all shape, tufts of slick red hair visible at the neck. He wore a dusty coat that came down to his knees although the weather was warm. She stiffened with the fright of impending altercation and, without even knowing she was doing it, she scrabbled in her satchel.

The man watched her closely, even leaned far forward in his saddle and peered down the road at her in an almost comic exaggeration of scrutiny. Then, as if the action he took was the result of some decision quickly made, he leaned sharply back and reined and kicked his horse's hindquarters so its forelegs paddled the air like some forlorn circus act. And as he did so, the man forced from himself a hyperbolic screech of hilarity that tore through her being with its weird familiarity. And the man disappeared as suddenly as he had come to light, up a sidetrack, his manic screeches fading along with the sound of his horse's hooves.

For a minute, she trembled in her saddle. Her fingers finally stilled to take possession of the pistol from her satchel. She did not need it now, but she sat there for another minute role-playing defiance as she pointed it at the empty road ahead.

# 4

# The Town – November 1842

'And then, the most extraordinary explosion of sound, almost as if a shell had been exploded.'

'How extraordinary,' said Lucy Bray, and Mary returned her stare of amazement. She had been in the colony nearly four months and had heard nothing of such a parallel world existing just beyond the view of the white man, beyond the reach of police. Cawthorne had made contact with that world, and now Matthew.

'I believe that to show power or to strike fear was the intended effect.'

'Some claim to territory, you say.'

'They are indeed disturbed by the very presence of these river people. It will work itself out one would hope, without bloodshed. I would be very sorry to see harm come to any of our fellows from the plains here.'

'We see them seldom in the town and they are always clothed and engaged in some form of employ.' Lucy could give work to a native girl. Her uncle would approve, but she could manage easily without anyone; she had Mary after all and she liked to do things herself when it was time make the stew or put out the sheets. A servant of any colour would make her lazy.

'Of course, we must not breathe a word of this. It is not permitted for the natives to assemble for the purpose of affray. The law will be upon us, and them, if a word is spoken.'

'I swear,' said Lucy with mock solemnity, her right hand raised.

'Upon my soul,' said Mary, crossing herself. 'But we are not the only ones who know of these things. Your Mr Cawthorne, of course. Watson the carrier, I would expect, for another. He goes everywhere and sees and talks.'

'Watson the carrier! He is famous for the news he transports as well as his goods. But he is rarely seen,' Matthew observed.

'Always on the road,' said Lucy. 'He should paint a sign on his cart, so we know who to approach for news. A shilling a story – he could double his income!'

'I must make his acquaintance if he is the font of all news. It could be of use to hear more of conditions in the north. But not today, as I must depart presently. I am to Mr Cawthorne's abode to meet two of his friends.'

'Friends, I hear you say,' Lucy enjoined earnestly, for she had heard that Cawthorne lived alone with his mother and entertained very little. 'I thought he had none, except for you.'

'His native friends. There are more natives who will visit the Cawthornes than there are settlers. I am to be introduced to Kadlit-pinna, the chief.'

'Ooh, now there is a fine one,' said Mary. 'I have seen him bathing.'

'Mary, you haven't.'

'I have. Every inch of him. When you are finished, you can bring him home to me.' She was silenced with a pantomime shoosh from Lucy.

Matthew's spirits were lifted as he made his way to Hindley Street. The veil of melancholy which crept over him in the long hours of his employ was gone and he was excited by what lay in front of him. And Mary's frankness: she was the salt and sauce on a cold pork chop and that was for sure.

'Ha,' he proclaimed, out loud, just as Cawthorne would. A man turned a startled head to look, but Matthew did not care. A world of possibilities was opening to him.

Matthew Larkin tapped three times at the door of his friend

Cawthorne and stood back to look again at the place. It was a dwelling made of brick and stone but it reeked of a depressed and awkward permanence, one that was not happy with itself.

On this day, the front door was opened to Matthew by an anxious little woman with a sickly and downcast air. When she saw him, she bowed so that he beheld the thinning part in the middle of her uncovered head. She held the door and stood back for him to pass. 'You will be Mr Larkin,' she mumbled in the accent of the south of England, perhaps Southampton or Portsmouth.

He stepped into a little parlour, which opened directly from the street with no entrance hall separating. There was no hook on which to place a coat or hat. The first thing he spied was a narrow staircase leading to the floor above and then on the left two more doors which were closed but which must have opened to very small rooms, so close were they situated to each other. He stepped into the parlour and Mrs Cawthorne took his hat from him and placed it carefully on a wooden box which stood in a corner, along with one other hat which he recognised to be that of Cawthorne himself.

As his eyes adjusted to the dim light within, he beheld an extraordinary scene. The tiny room was jammed uncomfortably with hard wood furniture, as if the occupants had moved in from a place of greater dimensions and had found it easier to place all their furniture into one crowded room than to dispose of it, as if one day their circumstances would change and they would move to a larger house again. Cushions were here and there, both placed in the chairs and strewn about the floor as if that were an accustomed place to sit. Standing against the fireplace (not in operation on account of the season) was a handful of native items: there were two spears of more than six foot each in length and taller than any man present, a kind of club for fighting or hunting, and a collection of short spears all hunched up like a bundle of sticks. Cawthorne had taken place in centre stage with an easel in front of him, and with a more serious, impassive air about him than Matthew had seen before.

Posing for Cawthorne was none other than Kadlitpinna, or Captain Jack, whom he had seen in the natives' camp with his air of authority about him; and on this day he was every inch the chief, dressed up as if for fighting, with a band around his head in which was stuck one white feather of a cockatoo, a string band around his waist dangling from which on one side was a mat of emu hair all fixed up hard with some kind of resin and on the other a tightly woven bag of several inches in which were gathered three more clubs, each one protruding with a bulb of hard and polished wood for cracking the skulls of man or beast. On his considerable girth of chest were stripes of white and ochre; in his left hand was a shield, painted the same way, and in his right were two more spears, these of eight foot in length if they were an inch. The whole gave him the most ferocious aspect, yet at the same time he wore a look of more simple pride, as if he were play acting some game, as if these weapons were not for hurting but for role play and if you did not see that, then there was something foolish about you. He was leaning slightly forward and one foot stood out a few inches beyond the other, to give the impression of movement.

In the corner of the room was another native man, slighter than Captain Jack, and grinning widely at all that transpired before him. When Matthew entered the room, his grin became, if anything, wider than it had been before.

Cawthorne's eyes were narrowed onto a certain patch of canvas, as if placing the final touch to some important section. His face was still, as if his features had been hewn in chalk, his eyebrows were raised, particularly the right, in what may have been concentration and what may have also been the very conscious portrayal of the serious artist at work. He was engaged in the great labour; he was not to be disturbed just yet. Captain Jack posed for Cawthorne, Cawthorne posed for Larkin, Mrs. Cawthorne appeared distressed by all that was occurring before her and the seated native seemed to still find the entire *mise en scène* to be simply hilarious.

Presently, Cawthorne finished a section of his work with a small flourish. 'Ah, Larkin,' he said, as if he had only that moment spied him, and his face dropped into his accustomed look of neutral civility.

Captain Jack relaxed his pose, placed his weapons on the floor and with a bow addressed Matthew. 'Good afternoon, Williamse friend.'

The other native man also stood up and began to bow enthusiastically. Matthew saw that he too was painted in some ceremonial colours.

'Good afternoon, gentlemen,' Matthew replied.

'Mr Larkin,' Cawthorne motioned to Matthew, 'allow me to present Kadlitpinna and Willa Willa.'

All bowed and smiled excessively to each other before the native men turned away to attend to Willa Willa's costume.

'I say,' said Matthew, turning to his host, 'your place is madly interesting.'

'Madly, you say.' Cawthorne allowed himself a rare, amused smile. 'I dare say you should engage my mother in conversation on this matter. Do you hear, Mother?' He raised his voice and turned to her. 'Mr Larkin finds our place madly interesting.'

At this, his mother only moved her lips and mumbled something that Matthew bent to catch, but could not.

'My mother finds the natives and their amusements at times perplexing.'

'Their amusements?'

'As we are about to see. Willa Willa here will shortly cavort for us in the native style.'

And indeed the grinning man was at that time placing a band upon his head, then some hoops around his waist made of knotted string; he was already daubed with the white and ochre stripes around his chest, but Kadlitpinna now drew white stripes on the other man's legs and arms as well, making him more skeletal, a visitor from the spirit world perhaps.

Once Willa Willa was prepared to his satisfaction, Captain Jack came back to Cawthorne and Larkin. 'We got them river fella come our place. Them crazy fella, mad bugger. They want to talk to Kaurna people why no go to meeting place in the mountain? All blackfella go there for meeting. But they come here – no good. We no like them.'

It seemed that these words were by way of introduction to the performance which was to follow, for Kadlitpinna immediately squatted down, took up two sticks from the collection at the grate and began clicking them together and chanting in a high-pitched wail that, though it was grating to the ears at first, was so insistent and repetitious that it soon lured Matthew into a kind of spell. At this, Willa Willa began to hop about from one leg to the other, and as he did, his arms were flung out and back repeatedly, his fingers extended towards the roof in an upward reach and down to the floor in turn. All his animated features were now gone and his face bore the most fixed and concentrated expression that it seemed embalmed upon him and his eyes were like miniature orbs set to explode were they only to be touched. Mrs Cawthorne pressed her back hard into her chair. Willa Willa leaped with his feet together and came crashing to the floor with his hands on his thighs and tongue stuck in maniacal expression. He held his hands together between his knees and brought them slowly upwards, his fingers wiggling as he did so. He half hopped, half walked in a shuffle across the room then turned and came back again in the same manner. The movements were repeated several times so that one ceased to concentrate on them when it was seen that the potentiality for variation was diminished; the effect was hypnotic upon the viewer – the thinking world did somehow cease and the eyes began to close as if on the application of some opiate.

As suddenly as it had started, Willa Willa stopped dead. Kadlitpinna's clicking ceased at the same instant and in the parlour there was a most pregnant stillness. Willa Willa stood with his arms outstretched, as if he had been carved from rock. Kadlitpinna was serious, as if some important deed had been completed, and Cawthorne looked on through slits of eyes like some inscrutable whaling captain surveying the distant sea for spume. Suddenly Willa Willa's pose was gone and he was there before us, wreathed in amusement again. Kadlitpinna was smiling and Cawthorne began to clap. Matthew followed suit enthusiastically, as it was the most enthralling performance he had ever witnessed. He noticed Mrs Cawthorne place the fingers of her two hands together three times in the soundless mime of handclap.

It seemed now that this was to be the time of departure of these native guests, for the most extraordinary thing occurred: each of them began to pull on a pair of moleskin trousers which had been placed behind the stuffed chair upon which Mrs Cawthorne was seated. Even as they were donning their European dress, they began to bow.

When their outfit was completed, their bowing became more enthusiastic to Cawthorne and Matthew. They smiled broadly as they did, Kadlitpinna saying, 'Goobye, Williamse', 'Goobye, Williamse friend,' before turning to the emaciated mother who still was seated in a chair in the corner, 'Goobye ,Williamse mother.' There was such a display of good manners that this could not have been a thing introduced or schooled by any white man, but simply the natural deference of a gentleman towards his dear friends.

As the door was closed upon them, 'Goobye, goobye' was heard, with Willa Willa joining in the chorus.

'What fine fellows,' cried Matthew. He was completely entranced. 'I have never seen such natural goodwill.'

'Fine fellows, indeed,' Cawthorne mused and allowed himself a small smile before his expression returned to its thoughtful public face. 'They may now use their time to fetch wood for our colonists, in exchange for trinkets, some sawn-off stick of wood or other.' Then he dropped some of his distance and turned his face to Matthew, as if only then remembering his duties as host. 'Welcome to our place, such as it is,' he said, with a self-deprecating embarrassment.

'I understand that you find it smaller than you would like.'

'It is all we can manage, my mother and me between us, and the few paltry fees from our school for the lower classes.'

Matthew looked about him at the size of the room and estimated that the other rooms would be much the same and as a consequence no fit place for a school.

'You may as well see everything, then you will know.'

Firstly he stepped across to the door which Matthew had noticed on the left of the entrance, and he opened up to show a room no more than the size that two kitchen tables might occupy when put together. In the corner, before the smallest of window openings, which were shuttered with a kind of wooden gate opening outwards, was a writing place little grander than a schoolboy's desk, and in the opposite corner was a small stuffed chair which sat low to the floor and from which a considerable effort must have been spent to arise. Between the two, against a wall, were spears and shields of the native, with clubs and string bags. On the floor stacked up were some flat wooden bowls as if for gathering fruits and there was even a curved throwing stick such as Matthew had watched the natives making only days before. Apart from this, there was just sufficient space for Cawthorne to stand; when Matthew tried to join him, the proximity between them became immediately uncomfortable.

'Snug as a bug,' Matthew ventured.

'In the summer months, it is like Hades in here and no escaping it, in the winter more bearable as I can shelter beneath rugs to read and study and to mark my tests. You can see the conditions I am forced to endure.'

Matthew did think of his own more comfortable circumstances: a stone house with ceilings of fourteen foot and walls of a thickness that kept the heat at bay for days.

'Come.' Cawthorne led Matthew out and into the next room on the left and there inside was a small bed with a dressing table and looking glass and such fittings as would befit a modest woman's boudoir. 'Mother's room,' he said grimly, and eased back from the doorway so Matthew gained the merest glance.

Along from that there was a little kitchen on the left, opposite a rickety stairway. At the back, an open door exposed a tiny yard, a rude paling fence and a string looped between two posts.

Cawthorne led Matthew up the stairs to another room, which was the size of the two downstairs together, but without the wall between them. At one end was a blackboard and a small raised section where the teacher must mostly stand, with it a high desk and a high chair from which the view of the labouring students below no doubt was unrivalled. At the back, incongruously, some kind of padded resting place with matted stuffing poking from its seams: a chaise longue of sorts.

Before this arrangement there was space enough for perhaps twenty chairs, although there were no chairs present, and for many fewer students if there were the requirement for desks. But there were no desks either.

'Are there no desks or chairs?' Matthew enquired, expecting that some practical solution there was, such as that they were all out to be dusted, or varnished.

'They must learn to sit, three hours together in the morning, and again in the afternoon, with their legs crossed. And they must pay attention, sir, or their ears are boxed, all ninety of them.'

'Ninety! Good God in heaven.'

'Yes, young Larkin, ninety of the roughest. The sons and daughters of blacksmiths and ostlers and labourers paid by the day.'

'Surely they cannot be all of attention, when you are turned to the board, for you must clearly write up there what you wish them to copy.'

'Aye, you have met my mother. This is her place,' he said, nodding at the chaise longue, 'and her with the strap and yardstick and well ready to use it.'

Matthew thought of the sickly, wan-looking woman he had seen downstairs. 'Your mother will thrash the children?'

Cawthorne looked away. 'The shilling and sixpence they pay up per month…'

'One and six!'

'In advance, mind,' said Cawthorne, with a raised and self-deprecating eyebrow. 'It barely keeps the two of us alive. To think, Mr Larkin, at Trinity Church not one hundred yards away, the boys will pay a pound a month. A pound!'

Cawthorne's face became animated for a moment at the thought of the money that lived within touching distance; his boys crossed the paths of those boys in the street at four o'clock each afternoon. Then he relaxed again. 'In the summer I join a surveying gang, in season I toss hay in farms, and a more comfortable bed is to be found in most of them than this,' and he tossed his head towards the chaise longue.

'That is your bed?'

He answered with a simple, 'Hmmph,' and then went on, 'I have done many things. I can do many things now to keep us alive. I thank God for that much, sir, but it is not the life I would cut for myself if I had a chance to choose.' He looked at Matthew now in a way that he had not done before. There was a hint of pleading anguish buried in the resentment that he expressed. 'To gain some recognition from the burghers of this town, to rise in the ranks of education, at the very least. But a master is not that which I was called to be. With a bucket of capital, a man can create oceans more in this place. But all I can do is write every day and paint as well.'

'As I have seen, and nobly well indeed.'

'Adequately well indeed, sir. But whether adequate or noble, my sketches of the native tools and weapons and of the natives themselves are sure to sell, if only there is a patron who will fund the first edition of my work. These paintings of mine are meant for a book, to be published for all the good ladies and gentlemen of the colony. And beyond, in New South Wales and even, may I say so, sir, in England itself, where exotic curiosities from the colonies are wont to create a stir.'

'Indeed they do, sir, most exceeding.'

'My name…' and here Cawthorne gripped Matthew by the shoulder and stared into his eyes, beyond his eyes, with an intensity that made Matthew shrink back for a moment, 'my name will be known. Matthew, I can be welcomed into salons I may now not approach. Doors which will open to such as you on the mention of your admiral father's name remain shut to me who must rise by toil alone. It is a long way to climb when the steps are made of industry and nothing else.'

He looked down as he said these last few words and would have wept had he not been as strong a man as he was. He had learnt long before that the shedding of tears would never help him. When he had made protest to his father years before about the state in which his mother had been left, he was regaled with such language as you would expect from such a rough type of seaman. He swore then that he would keep his mother all her life and at the age of twelve he had devoted himself to his duty. Tears, no matter how hard they were shed, would never become a leg of lamb for the table, dressed with a pound of roasted parsnips. Only long persistence would, and still then no guarantee. Cawthorne had consumed books, had educated himself and had absorbed whatever his genteel mother could give him too. But without the capital that had disappeared down his father's throat, there still could be a life of drudgery without end, a life of hopes and dreams that still one day may end up in the dust.

Matthew could do no more than place his own hands on Cawthorne's shoulder, where Cawthorne's had so recently been placed on his and say the words, 'I wish you well, my friend. May god be with you.'


The hazy heat of late spring was pushed away that afternoon when the breezes swung south-west to run off the sea in what colonists had come to call 'the change'. By midnight, the clouds burst on the township and by first light rivulets ran through the pounded-earth streets, leaving ruts and potholes behind them. Citizens woke to the dying of the drizzle and stepped out into a fresh cool morning. Once the menfolk had stirred and breakfasted, then gone out to their business, so too did the more adventurous of the women, among them Lucy Bray and her nurse Mary.

As they turned into Hindley Street, one cart was down to its axle in a pothole that had appeared overnight. There were five pairs of shoulders gathered to the back of the cart and another man pulling steadily at the horse's bridle while the poor beast struggled along with them all.

At length, a shout went up as the wheel bobbed out and the thankful horse peeped sheepishly around its blinkers at the men, who gave her encouraging pats on the rump and shoulders.

The colony had been in place for more than five years now, closer to six, and many of the shops had built boardwalks outside their premises and the ladies who braved the morning made good use of them. Lucy liked to do her own errands in the mornings, and her uncle encouraged it. The more she was out and being seen and becoming familiar with the ladies of the colony, the better. Mrs Woodhall was out early and she dipped her head and hat in acknowledgement of Lucy, then hugged her shawl around her shoulders as if to say that it was too chilly to stop and chat – which it wasn't, but Lucy creased her brow and nodded in aquiescence anyway.

They purchased some buttons and golden thread for Lucy's day gown, then inspected curtain material for the new Government House. In matters of taste, Lucy was prone to flights of fancy – everything in gold and purple, something splendid – and Mary gently pulled her back, pointing out that hundreds of people would be received at Government House before the curtains were done for, and perhaps something more restrained was in order.

'Of course, I am being silly, Mary,' Lucy said, and they took some swatches of material to recommend to the governor, or more likely Thompson, who would narrow his eyes and ask the price of each and record the details in his little book.

Once done with matters of state, Lucy and Mary made for McIvor's sweet shop.

'Isn't it wonderful out, Mary?'

The morning sun peeked around Lucy's bonnet. The street was full of lifted voices, vigorous shouts and cries; all activities were made complex by the muddy road; merchants and workers helped each other with deliveries and repairs. Some yards away, a suit-coated man had slipped and mired his backside, to which stain a damp cloth was being applied by a shop clerk.

'My goodness,' said Mary.

'I would not miss a morning like this for anything,' Lucy replied.

'My goodness,' repeated Mary, 'be watchin' your step now, miss. You can't be ending up like that gentleman.'

The gentleman in question now, sponged to his satisfaction, picked his way to the boardwalk in the direction of Lucy and Mary. 'Good morning.' He lifted his hat to Lucy, and nodded to Mary. 'Permit me to introduce myself. I am Stewart, Alexander Stewart. And you, I believe, are Miss Lucy Bray.'

'Well, so it is, sir.' Lucy was by now accustomed to being recognised, and discussed. 'And this is Mary,' she added.

Stewart quickly nodded again at Mary and turned back to the object of his interest. 'You are looking radiant this morning, Miss Lucy. The fresh air has heightened your complexion to such a rosy glow.'

'Why, thank you, sir,' Lucy replied with thin lips. There was something about the attentions of the man that she did not wish to encourage. 'Some early shopping,' and she inclined her head to the sweets store they were standing outside, by way of agreeable conversation.

'Ah, some sweets for the ladies. Excellent.' Mr Stewart was ready to be agreeable in everything that was needed.

'Actually, they are for the governor.' They were in fact not for the governor, but Lucy could not help herself from contradicting the man. As if women were the only ones who had a sweet tooth!

'Ah, I see. How marvellous. I am wont to indulge in a bonbon or two after dinner myself.' Stewart pulled a gold watch from his fob pocket and looked at the time. 'I am afraid my little mishap has made me late for an appointment – some papers to sign.' Stewart added, without need to do so, that the nature of his business that morning was, indeed, business.

'You slipped, sir?'

'Yes, my first wet morning in the colony. It is a very different road than it was yesterday afternoon.' He touched his hat and was on his way.

'A fine cut of a man,' said Mary, as Stewart strode away, sticking to the boardwalk this time. Mary watched him closely as he went up the street, her eyes following the patch on his behind that had been sponged.

Lucy allowed herself a glance.

'A fine cut of a man,' Mary repeated.

Lucy glanced again, then pulled her head away. 'Yes, indeed,' she murmured. 'Come, Mary,' and she took the arm of her nurse and life-long companion.

'Bought two hundred acres in the near south, he did – the best land. And barely bargained for it.' Mary shook her head. 'Only two weeks in the colony.'

'Yes, I heard,' said Lucy, and shook her head too, to call an end to the discussion. It was as if Mary was recommending Stewart to her, but that had already been done by others.

As she looked up from the boardwalk, she saw the figure of Matthew Larkin, talking to a tallish man with hooded eyes and self-conscious movements; his coat was decently cut, but shabby.

As Lucy and Mary moved closer, the stranger looked up to see their cheerful faces, then slipped quietly away with a nod to Matthew and with no greeting to them.

'Mr Larkin, you have a sweet tooth, I see.'

Matthew had in his hands a small bag of McIvor's peppermints.

'Miss Lucy, Mary. You are brave to be out this morning.'

'How could we be but out, with such excitement in the street?'

'Ah, yes, it is a spectacle after the rain, isn't it?'

'And you must tell me, who was that man you were speaking to? I have seen him before but have never been introduced.'

'Ah, that is Cawthorne.'

'Cawthorne, the somewhat famous Cawthorne!'

'Famous?'

'Your friend may be solitary by nature but his eccentric collections have made him somewhat famous. His artefacts. His native things.'

'And his friends. I met Kadlitpinna and Willa Willa yesterday – extraordinary chaps. Absolute gentlemen.'

'By the look of Cawthorne, his eccentricity may not be feigned, as it can be in some.'

Matthew looked quizzical.

'You know, all done to achieve some notice and to place oneself ahead of others. But Cawthorne, I observe, is not seeking notoriety.'

'Indeed, Cawthorne does not seek notoriety for his eccentricity. It is not feigned, it simply is.'

'Then what does he seek? All men are seeking something, are they not?'

Matthew looked closely at Lucy. As usual, her comments and questions made him stretch his thinking. 'Hm, well, recognition of his abilities, I expect – a form of respectability perhaps, security, acceptance – those things which many lesser men than Cawthorne secure at birth without blinking an eye.'

'Many men will seek favour by flattery and manners. A few will be more reserved in their counsel. I think I prefer the latter.'

'Flattery is a commodity not sold by Cawthorne. His is a straight line of work and steady advancement, which I fear his small notoriety may even obscure.'

'Ah, but notoriety can be gained in many ways,' said Lucy, her interest being more with the Larkin before her than with the Cawthorne at the end of the street. 'You have gained some small notoriety in the world of women, such as it is in this place,' she tapped him on the shoulder with her furled umbrella, 'but the men have perhaps not noticed you so much.'

'So be it.'

'I was hoping to see you today. There is an important personage coming up from the Bay this morning. I'm sure there will be a welcome tea before three days are out. I, of course, must attend.'

'Our Lucy is the vice-regal lady now,' Mary observed with a nod.

'And I think,' Lucy went on, 'you shall attend also.'

'Why should they invite me?'

'Why?' She laughed and then continued in a hoarse conspiratorial whisper, 'Because I tell them to, that's why! James too, of course. Powerful men will be present and it may be advantageous for you to know them.'

Lucy tied her bonnet up tight and bade Matthew farewell, Mary made a small curtsy and they were gone.

Matthew slid a peppermint into his mouth. Around him, the hubbub of a Hindley Street morning swirled; he seemed to be the only still person. He looked after Lucy, stepping confidently through the street, picking up her dress at damp patches, a word for all she encountered. He turned thoughtfully towards Government House and his place at work. There was a pile of orders to be made out and some reports to be copied. Perhaps if he worked well enough, he could take a walk at lunch, around the bend in the river, to the place where the natives had their camp.

Adela Peake's room was two streets back from the port where her ship lay at rest. The hotel was adequate, just, and, because its adequacy placed it in a higher class than others about the place, its rooms were often let to the gentler travellers from the ships. The bed was soft but squeaked when one flopped on it. The one window was divided into four panes, the bottom of which had been smudged by fingers, those of a child, she presumed, trying to gain balance on tiptoes to see the view. Through the top two panes, she could see the masts of the ships rising like a painted scene above the hotels and chandlers shops that separated her place from the quay. It was a peculiar sight: rigging, ensigns and masts appearing to climb incongruously out of slated roofs, always the reminder of movement and of where one was going – there was never rest. Would she ever rest again?

She braced herself once more for the squeaking springs, then lay down and closed her eyes; but just as in the very near skyline there was the physical command of the ships, in the street were the sounds of the port, overruling everything. After six weeks at sea, you would think a soft and steady bed would enclose one inexorably – that you would be born down into it, folded over – that sleep would take you like a narcotic into fields of asphodel.

Wouldn't you?

But Adela was restless; she had not travelled further than Bournemouth before, and here there were unusual sights. More than half the men in the streets were negroes. Tall, muscular, ebony like the keys on a piano – many of them with shirts cut away at the shoulders, for the greater ease of rolling barrels, she presumed. She admired them, not in any salacious or unseemly way, but for their earnest and intelligent expressions; and they, it seemed, accepted her in the same spirit of gracious equanimity. One tall, thin and dark man had even walked up the street dressed like a proprietor, in a gentleman's frock coat. Then there were Chinamen too, in long nightdresses of blue and grey, busy in their little establishments. Cape Town was indeed a place of its own. They said you could walk in half a day from the bay to the ocean on the other side – a cape indeed.

Adela raised herself from the bed; five minutes rest was all she could manage. She would be three days in the Cape and there was no urgency to see whatever there was to be seen. But she was rattled. On the way in, she had seen a tea shop at the corner of the hotel, as safe a position as there was from which to observe this place – to be both in it and outside of it at one time. She placed her hat upon her head and stepped down the stairs; it was not too late for tea and indeed, as she presented herself diffidently at the glass-paned door, she could see that the corner room was almost full.

The girl who came up to her had seen wide-eyed and disoriented travellers before – but few as bad as this one. In a minute, she had brought Adela a pot of strong tea with two scones and cream and strawberry jam. Adela stared at her plate as at an apparition. The tea she had expected: India being only days away, logic would say the tea could be even fresher and better here. But the scone was crusty on the outside and meltingly soft within, not floury as the cheaper ones often were. And the jam was excellent. Why indeed should the fare not be as good as at home? The Cape was now a metropolis of twenty thousand people, with dairies and cultivated fields. Why, it could be the centre of the world. The thought cheered her a little, that some place other than London could be that, and could provide nice jam too.

That she was away from the ship and not moving somewhere – that strangely gave her a moment to reflect in a way that she had not before. She thought with a shudder of the last six months in London. Mother had sensed her fear. She had never said that she need not come away, but such was implied in her mother's every movement, her every delay. And it would be wrong to say that it had not nearly worked. Her duty lay in South Australia, but her duty lay in England too. But if James had not gone away, then her duty and her pleasure both would have been in England – her joy, in fact. It had seemed so perfect.

She remembered the day that James had come to her, the engagement ring fresh on her finger a fortnight before.

'My father, the admiral, has decided that I…we, shall take up land in South Australia.'

She had sat quietly, searching James's face for irony, for his endearing playfulness, but found none there. It had been the absolute end of her world. The admiral had inspected her, had looked her up and down and given his assent. The admiral had approved the engagement, waited a month until the fact was notified good and proper, then announced that he had set aside funds for property in South Australia; the slaving had gone excellently in the last year and there was excess capital to be worked.

She was a good prospect; she knew that. Her hips were made for breeding; she knew that too. It had been observed a hundred times through her childhood and her teenage years: 'hips for breeding, hips for breeding'. It was her fate, just as it was that of men to go to sea and perish in the waves. But she thought with resignation that if she had to choose her sex, she would not change. She could not imagine firing cannon from thirty yards into a French ship and watching men blown in pieces. She had been close enough to ships to feel the smoke, the linseed oil, the disarray – the poor men in the streets with severed arms and legs, with one hand out for alms. Better to be a woman.

'Hello, dear, do you mind if I join you?'

Adela's roaming thoughts were abruptly pulled apart. She could not help but look around at the other tables; they were all full. 'But of course, please sit down.'

'I wouldn't ask, but the place is so busy. It's no surprise. They do a better scone in here,' said the woman, glancing down at Adela's plate.

The lady's voice was cultured, but at the same time was not. Her accent was peculiar and it took a moment for Adela to realise that the woman was not a visitor, not in transit, but had probably been in this part of the world for some time.

'So I have already appreciated. And the jam is excellent too.' Adela's voice was tired, so much so that she was afraid she might seem careless, to this woman. She reminded herself to lift her tone, in order not to cause offence, but the woman pushed on without caring or even without seeming to understand what offence could be.

'Well, it's really the only place, within a mile. I come in here sometimes, at the end of my day, as a treat, you know.'

'Oh, I see.' Adela rose to the requirement to make conversation. 'Do you have business in this quarter?'

'Oh yes, miss. I sell fancy things to the ships' providers here, you know. Lace doilies, tea cosies, antimacassars, a hundred things. You never know the things that ship's captains will buy for their selves, and them that are migrating to India or Australia too.'

Adela noted the ambiguity the woman had created over whether the captains were buying for their passengers or whether the passengers were buying for themselves, but carried on. 'Do you make your things yourself?'

'Ooh no, not now, I don't. I've got girls as I've trained. The Cape has been a good place for a woman with a bit of push.'

Adela did not doubt that the woman had what she called 'push'.

'It is my first day in the Cape. It is quite a sight.' Adela directed her glance to the busy mercantile environment outside their window.

'Oh, yes, you don't see many blackies in England, do you, nor Chinamen. Not unless you are down by the docks and then you'll see everything and I mean everything, but a lady like you might not roam so far. Nineteen years since I been there and I don't miss it. I was meant for a governess on a farm – in New South Wales. But I got this far and stopped. I looked in all these shops up 'ere and a bloke said there was money about the place and not enough nice things and so…'

'A farm, you say.'

'Yes, dear, looking after the children and teaching them how to read and count. I can do those things and make things too, that's why they wanted me. But as I say…'

'So why not go on? You might have done well there.' Adela would not normally interrupt anyone, as a rule of courtesy. But she was tired and the woman's voice trilled gratingly up and down and would not stay on the subject that was of vital importance to her: life on a farm in Australia.

'A girl on ship said she'd heard it was lonely on the farms and she didn't know what to do. The farms there, they've got another word for them that I can't recall for the moment. She said they are so far apart that you have to ride for fifty miles to get to the next one.'

'Goodness.'

'Now that's a long way to go visiting anyone, I say. And me, one thing I never knew that much about was horses. I like to get about and talk to people…'

Adela had readily observed.

'…and there was plenty of folks here, so when I came here, that's where I stayed. What's the matter, miss, you've gone all pale. Have a nice sip of tea.'

'It's been such a long time since I've seen my fiancée.' She wondered if this woman before her was the type of maid and companion that

James had written about, 'on every boat' is what he had said. 'Did you say fifty miles?'

'Not all of them. It depends how far out you go, from the towns, I mean.'

'I believe we are quite far out.'

'You are going to meet your husband! How lovely that is. I do hope you get on well, you and your husband.'

'Not yet. I mean, we are not husband and wife yet. How odd it all seems, to be husband and wife. And to be in such a place. And to be having children, and,' she looked at the woman opposite her, 'to be employing a governess, perhaps. I must say I am uncertain as to how it will all work.'

'You'll find your feet once you get there.'

The woman regarded her with sympathy, but Adela wondered if her sympathy was not a little patronising; Adela feared that she was too genteel, too full and peachy, too placid for the provinces, let alone a colony. She could see it now, all at once, even more than before. If this woman across from her was frightened, what hope had she?

'I expect so.'

'Perhaps you would like to be purchasing something, miss. To take to your new place. To make life comfortable. As a memento of your stay in the Cape. Why, there is a store just a few numbers up…'

'I'm afraid I may have already packed more than enough, things that may not be useful. I am sure I will be required to be useful.'

'But where is it you're going, miss? You haven't told me that yet.'

'To South Australia.' The words were awkward in her mouth. It was not her home. It was not home.

'Ooh, that's the new place. There are ships every week, at least one. Are you leaving tonight?'

'Oh no, we arrived only today.'

'Ah, but there is a ship going tonight as soon as the tide is right.'

'There is? Will they take a message?'

'A letter, dear? Of course they will, if you pay them proper. Anyway,

I must be ducking.' The woman drained her cup and bade Adela good day. She had been in the corner shop for tea and that was for sure, not for gazing out of windows and wondering why. The door opened and out the woman went with a whoosh.

It was only after she had left that Adela realised that she did not known the woman's name. Then Adela thought, with a further start, that she had not introduced herself either. How very peculiar, she thought. Her manners were all but gone, in six weeks at sea, away from civilisation. But, a ship leaving tonight. It would reach South Australia three days before her if the winds were even. She thought of her dear James, waiting.

'Oh, miss, would you bring me a sheet of paper and some ink? I must write a note, to South Australia.' She tried to get used to saying the words.

The girl nodded and went away, and Adela Peake fell into even deeper thought than she had before.


Matthew had been to tea since his arrival in the colony. But that had been for the purpose of introduction and inspection; it was really the world of women, with some men attached as if for the purposes of ornament and balance. But today was to be the world of men; he could smell the difference from half a mile away.

'We go to the house of Woodhall, the banker,' said James. 'Captain Phillips will be there, and others.'

'Phillips!' Matthew had heard of Phillips and seen him in the street. He was a small but fierce-looking empire man who had spent time in India. He had been made the inspector of police while waiting for the purchase of his selection, and was rarely seen off his horse or without his sword at his side. The women had tittered that he would go to the market to buy a bag of beans in his full helmet and cuirass, in case of rebellion or native insurrection. He seemed a cartoon character to Matthew, but on the other hand a powder keg.

'A man not to be feared, but respected and cultivated,' was James's ever-sensible verdict. He flicked the reins at the horse that was pulling the phaeton he had borrowed and looked across at Matthew to gauge the effect his words might have had on his brother, but saw nothing. 'And today there is another important guest who is but three days in the colony.'

'What guest?'

'You have heard of Angas?'

'Who has not?'

Angas had for six years in England encouraged the establishment of the colony, raising capital, making speeches, even establishing new banks and directing capital there, placing men from his church on the board of the company that was raised to break the ground in South Australia. He had a reputation for ceaseless industry and the kind of temperance which bordered on contempt for the excesses of ordinary men.

'His son has arrived.'

'His son. But which? I have heard that there are three, that two are as steady as you go and that the third is an artist by trade and not a coachmaker or banker which, by the ancient and immutable laws of succession, he would appear to have been destined to be.'

James paused to give Matthew a look which said he was a moment closer to cheekiness than he had a right to be. 'You speak of the very one, Matthew. George French Angas is here. And, yes, a different type of man to his father.'

'This Angas is a man of some importance, James, to have produced such high spirits in you.' Matthew was teasing for information; his brother's mood was high.

James checked himself for a moment. 'Is it that obvious?'

'It is, brother.'

'Then I should explain. The *Peston* returned to the Bay yesterday and I have received the mail this morning.'

'Adela!'

'Indeed. Arrangements are made for her journey here. At this moment, she is on the sea, following her letter. She could arrive within days, two weeks perhaps, depending on the winds and tides, whatever Jupiter would send their way.'

'That is marvellous news. James, I am happy for you.'

'We will be together for a very short time. Our property settlement is close. I have lost patience with the hard men who hold out for succulent profits and we cannot be seen to be sitting on our hands. We will be heading north, a good way from Adelaide. But you have heard of the township of Clare.'

'I have.' Matthew's heart leapt with excitement.

'Thereabouts, the land is a fraction of the cost and still provides an excellent pasture for sheep. With what we save, we will bring merinos from New South Wales. We will have them run across land from there.'

'Over land! That is audacious, James.'

'It is the new way. Because we are so far north, we will cut five days off the run. We will have a very large tract. We will provide wool for the empire, Matthew. Soldiers in India and Africa will bear uniforms made from our wool. The facilities of the town of Clare are few, but will improve. Some colonists fear the distance, but not us, eh.'

'Yes, it is far. Are there natives there?'

'There are natives. With patience and training, they may come to work for us, else they will be required to clear out.'

'To clear out?'

'There are reports of resistance, but my fervent hope is that the natives will be as conducive to influence and civilisation as are those of the plains here.'

'I have heard that they are fiercer. There may be fights!' Matthew's imagination was now consumed by the north and by what might be. It was a sweeping move by James, to go further out – into the bush. It was visionary. But Adela was to follow, out there! They would have their own land and make their own rules. It was freedom. The natives were wilder but he, Matthew, could bring them into a new world. His experiences in Adelaide would ready him for it.

'There may be. But look,' said James as he pulled the phaeton up in front of a vast stone house that stood out in the bare and open street, 'here is Woodhall's.'

Matthew looked up at a colonnaded portico of the most magnificent two-storey house. A hundred yards away in the direction of a dusty trail that led away to the hills, three emus pecked absently at the hard earth before them. They were incongruous now, where two months before they had been commonplace. As Matthew watched them graze, a shot rang out and one emu fell; the other two ran off and a man walked up to claim his prize.

'Yes, here we are,' said Matthew.


Although it was Woodhall's fine new house, and Angas the guest of honour, Captain Phillips still jostled for attention. His eyes probed the room in an edgy way, then would rest on a person of interest, judge and summarise. If his gaze was met, he would simply turn his head away to focus on another. He was like some magpie or crow, always picking, and he held his cup of tea for only so long as it took to hastily drink its contents, and then he motioned for the attention of a serving woman to get it away from him as a nuisance he had no business with.

French Angas, however, was born with saucer and cup in his hands, or so it would have appeared, and Matthew could see that, although he must have been only twenty-five or so years of age, he turned heads towards him through his serene confidence and articulacy in conversation. His dark hair was longish and swept back from his brow, leaving his face quite open for the world to remain in admiration of his fair features.

In nine months of travel, first to Sicily, then to southern Africa, he had seen military types like Phillips. They could be useful, but would never open up the world to him the way he wanted: all those regulations and duties were so sapping to the spirit. He had seen settlers in Natal – some were decent chaps, others less so – but all had come to play for profit and to improve their place in the world. They would take him to beauty spots to paint, but waterfalls and wave-lapped coves, like military men, were all of a type. So Angas was always watching for the muse who would deliver him some real local colour.

As the Larkins arrived, tea was being served; cake was laid out on a table with plates and forks. Also present was Mr Newsome, the protector of Aborigines, in conversation with Mr Hall the magistrate, and Mr Kendall, the accountant, who had come with Matthew on the voyage out. There were four or five others, some of whom Matthew had met in various places of entertainment around the town.

Lucy herself bore a china cup to Angas, then turned in feigned surprise to Matthew. 'Why, Mr Larkin,' she turned to James, 'and Mr Larkin. How good of you to come. I think you know most of the gentlemen present.'

'Some are of my acquaintance.' Matthew nodded cheerfully to some of the more convivial heads – others he ignored.

James had met almost everyone and his cheer-making voice accompanied much shaking of hands and slapping of backs.

They were handed cups full of milky liquid.

Mr Woodhall stepped in to make an introduction. 'You remember, Captain Phillips, James.'

'Indeed, I do, Mr Woodhall.'

The two men shook hands.

'My brother Matthew,' said James, 'this is Captain Phillips.'

'Good afternoon, sir,' said Matthew, in the jauntiest tone he could muster.

'Good afternoon to yourself, sir,' said Phillips in a burr that might have been Hampshire and with an eye that regarded him steadily.

'Captain Phillips has been a soldier at arms in India, and will most likely take up property near us in the north.'

Phillips shifted his weight from one foot to the other. 'Your brother and I came to the same decision about prices. Some of those who bought up and will not sell on are nothing short of scoundrels.' Phillips did not bother to lower his voice. 'And so we are to be neighbours.' He delivered this as a piece of news, neither joyous nor aggrieved – simply fact.

'Ah, how excellent,' Matthew said, in spite of the reserve he felt immediately about the fellow.

'And you,' Phillips went on, 'have made yourself known in this town. I've heard of you.' The man's tone and his manner of pointing his forefinger did not inspire confidence that the notices obtained had been completely favourable.

French Angas drew near, with Lucy close in attendance, and James sought to draw him out, if only to place Phillips in the background for a time.

'It is an honour that you could come to our colony,' James began, once introductions had been effected, 'and in advance of your own dear father whose zeal for our adventure is unsurpassed.'

'My father's zeal for South Australia is only surpassed by his contiguous zeal for banking, investment…such matters,' and French Angas waved his right hand, like a careless orchestra conductor, while balancing a half filled cup, a saucer and a spoon in his left without effort.

'Ha, ha,' someone invented a chortle, and all joined in, whether they understood the word 'contiguous' or not.

For a moment, the room was filled with rounded men of the world who were of the nature to keep business at arm's length, where it belonged.

'Of course some people have to make fortunes for themselves, while others have them made for them.' Phillips could not restrain himself from a moment of colonial bluntness.

'Of course your own interests lay in other matters, sir, eminence in the world away from finance,' Mr Kendall cut through diplomatically.

'It appears one can accumulate capital and purchase land in South Australia from as far away as London. Indeed, it would appear that it is in some instances preferable to do so from there. However, my own interests require a more, shall we say, first-hand contact.'

'Mr Angas is to paint our colony,' Lucy put in by way of explanation. 'He has been inspecting some promising places already.'

'Yes, to paint!' Matthew cried, emboldened by Lucy's presence. 'How marvellous.'

The others smiled at his unrestrained enthusiasm.

'Ah,' said French Angas, waving his hand again, 'do we have a young artist present?'

'I have tried my hand, in England. I am sure there is a ready market in London for subjects from the newest colony. I have been here little more than six weeks, sir…'

'I but fewer days, ha ha…' and all joined again with the wit of French Angas, excepting Phillips, whose moustache twitched up and down from left to right, reflecting the grimaces he was making underneath, '…and there are many fine places that I have seen. In two days riding with Mr Gilles here, I have seen rivers, hills and coves of unsurpassed beauty, and already have begun to paint.'

'You are a model of industry, sir,' said Mr Woodhall, handing his teacup to a serving girl and wiping his own neat little moustache with his forefinger knuckle.

Indeed, Angas had stepped off the ship at Semaphore and immediately set to work, scouting for places and sketching his first impressions. '"Idle hands are the devil's work," or so goes one saying of my father's that has rather stuck with me. I have spent three weeks in Sicily, a most diverting experience. The light there was of a brightness unsurpassed to my eye, but in this place, how shall I say it…young Matthew has been here six weeks, what say you, sir?'

'Dazzling is the word I would use.'

'Dazzling,' repeated French Angas with a raised eyebrow. 'Indeed, sir. Perfectly spake. The hills so blue, the grass so…how can I say it…?'

'The grass is not green as in England. There should be another word to describe it,' Matthew observed, excited.

'So there should. And very well spoken once more, young Matthew.'

Young Matthew was how he felt before this man, just two or three years his senior.

'Mr Angas intends to find some subjects among the native population as well, Matthew,' said Captain Phillips. His eye now regarded Matthew as would that of a knowing cockatoo.

Matthew turned back to Angas. 'Oh, but there are some fine black-fellows,' he said. He felt a cautionary touch from James at the back of his right elbow.

'Indeed, Matthew,' said Newsome, the Protector, 'some of them are coming closer to us, and performing labours for which they are fairly paid in kind. Captain Phillips, would you agree, there is hope that the native will become civilised?'

Phillips thought for a moment. 'There may appear to be some small hope for a proportion of them.' With Angas present, and Newsome, he had for once to restrain his views, which were said to be for providing the natives with bags of flour laced with strychnine – a loss of flour, he would say, but a saving in bullets. 'However, it is paramount that order is maintained and an appropriate structure of society with it.'

'The natives of the town,' Newsome went on, 'are coming to us. To have a shaven face seems to have become quite the latest fashion in the native quarter.'

This brought smiles of recognition to many nodding faces.

'Indeed, if I may say so,' said Mrs Newsome, 'our Debbie has en-gaged one native lad to bring armfuls of wood from wherever he can collect them, in return for a shave and a trim. He left the place as happy as the meadowlark. In time, what could he not do?'

'Indeed,' said Lucy, and eyes turned towards her; she was not only an intelligent girl, but also the governor's niece, 'it is a process which must be taken one single step at a time. The natives here are subjects of the Crown, and must be brought into our society.'

'Most amusing and most interesting,' said Angas. 'But the toting of wood for pay in a shave or a bag of sugar is not the subject for a paint-ing. I have painted peasants at work on the foot of Italy, I think with some success. Here, I have found a number of very good places. And in the street the most stimulating array of fellows. This morning, I have seen Irish women in their bonnets, Germans in their most picturesque national costumes, Chinamen with their wide trousers, Catholic priests, English country bumpkins in their smock frocks.'

'Our colony is a paradise of dissenting views, Mr Angas, as I am sure you know. Freedom for all.' Lucy had already become a devout colonial.

'Indeed, it is a sight to behold, a walk down your Hindley Street. But people in England will not pay for my folio to be regaled by a Scotchman in his kilt. I have not yet found the colour that I need, the exotica that I seek.'

'There are some marvellous painted natives here,' cried Matthew.

Mr Newsome stepped in again. 'The native is under full protection of the law, Mr Angas, and the better they are treated, the better will be our relations with them in the future. It is the outlying areas that concern me. One never knows what is happening there. What news we get is stale, and what tracks there were are gone.'

'Gone as are the Whigs from government now at last,' said Phillips, looking around him for support among his fellows, but finding only non-committal pucker. 'But their law remains and no man has the will to change it. Whichever way, civilisation will push on.'

'All the greater need to capture the ancients now,' Angas mused aloud.

'I have seen one in Cawthorne's own parlour.' Matthew could not restrain his enthusiasm. 'Two really.'

The group of six or seven faltered in its animation for a moment.

'Cawthorne!' Captain Phillips was the first to speak. 'Oh, yes, Cawthorne.'

Angas looked around him with amusement at the change which had come across their little gathering. 'And who is this Mr Cawthorne, who can make a cup of tea turn cold in our hands?' he said.

'Mr Cawthorne lives,' Mr Newsome explained, 'off the end of Hindley Street. No more than a stone's throw from the river, around the bend of which lies a natives' camp.'

'I say.'

'Mr Cawthorne has taken to befriending the native.'

'I double say.'

'And, I am led to believe, has commenced a collection of native artefacts.'

'Why, I do declare,' said Angas, placing his cup gently in its saucer.

'He has listed thirty two different items already,' Matthew said, 'and sketched them.'

French Angas's gaze was lowered on him now with added interest.

'And he has learnt their language,' Matthew said, with pride.

'Mr Cawthorne is a peculiar fellow, one of a handful here who have come close to the native.' Mr Woodhall's voice was flat, neutral. 'I feel that his talents could be of some use to this colony one day, if disposed in the appropriate manner.'

'I think they could be of use to the colony directly, if this collection of his is used in the manner most beneficial to all.' Angas hesitated, 'I mean to say, if his collections can be made over into the promotion of the colony, there could be signal advancement for many.'

'We have a boat in the harbour each week, and land taken already for fifty miles in every direction. What need have we of promotion?' Captain Phillips gave the view of the police. 'And more disorder every week from those who come with not land but labour as their object: a good day's pay and plenty of cheap grog in view and little else.'

'Indeed, the colony is expanding,' said Woodhall, 'and our new governor is pushing this element out to work the new stations. Expansion is our safety blanket, captain.'

'Indeed, Mr Woodhall,' said Phillips, 'you have a point. This may be the new governor's first move that actually is of benefit to us all. But hush, we have the governor's man among us. What say you, Matthew? Is the governor right to shove the layabouts into the regions?'

'Oh, indeed, sir.'

'And will this not hasten the demise of the natives of whom I hear you are so fond?'

Matthew had not thought of the question in this way before. 'I believe we can live side by side with the native, sir.'

Phillips and Woodhall grunted.

'Cawthorne has already begun to paint Captain Jack himself,' Matthew went on, turning to French Angas.

'I do say, Captain Jack, what! Now there's a name to conjure with.' French Angas put the thoughts of Phillips and Woodhall into the background; the future of the colony could be left to itself.

'A chieftain. And all daubed in paint he is, and with a shield and spears!'

Angas surveyed the room as all returned by degrees to a composed equanimity. The ladies came in with more tea.

'I say, this Cawthorne of yours becomes an interesting chap,' said Angas, taking another cup, and smiling at the expectant faces around him.


That night, Lucy laid in her bed, too tired to read, too excited with her day to be asleep. Since the news of the nearness of Adela's arrival, suddenly marriage had become more than a game of speculation that girls and matrons engaged in, and the men too if they would admit it.

Adela was really coming. A friend.

The news was too stimulating: a friend besides Mary. A friend she could sit with, and talk about everything that concerned her in the way that women of education would talk. And Mary could be there too. And Adela would ride; she must ride. She would ask James how well Adela was with a horse. They could go away from the town together. In numbers, there would be safety. Surely that would be permissible; she would find another girl to make three – impregnable! She must speak to Uncle immediately.

And the game of marriage: if one of the Larkin men was to be married, then why not the other? Would it be the thing to do? If her mother had been with her, she would have known the right answer without even having to think consciously. She would have sensed it, but yes, it must happen, in time.

She thought about her night. As if the afternoon with Angas was not enough, there had been dinner with her uncle and some newly arrived sea captain. What stories he had told. Her stories too, of the bush and of the wildness; just as much exaggerated as were those, she presumed, of the captain. Her uncle had raised his eyebrow to her across the table as she rattled on.

That night, she had spoken of the peculiarities of the bush, of natives and bushrangers, of men too long away from the town, too long away from the law. The stories were in her spirit, even if she was not in the stories.

But they were just other people's stories, and indeed she was not in them. She had been no further than the Bay and tomorrow she would go to Klemzig, four miles away. Adelaide was like a cage with the hills and the sea and short boundaries to north and south.

The captain had been to the colony before, had dined with the previous governor, but had not been so royally entertained. He made a gift to her: a small pistol, tiny. American, he said, a lady's weapon. He would not say how it had come into his keep, but he would give it to her, for her protection, to remember him by. He had called her 'my dear'. He would return to the colony in a year, most likely.

The pistol was in her drawer now, beside her bed, with five rounds which had come with it. It thrilled and frightened her; it was like a passport to a foreign place. She lived close to the edge no longer. She could go over the edge. Into the wild.

Adela. Marriage. Her pistol. The endless hills and the grassy plains and wild men. The rough characters and the genial scoundrels who came to town to stock supplies for prospecting – all away, past the hills, just out of reach.

Lucy waved away her thoughts. She passed her hand before her face two, three times, as if to shoo away a fly – such were the annoyances of sea captains. The candle by her bed flickered for a moment with the disturbance in the air, and on the sand-coloured wall of her room ghostly shadows formed in the half-light that it shed. She made her hands float like a wave before her and their image played on the wall as she did. Her sea captain was jostled and threatened by her mercurial knuckle shark fins.

Her mother had played shadows on the wall for her when she was a child – as if she were not a child still, nor even some child-woman caught between the two.

'Oh, Mother,' she cried out loud, and formed her arms into an arching embrace that was reflected upon the wall. The candle flickered for a moment more and the shapes came like Gothic cathedral spires that arced and dodged about the room all around her until she became confused and held her head in her hands and looked upon the wall no longer.

'Mother, help me,' she said again, to herself this time, in a whisper, and her mind began to form images of days gone by, of her mother and England, of ponds and ducks and lilac trees – careless days. After several minutes of such childish thoughts, Lucy drifted into a light and fitful sleep.

On the day of the trip to Klemzig, Lucy was up with the sun and had breakfasted on eggs and tea and solid, dark bread by the time her uncle even gave the word to call her. The news of the absence of Larkin and the inclusion of Thompson had been accepted without complaint. She was going out riding and that was enough. The pity was that she had wanted to show Matthew her pistol and even to fire a shot and perhaps bring down a bird.

She decided to leave the pistol behind.

But then what good was a pistol if it was not taken on a trip into the country? Even though Klemzig was barely four miles out and was surrounded by vegetable gardens and grapevines, it could still be considered the 'bush' if a point was stretched. Her uncle had not forbidden the pistol, but he had not had to; a lady would not normally go about armed so the question never occurred. But what if there was some emergency and she could have saved the day, but for the lack of a pistol?

She opened her satchel. There was plenty of space. Without thinking any more, her hand reached out and opened the drawer of her bedside table. The pistol slipped in as if of its own accord and the buckle was fastened. It was the work of a moment.

Lucy had saddled her horse and was ready waiting in the yard when her uncle emerged with a 'Yes, yes' as if she was hurrying him on, which she was not, and a solid 'Hrrmph' in the direction of Thompson.

He settled on his horse and smacked his short top hat into place. Thompson quietly mounted and positioned his side-satchel, then signalled ready to the governor with a lift of the chin and a raised eyebrow.

The ride to Klemzig was pleasant in the morning sun. All around them, parrots of red and blue and green took to the air at the approach of hooves and Lucy's persistent commentary; there was a shower of colour overhead at every turn. The track went alongside the river, which one moment was close to them so they could smell the cool water and then bent away from them around and beyond ancient gums that towered white bark citadels above them; and then the river came back to them and then bent away again in an endless dreaming game.

The track became a climb that was so gentle that not even Lucy noticed it until she turned to look at what was behind and saw that the trees they had left behind ten minutes before were now below them and that in the distance beyond could be seen the strip of blue that was not the sky and so could only be the sea, never visible from the plains. The track then bent decisively away from the river and made its way for the last two hundred yards towards some wispy columns of smoke that were the remnants of breakfast fires and then there was a bend in the track and, quite suddenly, there were rows of neat wattle and daub huts and five men sprang to greet them.

They all wore smiles of welcome that reflected the genuine pleasure they felt at the governor's visit. To have left their homeland had been a decision of great moment. To be allowed to build their own church and to practise their religion freely was the realisation of long-held dreams. Little wonder their dedication. Three of the men wore beards that followed the line of their jaw, trimmed short by scissors, while their upper faces were shaved clean in a fashion Lucy and the governor both thought, quite separately, would never catch on in Adelaide.

After much smiling and greeting, the little inspection party was taken around the village. The huts were as clean as it was possible for them to be and Lucy was taken off by the women to view the clothes washing and other arrangements indoors. The water supply this far up the river was clean; the question which occupied the governor's mind was how the Germans were disposing of their rubbish. The head man took them to a place where holes had been dug and waste was covered over. Vines had been planted further up on high ground before the ridge that was the beginning of the ranges. It was cooler there and was the place for their Riesling grapes and the site of more waste problems once vintage came. As all appeared to be in order in the village after an hour or so of walking about, and being interested in the future of viticulture in the colony, the governor suggested an impromptu party of inspection, to which the Germans proudly assented.

Lucy had been taken by the women for tea, or so it was thought, to the hut of Frau Kuchenmeister. As they approached the place, loud cries could be heard from the rear of the dwelling, as from the barracking of some contest. As the men turned the corner to the rear of the hut, they beheld Frau Kuchenmeister in the act of splitting in two a sawn log nearly six inches thick, to the approbational murmurs of the crowd of six or seven women gathered around. The axe was then handed to Lucy, who swung the blade with surprising confidence and, swivelling the handle with her wrists at the last moment, split the half log into quarters.

She turned and smiled widely to the men. 'There's quite an art to it. They've taken a minute to teach me. Now Frau Kuchenmeister and I are having a contest.'

'A contest?'

'To see who can get the smallest piece.'

And duly Frau Kuchenmeister swung the blade and got the quarter piece down to an eighth.

'This is where it gets interesting.'

Governor Bray looked around to his German friends to assess their response to this turn of events, but their faces were full of keen admiration for the girl.

Lucy stepped forward and licked her hands before picking up the axe. 'Best not to spit,' she confided to her uncle, indicating that she retained her grasp of vice-regal decorum. Then she put her full five-foot-two-inch frame behind the axe, her weight shifting from the right foot to the left as she swung.

The blade flashed down, slicing the eighth piece at its pointy centre and sending a shard of wood into a spin but leaving most of the chunk standing on its block.

'A technical hit only, I'm afraid. Not very good.'

Approving sympathy rumbled around the little crowd.

'Here, Mrs K, finish it off.' Lucy handed the axe to Frau Kuchenmeister, who casually swung through the wood, splitting it perfectly into sixteenth pieces, which spun off the block in pleasing little arcs.

'Brilliant,' cried Lucy in admiration.

Frau K stepped up and clapped her arm around Lucy's shoulders. 'Ya,' she said. 'Good girl, good girl.'

'How marvellous,' said Governor Bray, stepping forward to claim his niece, and addressing the whole gathering as he placed his own arm around her. 'It gives me great pleasure to observe that there has been more splitting logs than there has been splitting hairs in our dealings with the German community this morning.'

Those who understood English chuckled broadly with the governor's minute witticism, those who did not smiled along anyway.

'I must say that the community here has progressed significantly since my last visit and is a credit to the hard work of everyone here and, might I say,' he said, bowing his head to the men who accompanied him, 'to the excellent organisation of its leaders.'

Whatever their language skills, the approving sentiment of these remarks was not lost on the gathering.

'And now, my dear, we are to be taken to view the plantings of vines further east in the foothills. That is, if you are quite recovered from your exertions…'

'I feel I could do it again.'

'Another time perhaps. Let us now place ourselves in the care of these gentlemen, who will guide us. Thompson, if you could bring the horses.'

And Thompson glided away to attend to the matter.

William Cawthorne closed the door of his house and stepped up to the square of land that had been set aside as a park at his end of the town. Here, he sometimes paced around after dinner in the summer twilight; occasionally, he would sit on the fallen branch of a gum tree and gaze down the little hill over Hindley Street, across the river and its scrub surroundings to the place where smoke from the fires of the blacks' camp trailed into the evening blue. Possums and other small marsupials had found a way to live among the settlers and sometimes they stared at William from the trees with their great dark eyes, their foraging and retrieving done – living off the leavings of humanity, their little families satisfied.

The question of family had become a weight on Cawthorne's mind. His little school would close soon for high summer and he was bound for the farmers' fields, baling hay and sawing wood for fences most likely – a day labourer, no better than the fathers of the brats who descended upon his school each morning. Or would he go to the port to unload provisions and stack them on carts for the town? As the days grew longer and melted into his fourth summer in the colony, Cawthorne felt deeper and deeper the disgrace of his lowly position.

His hope was to raise capital to go into some business. He had tried surveying during the year that the colony was being mapped. It had been amply to his liking and the lure of real estate was strong. But now the most he could hope for was to rise in the teaching profession and to gain some security from that. He thought of his hothouse school-room and its ninety students. What use were Plato and Paine, Sophocles and Coleridge, with students who came to him with little more knowl-edge than the spelling of cat and dog? Each day brought fresh agonies; his hard-won knowledge mocked him with its futile inefficacy.

It was time for him to take a wife, someone to help him with his mother as she aged; though only fifty three years, she was stooped with excessive care. Again, his very lowness laughed at him.

That evening, he had walked to the natives' camp to sit on the tree stump stool. At length, a group of women climbed down the bank and waded into the river – five or six young girls and two older ones.

The smiles they gave each other were broad and the teeth they displayed were large and round, white and awkward, a row of pearls carelessly shoved into their mouths as if by a god who was in a hurry, off to lunch. Artlessly, they waded into the river, in nature's clothes each one of them, and unashamed to be before him, seated dolefully as he was on the opposite bank with his pipe. The young women transfixed him, their small buds, their legs arranged so differently to European women as they swayed left and right into the stream.

They were so innocent and unabashed that he felt as a man would who had seen the Garden of Eden, before the fall, before the knowledge and the apple. The girls had splashed each other and washed themselves in the cool waters of the river. Some of them glanced in his direction, and splashed more, then looked away and then back again until their peals began to scare the magpies off their perches. And then after some minutes, they all rose as one, by a signal unseen and unheard by him. The sight caused him consternation as he fought within himself. One manly half of him would leap into the river as if in some ancient baptism, engaging in the Dionysiac abandon which the Greeks took to be required for good health. But the other half was restrained, was civilised, took its hat off to the rules of his society, and paid homage to his dear mother whose life was in his hands. No mad diversions for Cawthorne.

And in this moment of the full agitation of his divided nature, these girls climbed back to their places and he saw upon two of their brown and glistening backs the unmistakable pitted marks of smallpox, and he was filled with sorrow. The deadly disease had been transmitted first from white man to black woman, no doubt, then through the communities along the river system from New South Wales as they traded and fought and interbred, but mostly when the Kaurna people hosted their conferences it came from anywhere and lived on and killed among them. It reminded Cawthorne of the way a gentleman will send a servant out with a calling card, to precede him in a town; in the same way, the white man had sent his smallpox ahead to announce his arrival. The people of the plains here had been hit harder than any other place.

Cawthorne's mind could not stay at ease and he began to walk. Even when he greeted Matthew Larkin in the street, he was still filled with confusion.

'I am bound for your house. Are you in?' Larkin said jokingly.

'Always in, except when I am not.' Cawthorne saw no benefit in trying to conceal his cloudy moods from Matthew.

'At the river, of course. But I must say, you seem as weighed under by it as I have ever seen you.'

As Cawthorne turned his eye back on Larkin, it was almost as dark, the eyebrow nearly as fiercely raised, as that of Captain Phillips himself. 'I have seen the girls,' he ventured, believing that Matthew would know what he was saying, 'at their bathing.' He cast a knowing look at Larkin and then stared away.

'I have seen them too,' said Matthew. 'They disturb you as they have me. The last time, I lay awake at night, remembering them.' His own face became nearly as disturbed as Cawthorne's.

'In the provinces it is said that coupling occurs.'

'I have heard it.'

'It is an abomination.' Cawthorne spoke with the consciously furious certainty of the scholar and of the man who was locked in the city. 'There is a Form, Matthew. There is a true Form of Beauty.'

Matthew cocked his head at this peculiar utterance.

'Have you read some Plato?'

'I have heard…a little.'

'There is a true and absolute Form of all things. Of Truth, of Good, and especially of Beauty. There is a beauty which is above and beyond the forms of convention, which are merely the fashion of their day. The knowledge of the Form of Beauty is buried within us, but is confused by the way it is dressed by society. It is God's work to find that form.'

Matthew grasped Cawthorne's arm before he walked away. 'I saw a mulatto woman, in the slave market at Rio, who possessed that beauty.' In the two-day stop at Rio, they had visited a series of small dark houses in narrow and miserably paved alleys that led off a street called the Vallongo. Here were the wretched slaves straight off the boats from Africa, lined up sitting in cramped rows in tiny rooms, fifty or sixty of them in a single space that had been built as a child's bedroom. Dark and brooding, menacing power Matthew had sensed in that room, and all of them still chained together.

Then, as a wealthy burgher had died and his slaves were set to be disposed of, there was an auction which they had attended in a large hall, spacious enough to have been a guildman's meeting place in a Lancashire mill town. Males and females were offered alternately. A table was placed in the middle of the room and a packing crate beside it for each slave to mount for inspection. Men had arms and legs bare; muscles were felt for their apparent power, teeth inspected to determine age and health. Accustomed to their situation as they were, these men and women seemed placidly accepting of their lot, except one.

A mulatto woman presented for inspection was so perfect of face and shape that allusions to the mythical nymph Calypso were made. About twenty years of age, her dress of pure white was cut to show her perfect figure to the best advantage. Immediately, the desultory manner of the bidders was replaced with the most enthusiastic interest. As the ante was raised, the look on her face became one of contempt, of disdain for her situation, her fears perhaps born from experiences at variance to those of the other slaves offered. Then she began to shake visibly as the furore in the auction room rose to a crescendo, so that when the hammer went down and a wealthy, portly middle-aged merchant stepped forward to write his cheque, she was led away a tearful, trembling wreck.

It had been the wish of his father that Matthew see the slave markets of Rio; it would be a dose of real life that the boy needed. If he were to be a man of the world, as he had said that he wanted, then he should see everything there was to be shown, and no single person would stop at Rio without looking at the slaves; it was reality.

'All who would purchase her were afflicted by it, though they barely knew it themselves. They were driven forward by it, into a kind of frenzy.'

'The frenzy of the weak – the mania for possession. And you, did you throw yourself at her?'

'Indeed, no. I was simply transfixed.'

'The girls at the river…' Cawthorne broke off and stared into the distance.

'Yes, Cawthorne, what is it?'

'Some of them are quite piteously marked – by us, and the disease that we fling before us. That disease arrived ten years before any colonist here in South Australia. Our knowledge of the Forms is innate, Matthew. It lies within us and we must be strong to seek it out. But we must abide with it and allow it to inform us. If we own it, we destroy it.'

'When I was eleven years old, I read the story of Scheherazade.'

'The Arabian tale.'

'That young woman possessed the Form. She had wisdom and beauty. She told a thousand stories and saved the young women of her town. She was never possessed, even by the sultan whom she changed and who surrendered to her. There must be a higher cause than running sheep and digging ores from the ground, seeking wealth. In my move to the north, I may find something of it.'

'Perhaps,' said Cawthorne wistfully, almost miserably, 'perhaps. If there is such a cause, I know not whether I have the strength or the position to pursue it.'

'You spoke to me of Plato's cave,' said Matthew. 'It is the true philosopher who must find the light, to bring it back to the bottom of the cave, to change the fools who will not see.'

'Aah,' groaned Cawthorne, 'it is not for one such as me.'

'It is a duty.'

'Matthew, I have duties enough.' He gestured up the street, to his little house where his mother waited, slicing boiled mutton for his dinner.

'Of course,' said Matthew, and in his mind there grew some notion of his own duty to the Form and the Truth, and that if Cawthorne could not pursue it, then it must be he who did.

At Klemzig, the official party walked their horses up to the Riesling grove while two of the German men accompanied them on foot, along with a boy named Franz, who walked alongside Lucy's horse and asked her questions in his native tongue. He had been very taken with her log-splitting form in a wide-eyed wondering way and now needed to know every detail about English trees and the uses of their timber.

At a small clearing, the Germans stopped and looked back towards the view which spread out behind them. They had reached such an elevation that when Lucy turned her horse she could see the whole plain spread out before them ten miles to the silver sea where dots of ships sat like little caterpillars, their antler masts sniffing the air. On the shoulder of the hills were the German huts, then the river snaking through the town of Adelaide. The most impressive of buildings among the trees was Government House.

'Uncle, the view would rival the hills of Tuscany.'

'Yes, it is quite a sight. Look,' and he pointed away to the left, 'you can see the curve of the Bay all the way to the southern hills and the Fleurieu Peninsula.'

'And Government House is there,' she pointed, 'where Matthew will be at work.'

'Ha,' cried the governor, 'if we are lucky.'

While Lucy was projecting her thoughts towards Government House in one manner, and while the governor's were occupied somewhat differently, there was a muffled sound of hooves scuffling around the boulder which marked the turning point in the road to the foothills vineyard plateau. The Germans were the first to notice and turned to face the intruders while the other two were still rapt in awe of the splendour of the Queen's newest Antipodean home and in contemplation of its most interesting inhabitant.

'Ho, there,' cried a rough voice and at last they turned.

Confronting them were two men on horses. One wore a huge red beard that framed a wild countenance with alert, amused eyes. The other was thin and sallow, his face that of a poker player, his hat pulled down to obscure his face, his beard dark, thin and wispy. While the party was being addressed, he walked his horse a few steps around the clearing, to the left side of Lucy and the governor, watching, but still in touch with the path to the hills.

'Generally, the term of salutation from vagabond to victim is "Bail up," cried out in as rough and frightening a manner as a man can muster. But as ye folks have been good enough to bail yourselves up for us without bein' asked, I'll just bid ye a very gentle good afternoon, then.'

'You are Moran,' said the governor.

The bushranger bowed his head by three inches in gracious acknowledgement, tipping his pistol to the brim of his hat as he did so.

'And by the sound of that voice and by the finery of your equipage, you would be the governor himself. The new man, come to save the colony.' And he added in a conspiratorial aside, 'Ye'd be surprised how much gossip creeps up these hills now, sir. And long may ye prosper,' he said, returning to his booming delivery. 'It is sure that what we need is a man such as yourself to keep the colony prosperous and me friend and me in gainful misemploy, now, isn't that right, Danny?'

If the other man was named Danny, he made no recognition of the fact, nor did he allow any expression to escape the shadow of hat brim that was over his face.

There was an irony in the voice of the big man, close kin to sarcasm, and Lucy found herself drawn into it, almost as if it were against her conscious wishes. This barrel-chested knave looked as though he should be out shearing sheep or lifting barbells in a circus tent, and here he was making fun of her uncle. But not just rudely, he was doing it with a peculiar, impudent intelligence.

Lucy felt an urge to push back. 'My friend and I,' Lucy blurted.

There was silence in the clearing for a few moments. None dared move while Moran regarded Lucy with interest.

He walked his horse two paces closer and made as if to peer with squinted eyes, although he could see her plain enough from where he had been. The man was clearly one for theatrics. 'Well, well. It seems the governor has brought his private schoolmarm with him to amuse us this afternoon, Kenny. What do you say to that, Kenny?'

The other man pulled his hat an inch lower over his eyes.

'What was that you said, Kenny?' Moran cocked his head in the direction of his accomplice, but still no reply. 'Ohhhhhhh,' said Moran, as if some withering insight had been relayed to him, though not a word had been spoken.

Since the appearance of the bushrangers, the two Germans had held their hands up in punctilious prisoner propriety; they stared wide-eyed and anxious at the pistol that Moran waved around as he spoke. They had never seen a madman like this before and had no idea what he was capable of doing next. Only the boy, Franz, was not afraid; he was rapt with wonder.

'I think you have disarmed Kenny, miss, with yer dazzlin' beauty, not to mention the superior nature of yer education.' He tapped his temple with his gun barrel and winked. 'Oh, and by the way,' he went conspiratorial again, his head bent forward and winking at her, 'his name is not Kenny neither. That was one I just made up to put yer off the scent. Oh, ho, ho, ho.' He rocked back on his horse in pantomime hilarity.

'You have an original sense of humour, Mr Moran. I'm sure we could all learn a great deal from you.'

'Ha, ha, ha, ha,' Moran spluttered on his horse, almost choking in real amusement now. 'Now it is me you have disarmed, miss. I am under your command.' Moran put his two hands up – the left holding the reins of his horse, the right handling his pistol – in a gesture of surrender which seemed to amuse him even more. For the first time, he held his hands in one place for three seconds.

Suddenly a shot rang out. A small shot from a very narrow-gauge pistol such as none of the men present had ever heard before – a ping more than the accustomed pistol crack. The miniature bullet cracked the middle finger of Moran's right hand and the impact and the shock made him drop his weapon to the ground, where it was quickly fielded by the German boy, Franz. With equal speed, Thompson bent from his horse with his hand out and quietly took the pistol from Franz. The balance of power in the clearing was dramatically altered. Expressions of shock remained on the faces of all except that of Franz, whose eyes were excited, as if he could not wait to run and tell.

The shadowy accomplice was now at full attention. His horse stamped its hoof and seemed to be demanding instructions. The governor was a man of action, but even he was too astonished to move; Lucy's determined face wore a small smile of victory; Thompson's resembled that of the cat that got the cream.

It was Lucy who spoke. 'There are five of us here to your two, not to mention the boy, who did well.' She inclined her head towards Franz in appreciation. 'More importantly, we now have three weapons to your one, since you have surrendered yours to the very capable Mr Thompson. Yes, my uncle carries a pistol, of course, and you counted that as long as he was covered, you were safe. But in all your calculations, you didn't consider me, did you?'

There was silence in the clearing for ten seconds as Lucy's words hung in the air. Then, without answer, Moran swung his reins and kicked his horse and so did his shadowy accomplice and the two wild men made a gathering of dust and were around the boulder and galloping up the path to the hills and were gone, not to be seen again. Bray made a show of opening up his satchel for a pistol, but too late.

There was a breathless moment as all came to the understanding that the danger had passed. The governor looked with shock upon his niece and found it difficult to speak, so confused was he as to the appropriate words to say. The two German men exhaled deeply and gave thanks to the lord. Franz ran away down the hill to be the first to tell the news to the villagers who would already be hurrying up the path on account of the shot that had been fired.

The story of the rascalry of Mad Moran the bushranger would be retold a hundred times in the coming years and young Franz would dine out on the story for decades to come. For his part, the governor mused on the wisdom of his decision to bring along the sangfroid of Thompson rather than to be burdened with the charming chaos of Larkin.

For her part, Lucy gloried in the notoriety this would now bring, not so much to the ears of the colony in general, but to those of Matthew Larkin in particular. For his part, Thompson would be licking cream from his lips for weeks.

And Mad Moran lived to encounter his unlikely assailant on another day.


*She came across a farm that was set, not back in the foothills like the others, but off the road, a hundred yards back. Outside the place, there was a man out cutting grass for hay. His little whitewashed hut of a house looked like it had just two rooms – perhaps there was a wife inside, or in the fields shepherding the sheep that wandered there. Further out, towards the shadows of the hills, there were some cattle, but no fences, not yet. Beyond that, the hills sprang away east to become the Barossa Ranges. The man's shirt was white against the yellowing green of that which he cut.*

*She stopped in the road outside this house and the man stopped in his work to gaze upon her. From one hundred yards, she could see him thinking – was that a woman on that horse, dressed like a man and riding like one too? In England, it would be an offence to go about so attired.*

*'Good afternoon,' she sang out.*

*The man took three steps forward and bent his ear as if to hear her better. 'Oh, I say, miss,' he said in the rough and friendly tones of Dorset. 'Are you all right?'*

'I am very well, thank you. Is this the way to Kapunda?'

The man's face brightened, for to him this was a simple question and he had feared that the woman's appearance might produce for him some more problematical enquiry. 'Oh certainly, miss. It is the only way, the only track you can take. Just follow Mr Watson's wheel ruts and you will be taking yourself there and that is for sure.'

'I see – the ruts of the redoubtable Watson. It seems I must follow not only his advice but his ruts also.'

'I'm sorry, miss?'

'Mr Watson would seem to be quite central to my story.'

'Oh, er, I wouldn't know about that, miss.'

'Of course not. Thank you so much for your assistance. You've set my mind at rest, sir.'

At this, the man's face lightened again, for he could feel the successful conclusion of this surprising business and the impending departure of this confusing and gamine apparition on horseback. And indeed the girl kicked her horse to a trot and proceeded, waving her hat, along the road to Kapunda.

**5**

# The North – November 1843

The sun was well up and climbing by the time the Larkin brothers rode up to the homestead of their neighbour Charles Jenks. They slowed their horses down the hill that led to a stream that bordered Jenks's home acre and as they reined their mounts around the hill they were greeted by the vision of Sylvania. A stone and mortar building rose two storeys into the air, as majestic a sight as there was for fifty miles in any direction. That Jenks had preceded them in the valley by one year and a half and that he had begun with capital and a plan was obvious to any who gazed upon his domestic masterpiece. The upper-storey balcony was fringed with lattice that had been imported from Birmingham and was painted a shade of grey that set off the dark stones which had been sawn to a nicety; then the neat white grouting gave the whole situation an attitude of rectitude and permanence.

The Larkin brothers sat their horses and looked but shared no word. There was no need for words when they both were thinking of what might be theirs, what would become theirs, in their own place, in time. James's thoughts were of Adela and a dynasty, while Matthew's were more complex and ambiguous; he was working towards an idea of what he wanted but his thoughts were still confused and open to being shaped by the course of events before him.

Before the house there was a levelled area, shored up on one side with enormous pearly stones, taken from a river bed whose waters had worn them away for five thousand years. This new area had been raked and grassed and cut smooth to resemble the forecourt of some English country house. On the grass, there were hoops for the game of croquet and lying at the side were mallets and orbs of wood, not yet collected by the servants from the morning game. As their gaze lifted back to the latticed balcony, a woman and child appeared from the passage there and the child pointed out the new arrivals to the woman, and they both began to wave and to call out greetings.

And so they kicked their horses and, as they approached, Jenks himself appeared from the ground floor entrance, rigged out in the nature of a fox hunt. Tight cream breeches were tucked into riding boots of soft leather, his red jacket was cut away at the sides and sported lapels of soft black nap. Jenks stepped forward hale and generous, a man of the world bent on entertaining his neighbours with the fruits of his success. Behind him teetered a man of over sixty years, wearing white stockings and a blue coat with large square gold buttons, an item of livery that would have looked the perfect part forty years before. This servant carefully bore a tray upon which was a decanter containing some viscous tan-coloured liquid and some crystal beakers which might once have been intended for the serving of water.

The Larkin brothers dismounted and, as they did, both noticed four or five horses bending their noses to each other, loosely tethered at the lower side of the house where the ground began to slope away to the stream.

'Er, Simpson,' said Jenks to his man and waved him towards the newly arrived brothers.

'Sherry?' said Jenks, observing as much as asking, but also as if to say 'what else'.

Simpson came forward and filled two beakers three inches deep and handed one to each of them, grunting, 'To your health, sir,' as he did.

Taking his glass from Simpson, Matthew looked up to the latticed balcony once more but the vision of mother and child was gone.

'I hope you are ready for a rousing morning,' said Jenks. 'The sport on offer promises to be most amusing…'

James and Matthew saluted their host. 'To your good health, sir.'

'…and profitable, of course, if the long run is to be taken into account. I am obliged to you for your attendance.'

'Your works here have continued apace, Mr Jenks. Your place is like paradise.'

'Thank you, indeed. We have done what we can. But I am sure that you are on the way to establishing your own heaven on earth. But of course first we must clear the land of all its pests in order to make use of it to the extent that God intended.'

'Aye to that, sir,' said a voice behind him and Jenks turned around with a welcoming 'Aha', for now there shambled from the building four other men with the appearance of being bright with the morning drink. They were headed by Phillips; with him was Bright from Spalding and Jones the Welshman, whose place bordered the Larkins on the west, as well as one other not of their acquaintance.

'All seven present,' said Jenks. 'Excellent. A fine number, seven, to ride. A lucky number. Hmmmph. Seven of the finest men.'

At this, Phillips looked at the new arrivals and fixed his gaze on Matthew in particular. 'A fine bunch indeed, Jenks,' he said, with a twisted irony in his voice. 'We must work as a team and all pull as one this morning, Jenks, for our party to remain intact. There are some that are taken by chance in these climes, sir, as should not be, and some who remain on this earth who would be better taken.' Phillips's face then abruptly relaxed into that of the Sunday morning guest, in a transformation that was remarkable.

'God moves in ways that are not for us to fathom,' said Jenks with sympathy, passing smoothly over the malevolent inference in Phillips's speech. 'I trust that He will be with us in the undertaking of this morning. Whenever you gentlemen are ready,' he said to the Larkin brothers. 'Your shoulder, Larkin minor,' asked Jenks by way of conversation as the Larkins took a swig of their wine, 'is fit for the fray?'

'I have been riding for a fortnight, Mr Jenks. Tibbs declares me fit enough and I would not miss this morning.'

'Ah, you show good spirit. Excellent, excellent.'

'We have not ridden far,' said James, taking a good drink of sherry. 'The horses are just warmed and ready.'

'Very well then, let us toast to the success of our morning of sport.' And Simpson duly went around and provided each member of the shooting party with a further splash of sherry to join in a toast to their mission.

The woman and child now appeared at the door, to smile upon the assemblage and to bid them farewell. Matthew winked and drew a shy smile from the lad, who turned then to his mother to acknowledge the small acquaintance between them. At this, Matthew noticed that the boy was awkward in his movement; he shuffled somewhat on his right leg as he turned to take his mother's attention.

'We will be quick and clean,' said Jenks to his men. 'Surprise will be everything to us. The enemy will have no particular knowledge of our intention but I must say that with time they have become more cunning, more difficult to pin, what with their weekly movements of camp. They have become more likely to stand and fight, more likely to have their arms at the ready. But they are also more likely to be dining on stolen property at this moment. To horse, gentlemen. The maids are lighting the fire as we leave. A side of best roasted hogget awaits us in two hours, haha. Let us away.'

At that, Jenks led the way to the horses by the side of the house and lifted himself into the saddle. The sad-faced Simpson trudged inside with his plate of glasses. Behind him went the mother and the lad, who dragged his foot behind him in his gait. The men mounted and trotted around the croquet lawn and Matthew lingered to watch as the boy went inside and made immediately for the stairs to return to his position upon the balcony. The boy mounted the first step with his left foot and dragged the right behind him on to that same step. Then the same procedure with the next step and the next, his mother at the bottom of the stairs. As she mounted the first step herself, she turned to see the odd young man watching her still. The brief smile she gave him was sad and understanding, full of the knowledge of the pitiful nonsense of their position, and of the inevitability of what must be done to maintain it.

'Come, Matthew,' the patient but urgent voice of his brother rang across the croquet lawn and Matthew turned his mount and was away with the men.

Jenks led them back across the stream and up the winding path and then along the brief escarpment that ran around the hill away from his fields and into the disjunctive knots of native territory. In the valley below, the homestead of Jenks sat solid, but like a toy against the blue green of the hill behind it and, with the croquet lawn before it, there was an incongruous air about the place, as if a palace from some nursery rhyme had been dropped by a god above. From the chimney, a wisp of smoke now penetrated the air like a violation, and on the balcony the two figures still stood waving like little clockwork figures.

As he rode away behind Jenks and his mates, Matthew clung to the image of the boy child and to his pitiful attempt to scale the stair, dragging his foot at every step, cheerful and brave in his lameness. The boy would never become one of these men, would never be a true heir to his father's estate. He would have to go away from the valley, to the town, to a university perhaps, to mark his mark in the world while thriving on the receipts gained from the crimes of others. Matthew thought now how fortunate this boy was, to be lame in body and to be absolved from all the expectations that went with fitness, and to expect a life away from here. But for now the seven men who rode were the boy's protection and were the creators of this system of safe passage, and in their thinking the mission they were undertaking was not an option that they had taken, but a thing of nature and transition, as inevitable as the coming and passing of the seasons.

The track dipped and the seven thundered down it, their mounts eager for the work. Seven horses and seven men. Into a raised valley now they leapt across a small stream which was a tributary of that which flowed past the house of Jenks. Great gums hung over them; those that were in the shade of the hill still hung on to the dew of the night and the men were all as wet as apple pickers before ten minutes were out. But on they went to another valley, then another hill, past acacias in bloom whose sickly golden flowers stuck onto their damp coats. At the top they paused to survey the country around the place and sighted woodland that stretched away into a morning haze as far as they could see; woodland that would be a patchwork of fenced-in pasture and crops before their days were out, or so every movement of their bodies seemed to say as they gaped to north and east.

In the near distance, two plumes of smoke arose like orisons in the still air. One was off to the left closer to the sea, and was in deep woodland and away down a steep embankment. The other was more distant, to the right, inland where the cascades of hills had flattened to a plateau which led along to mile after mile of the wooded land. In some places, there were treeless openings filled with rich grass: the spearing grounds of the blackfellow's own paradise.

'Let us rest a minute,' said Jenks, and produced from the pocket of his huntsman's jacket a small pipe, which he proceeded to stuff with tobacco and to light. 'I will give you gentlemen a moment to survey this scene, and then to tell me what you think.'

A flask of water was passed around and they found stones or fallen branches on which to rest. A couple produced tobacco and proceeded to roll cigarettes.

'It is God's country,' said Jones the Welshman, unable to wrest his eyes from the haze in the distance and the Arcadian scene which lay before it. 'And that's for sure,' he finished with emphasis, giving hint enough of the visions and dreams that he harboured.

'Aye, but do we take the high road or the low road to get to it?' Phillips emitted his characteristic impatience. He was for riding out each Sunday until the job was done.

'I am no master of this country and would leave that decision to Jenks himself…' said Jones, conscious of his own status but wanting to remind Phillips that he was not the master of the expedition either.

'But what do you say?' Phillips continued, testing the man.

Jones looked at Phillips for a moment, as if in question of whether to remonstrate with the man, then, as Jenks waved his pipe and grunted encouragingly, he went on, 'I say the high. It is further from us but the track will be easier and our approach will be less noticed.'

'Aye,' said Phillips, 'so it is. Your thoughts are keen enough.'

The other men nodded their assent.

'Jenks?'

'There is no question that the Welshman has it,' said Jenks. 'There is no doubt in my mind but I wanted there to be no doubt in yours as well. We shall slow our horses and approach with caution.' He spoke carefully, quietly and deliberately, so every man would lean forward in his place to hear him. His sense of authority was not that he should direct, but that men should be bent to follow. 'If we gallop in, they will hear us from a mile and will be bounding into the bush in a moment and all is lost. We will look like fools. So we must approach with stealth, then fan out to approach them from three directions. If we put our horses on the burst from two hundred yards, we will catch them with their knives and forks still in their black mits.'

This last was greeted with uproarious applause and mirth from the men, for all there knew that the blacks used no knife or fork but ate their meat with their hands like all uncivilised folk. Jenks knew the way to win his charges over.

And so it was decided: the smoke plume to their right would be their target and every man went about his business now in a quiet and sober way, for this was a Sunday morning ride no longer and the final act was upon them. They could smell the sweet odour of blood and feel it sticky between their fingers. Matthew had been silent through the discussion of tactics; his head nodded and he grunted assent in the places where that seemed appropriate. This was Jenks's mission and somehow it was Phillips's too, for Phillips's status had risen, not just because of his tangible abilities, but because he had lost a son. He was more important now, and his taste for vengeance would be appeased.

And so the men remounted after a time, their horses freshened by rest and water. They walked quietly, almost silent. Acacias flowered golden by the side of their tracks and sometimes banksia and callistemon. Low, wiry bushes sprouted tiny red flowers and colours jumbled together in a living potpourri. And then the highest gum that Matthew had ever seen, set down by the bed of the creek so they were almost at eye level to the lowest of the hundred or so white cockatoos that sat upon its branches. It was as if that tree had blossomed massive shimmering white flowers.

Matthew turned to his brother and would speak to share his joy at the sight but James knew him too well and held up his right hand to say, 'Quiet, not a word.' And then he nodded to his brother to show that he shared his appreciation.

The cockatoos sat squarking and chattering to themselves in their usual manner, and allowed the men to pass without taking to the air, as if this was God and nature giving their sign as to the goodness of the operation that was before them.

While the men's eyes were on the smoke that plumed ahead of them from the natives' campfire, they also watched for rocks and rivulets beneath the horses' hooves; and all the while their eyes scoured the bush for native sentries and their silent spears.

But no natives came; no sentries were posted. No head man would believe that the white man could come this far for them, to the forest, to the outer limits of their land. No lawman warned of their coming or had seen it foretold in the stories of their ancient heroes and dreaming ancestors.

Presently, the plume of smoke was so close that the men could smell it and they all sat their mounts while Jenks motioned with his right hand and Phillips and Jones walked their horses through the light scrub, their heads bowing beneath the low-hanging branches of the gum trees there. At another motion from Jenks, Bright from Spalding and another man moved away to the left and took up their position on a small rise eighty yards from them. And so they proceeded to encircle the spiral of smoke and the camp of the natives.

But as they closed in, they caught sight of a boy, rummaging about in the scrub at the foot of a tree. What he was doing the men could not

be certain, but perhaps he had been looking for a possum or was collecting grubs from a hollow log or berries from some bush; still, at the
sound of the approaching horses, his head shot round and he held the
men in his gaze for some moments. He might have been eleven or
twelve years old and perhaps he had never seen a white man before, but
he stood in wonder for some time as they approached, as if he was assessing all the stories that had been told him; and he could not take his
eyes from the strange beast, the horse, which he had been told was not
attached to the man, although there was no telling at this moment that
it was not.

And so the boy gazed upon the white man for a moment as they
sat their horses and smiled upon him. Then some instinct in him turned
to fear as the white man slowly eased a smooth grey rod from the pouch
at his thigh. The fear rose from the pit of his stomach to his chest; the
boy turned and ran in the direction of the camp, yelling as he did.

'Charge,' Jenks shouted, only as loud as he needed to carry his order
to the men on the higher ground eighty yards away, and as he did he
spurred his horse, ducked between the trees and took aim at the running
boy. The shot went through the back of the boy beneath his right shoulder and he went immediately to ground and was trampled beneath the
hooves of the horse of Jenks and by those of the Larkin brothers too.
As he passed over him, Matthew saw the horribly disfigured boy, his
head crushed by the hind hooves of his brother's horse, a spurt of blood
counterpointing the colour scheme of the fallen leaves of green-grey
gums and the faded red flowers of callistemon.

All at once, it seemed they were upon the camp of the natives and
a rude and temporary one it was, with sheets of bark leaning against
trees for shelter and nothing like a permanent hut in view. There was a
campfire and a dozen to fifteen natives of all ages about it. Young naked
girls of fourteen or so stood up in their places, their mouths open in
amazement. Old men stood too and the younger grappled with spears
and clubs that lay about. One man raced for a lean-to and was ferreting
about for spears that were there as in some kind of arsenal, but as he

bent, the fearful noise burst out and he fell where he was, his hand grasping a fighting club that he would never use.

Matthew raised his gun and it was a girl who stood in front of him, her eyes betraying her fear and shock. Matthew gazed into her and he could not focus his mind to pull the trigger when her whole face disappeared before his eyes and there were splinters of bone and the dripping gore that clung to her skull. Her trunk fell to the ground, arms flung outwards and Matthew gazed upon her small breasts and the pouch of fuzzy black hair between her legs.

'Get the breeding stock, you fool,' Phillips was hissing in his ear, and he rode away in pursuit of another girl, whom he shot in the middle of the back, and she fell forward on her face. All around was shot and screaming and the acrid smoke of gunfire. Beside him, Jenks was taking cool and careful aim at those who fled. One of the last was bounding into the bush and Jenks trotted his horse to the edge of the clearing and took a full three seconds aim and fired. His expression after the exchange was one of satisfaction. Matthew felt a spear pass by him and like a fool he looked around to see it stab into the ground at the base of a gum tree at the edge of the clearing. When he looked back, the same old warrior who had thrown at him was picking up another spear and he hurled it towards Matthew. The spear sliced through Matthew's forearm then lodged in the neck of his horse. The old man who had thrown the spear now looked around him but there were no more spears. Matthew fired his revolver and the man went to ground clutching onto his stomach.

Matthew now was gripped by panic as his horse tossed his head up wildly in a vain attempt to dislodge the spear that still stuck in his neck. The screams of the horse were like none that Matthew had ever heard before and brought nothing but fear and panic and tears to him. He had not long to wonder what to do as the horse now collapsed its weight on its right leg and it fell, bringing Matthew heavily to ground with his right foot crushed beneath.

The men now wheeled the horses together in the centre of the clearing, for there were no more natives left to shoot. The old man whom Matthew had shot rose from his daze upon the ground and knelt while still holding on to his stomach, but not for long, as Phillips leapt from his mount and picked up the hunting club that laid on the ground next to him and bashed him once, very hard, across the temple and he went down and moved no more. Phillips tossed the club to one side and turned back to his colleagues.

'Keep the club, Phillips,' said Jenks, 'tell your grandchildren about it.'

Phillips scowled at Jenks for the mention of grandchildren, for his first son was lost and only one remained.

'Ah, yes, my apologies, old chap,' and he touched his hat in accentuation.

But it was the plaintive whinnies of Matthew's horse that now attracted them and they gathered around the sorrowful sight. The horse continued tossing its head and trying desperately to regain its footing.

'Don't you know what to do even now?' said Phillips, scowling at Matthew. 'Will you write a poem?' He drew his pistol and fired one shot into the horse's head and its fearful struggle was over.

Around them were eleven grown bodies and two babies whom shotgun blasts had carried off along with their mothers. The arm of one infant moved slowly as the blood drained from the wound in its throat from the shot that had passed through there on its way to its dead mother's heart. Its hand stopped on the woman's breast and moved no more.

And then there was the boy who lay out in the bush; he had to be counted too.

'Fourteen,' said Jenks, completing the arithmetic in his head. 'An excellent effort, with only two or three run off. Capital form. Now to help out young Larkin.'

But someone had already produced a couple of stout branches from the bush nearby and was knifing away their lateral shoots to make a lever that could go under the horse. With one such wedge under each side of Matthew's foot, the horse was prised away and Matthew dragged to safety and his boot cut so the foot could be examined.

'A bad sprain at the least, perhaps a bone is broken,' said James.

Matthew tried to stand but could place no weight upon that foot.

'The spear wound has not hit a vein, but it is a decent slice. If we had a native medicine man, we could treat him here.'

'Native medicine? You would let a nigger lay hands on your brother?' said Jones, and spat into the embers of the fire.

'Grace,' said Matthew – that one word.

'It's not that bad, lad,' said Jones, alluding to the ambiguity of the word, potentially referring as it could to a state of being as much as a person's name, and all joined him in laughter except Phillips.

'I know what he means,' said Phillips, with a face that looked like it had bitten on a lemon.

And so a wintry smile of knowing came over Jones as well and the other men too wore looks that men take on when they smile in the face of unpleasant things.

'We will ride two to a horse,' said James. 'Can you do it?'

Matthew nodded with certainty.

'We must leave the horse to the crows,' said Jenks.

'…and the natives.' Phillips, it seemed, needed to point out, 'There is meat there for them to last a month.'

'Those that are left of them.' Jenks reminded them all of the relative success of their mission and the men brightened and took their cue to wink and nod at each other. 'A horse is a horse,' Jenks finished enig-matically, but the men still nodded that they knew his meaning and even Phillips was induced to gain some pleasure and to shrug and join them in their high spirits.

And so, after the gathering of souvenirs and putting out the camp-fire, they dragged the bodies of the natives to a gully ditch and covered them with stones and dirt. With thoughts of home and hogget foremost in their minds, the men mounted their horses with the Larkin brothers together at the head of the assemblage alongside Jenks.

On the endless trek, Matthew Larkin thought of the slice in his arm that was beginning to throb in time with the beating of his heart; he thought of the naked native girl, her face disappearing under the shot from Phillips's gun, the half-formed breasts and black fuzz of her headless torso leering at him as he stared in horror.

The shooting party returned to Jenks's house and by the time he was transferred to one of Jenks's ponies, Matthew felt a lightness of head and the first beads of perspiration on his forehead. But that could have come from the exertion of the ride, and he summoned his strength for a stout salute to Jenks and the other men as they set off for home. By the time they came to the Lingalee and stopped in front of the house, he was leaned forward in the saddle and sweat was bursting from his forehead as in a Swedish bath. His face was flushed and red – not the red from the sun but turning to the dark and mouldering maroon of a bruise.

The native girl Grace scampered up from the hut when she saw Matthew's slumped body. She shouted out from thirty yards away in her anxiety. The men were aware that Grace had knowledge of the plants of the hills and that she was thought to trade with men from distant places for special herbs. When she arrived there with her cousins and the boys, she had carried a shoulder bag made of flax that held grasses and dried berries.

The men who had come out to greet the brothers now looked to James for guidance. He stood back to let Grace through and the others did so too in the proper deference that was due to a healer, no matter of what colour or culture.

Grace examined Matthew's wound then looked into his eyes and made her diagnosis. 'Them blackfella put spear in bad things,' she said.

They had heard stories about the men of the hinterland – of sheep's intestines left to sit for days in a pot and when the liquid stopped moving and had distilled down to an evil black sludge like hemlock that even the flies would touch no longer, then the spear tips were dipped

in it and all was ready for battle – the white man's own property returned in poison.

'I come back,' said Grace and she went away and they carried
Matthew inside and laid him on his bed.

'We must send for the doctor from Clare,' said James.

'Grace will tend me,' said Matthew.

'It is my duty to send to Clare and I shall do that. In the meantime,
Grace may tend to you, I am sure.'

'It is fifteen miles to Clare, brother. Save the horse.'

'It is eleven miles to Clare,' James smiled.

'Send me Grace,' said Matthew.

'She will come, I am sure.'

In ten minutes, Grace returned. Over her shoulder was a smaller
finely woven string bag, its strap cut between her breasts ,which were
concealed by a man's loose calico shirt that lapped the tops of her thighs.
Beneath this makeshift western regalia she wore a pubic tassel that was
tied around her waist with flaxen string. Clutched to her chest there
was a smooth stone and a low-sided bowl and in her right hand a
wooden mug with water. She did not knock upon the door, for she
knew little of doors and the etiquette of security and privacy, but had
seen that white people observed many strange and unfathomable rituals.
But those rules did not apply to her. James made way for her, having
been able to do nothing in the meantime but hold a clean wet sheet
over the wound and wipe his brother's face.

Grace placed her hand upon Matthew's brow and felt the heat inside
and the cold of the sweat that sat upon it. From her bag, she drew a
handful of sticks with withered leaves, snapped long ago from some low
desert bush.

'*Pitjuri* plant,' she said to James. 'From my father country. Make
him good. *Thalgi* too.' Without hurry, she crumbled the dried leaves
into the long flat bowl and applied the grinding stone to this mixture.
She ground it all up and down in a motion that was not simply of the
hands but of the whole body. Her shoulders and her backbone moved

as she ground and after a minute she began to moan and sing in a tongue that neither Matthew nor James had ever heard.

The moaning of Grace was hypnotic and in his fevered and half-dreaming state Matthew thought himself in the parlour of the Cawthornes with the dance of Willa Willa that had startled him at first and then became a lulling soporific thing. And as Grace moaned and sang and as the fever worked through his body, he felt himself crossing over some invisible line, as if into another world.

He drifted into a sleep. In his sleep, he dreamt of his horse. His horse was riding above him somewhere, in the sky, just out of his reach. The horse looked down to Matthew and said to him, 'Come to me, Matthew. Come to me now.' And then he turned and steepled away into the sky and was gone into the clouds, like some centaur returned to his alpine cave. And Matthew's arms were beating at the air as he tried to progress through the clouds as would a swimmer in the ocean but he made no progress and the horse disappeared into the mist and was gone and Matthew was left collapsed on his pillow until he was awoken with a stab of pain.

Grace had pulverised her sticks and leaves and tipped some water into the flat bowl. Then she dipped her finger in it and made a paste which she slathered directly onto the outside of Matthew's slicing wound. While James held down Matthew's arms, she took a length of the most delicate flax twine, then slipped it though a shard of bone that had been split from the chest of a duck and then she stabbed it into one side of his wound and drew it all the way through to close the gap partly over. A thin film of the brown-grey mixture was cohering the sides of the wound as she worked. Matthew started up from his swoon and was held down by his brother.

'Grace is sewing up your wound, old boy.'

At these words, Matthew calmed himself and sighed and collapsed back down upon his bed and closed his eyes.

She then passed the bone and flax all through the wound with seven fixes and made it closed and safe. This was covered over with more of the mixture she had made and smoothed with her hands. Then she dabbed some water on Matthew's forehead and continued to murmur her orison, over and over and over again, and while she did it, Matthew slept the healing sleep, as deep as death almost.

Grace regarded her work with quiet approbation. James had watched her throughout and was filled with wonder. He thought of his father the admiral and his certainty of the scheme of things – the Pyramid of Civilisation with the king or queen at top and with Aborigines residing with monkeys and other primates at the bottom. James thought now of his own puny nature in the scheme, of what he knew and what he did not. He regarded the girl differently now; he could never again treat her indifferently as he had, for she had given her power to him as a gift and he had taken it from her as a gift and now he was beholden to her in respect at the very least.

Grace turned to watch James watching her. There was silence between them for a half a minute as they looked at each other, but both were listening to Matthew's breathing. It was as if Grace could read the thoughts of James. She bent her head towards the floor in silence for a moment and when the silence was broken it was profound, as if rules had been written there, in that moment, and not on a tablet of stone on some mountain long past, not even in a great book in Westminster or Adelaide or in any other seat of wisdom with its dignity and fraudulent air of permanence.

'You go now,' Grace said quietly. 'I stay.'

James Larkin was swept by the feelings of his own inefficacy in the face of this girl. He could have her ordered away, now that her job was done; many would, but he would not. He bent his head in one nod of assent and left the room, closing the door quietly behind him. Grace turned her attention to the wound once more and, finding that all was satisfactory, she pulled the blanket up over Matthew's naked shoulder. She stood beside the bed and released the two buttons at the top of her shirt and pulled it over her head, then held it in one hand. She pulled back the blanket with the other and lay next to Matthew, her breasts soft on his chest, her arm around his waist, light as a dream. When beads appeared on Matthew's head, she wiped them clean away. And there Matthew slept while Grace lay with him, and in her half-waking half-sleeping repose, she dreamt her own dreams of a life that was to come, and of the caring and healing that she was born to administer.

As the sun went down, James returned to Matthew's room and tapped very quietly on the door. As he approached, he had noticed that no candlelight showed beneath the door. He listened carefully for a moment. There was a rustling of sheets or garments, possibly both, and then a soft footfall on the new floorboards. He waited a full minute and the door was quietly opened and Grace was there, her eyes lowered. James shuffled his feet on the threshold, for the moment not knowing whether the room belonged to him or to Matthew, or to Grace.

'Him good. You see.'

James heard the pride that was in Grace's voice and also her note of propriety.

Grace pulled the candle back to open the way for him and James could see that her shirt was crumpled, misshapen, stained with sweat. He walked the few steps across to Matthew's cot and knelt next to him.

'Brother,' said Matthew weakly.

'You are awake.'

'Just now. I slept the afternoon away. Did you stay for hogget?'

'Of course I did not. I brought you back, on Jenks's pony.'

'You did? Of course you did. You would. It was you there. It seems so far away now, so very far away.' The memory then splashed into his mind: the native girl, her face and head blown away before his eyes. Flat on her back with her arms spreadeagled; her young womanhood on show and nothing more.

'Oh my god,' Matthew groaned and he began to cry, just little sobs into the back of his left hand. 'What is to become of me, brother? What is to become…?'

James was at a loss to respond. His brother might be of a Romantic inclination, but he had never seen tears before. And with tears James

had no experience of coping. His older brothers would never have allowed their faces to relax from the fixed determination the admiral had
taught them; even Adela was of a solid, even disposition, taking things
as they came, perhaps wavering and doubting herself, but he had never
seen her cry. The British temperament was the envy of the world and
the empire had not been built on tears.

'…of us. What is to become of us, James. Of us, of us, of all of us…'
Matthew held on to James's lapels and threatened to bury his head into
his brother's chest.

James turned to where Grace stood. She had now dripped wax into
a saucer and was holding a candle erect with her palm spread beneath
the china; her hold was calm and comfortable, her face serene, almost
glowing in the half-light of dusk. James stood and Matthew withdrew
his hand from James and let it flop upon the sheet. It seemed to James
that whatever remained to be done, Grace would know how to do it.

'You will remain?' he said to her.

Grace cocked her head at him, uncertain.

'You will stay?' he said, choosing a simpler word.

'Me stay. Me stay.'

'Oh yes, James. Grace will stay. She must stay.'

'Yes,' said James. 'Yes, she must stay.' He knelt once more by
Matthew's bed. 'She may stay as long as…as she is needed.' James
pressed once more, firmly, on his brother's hand. 'Goodnight,' he said,
and turned to go. 'Thank you,' he said to Grace in a gentle way that
she had not heard before from him or any other white man beside
Matthew.

At the door, he stopped, hesitated, as if he were on the brink of saying something he had been contemplating. But then, 'Goodnight,' was
all he said, and he quietly closed the door.


The Larkins' man Joe had arrived at nightfall – too late to embark on
the return trip. The news that he brought caused deep concern for
Tibbs. He had heard of cases like the one before him: native poisons, a

young settler, a guessing game. A broken leg would present him with a routine solution. But fever from a native spear wound? It was poison, and poison was a mystery. Matthew was an isolated figure in the valley – the inessential younger brother of James Larkin, he was not immediately respected. He had been wounded and that brought him notice, had lifted him one step higher. The conversations he had had with Matthew in the crude taverns of Clare had been interesting, even enlightening. The young man was well read and gifted with words, two facilities that were probably of limited interest to any other in the valley besides Tibbs himself. But the lad was perturbed, and in his cups had told Tibbs about shooting the skull off a native man, and now came this story of native poison. If Matthew survived the night, he might have a chance; but if so, what would Tibbs prescribe?

Tibbs and Joe covered the ground briskly and it was not yet nine when the homestead came into view. There was the hut where the Larkins had lived for the first six months at Lingalee, and now a stone house was taking shape a hundred yards further up the valley. The doctor absorbed it all. A man had been posted at the gate and trotted inside at the moment of their approach.

Presently, out came James Larkin to greet them. 'Doctor, thank you for coming straight out.'

'My duty, dear boy. And a pleasure to see how well your undertaking fares. But what of the patient?'

'Surprisingly well, it would seem.' James was not certain how he should relay this news to the doctor. He had allowed a native girl to treat his brother. He could not hide the fact; the ointment was there to be seen. He had decided that the doctor might as well see everything.

'Fever?'

'Abated…considerably.'

'On the slide? In – what? Less than twenty four hours?' Irrelevantly, the doctor took a gold watch from his fob pocket and looked at it, as if some surprising answer was to be found there. 'Three days, I would have thought.'

'There has been fever in the night but he is much improved this morning.'

'The devil you say. Have you given him anything?'

'It is best you see for yourself.'

The doctor was taken aback, 'You mean you can't say? And what of the injury to the foot?'

But they were at the door of Matthew's room already and James pushed it aside and motioned the doctor through. The room was square and clean. There was a bed in a corner with Matthew propped up in it, and a chair. Next to it, along the side of the wall, there was another cot, a low bundle that might have been stuffed with leaves and worn sheets and which could be rolled up and moved in a moment. Upon this bundle squatted a native woman, a large calico shirt pulled around her thighs and with an interested proprietary air about her that set the doctor back for a moment, so unlikely was it to be worn by one of her kind, especially in such a place.

'Wha—' The doctor turned in surprise to James, who smiled him through to his patient.

'Good morning, doctor,' said Matthew weakly, gathering strength and sitting up on his elbows.

'Good morning, Matthew. You are…improved? The way your man would tell it to me last night, you were lucky to make it through. Stories of native poison and spears and broken feet and I don't know what. Were it not for the impenetrable dark, we would have set off immediately.'

'We have my native nurse to thank.' He glanced towards Grace, as if he had any need to draw the doctor's attention to her. His spirit was lightened. He had been injured, it was true. But it was only a slice perhaps, and the event had brought Grace from the hut into the house in a way that made her more than simply useful. She had saved him and gained a kind of status.

'Is that what you call it?' cried the doctor, glancing down at the cot against the wall and taking a moment to sniff the air. 'Now let's have a look, then,' he said, remembering his duty.

Matthew drew his shirt down and the doctor leaned forward for fifteen or twenty seconds while he observed the stitching and the ribbon of ointment that seamed the wound and now resembled a remarkably flexible glue. He felt Matthew's wrist and timed his pulse. He placed his hand on the boy's forehead. When he sat down again, it was heavy, almost a collapse.

'Well, I'll be blowed. There we were, fretting all night, Joe and I. Up and away at first light. Death's door, all that kind of thing. And here you are, beaming away at me – weak of course but very much alive. Man doesn't know what to think.' He sat with his hands upon his knees, wondering what he should do next.

'*Pitjuri*,' said a quiet voice behind him.

'What, what's that…' said the doctor, turning upon Grace, then looking back at James.

'*Pitjuri* is the native medicine,' said Matthew, 'not available here. It must be traded for, with the men from the north. Grace possesses many secrets. Her grandfather was an Arrente man.'

'What the devil is that? Some kind of witch doctor?'

'The people from the desert lands. Arrente. It is their…clan, as it were.'

'Oh, I see,' said Dr Tibbs, not seeing at all. 'Well, let's have a look at this foot then. No use curing something that's not wrong with you, eh.'

And so the doctor observed the swelling in Matthew's foot and prodded him until it hurt. 'Hmph. Bad sprain of course, but there's a broken bone in there too. Set a caste if I had the plaster, but out here…' His voice trailed away and he shrugged. He produced a bandage and strapped the foot and secured it tight with a pin. 'Best I can do under the circumstances. Is it painful when you stand?'

'Exceedingly. Will I be able to ride, sir?'

'Ride? I expect so, but it will take some weeks. As long as you hop to the horse, ha ha.'

James smiled and raised a lightly clenched fist to his mouth to indicate the suppression of a titter.

'But what of the other one, the shoulder?'

'Oh, yes, I do feel it terribly in the cold mornings.'

'Not surprised. Looks as if the left shoulder and the right foot will have to balance themselves out, eh.'

James obliged with an amused grimace once more.

'As long as the horse understands, ha ha. But there will be no more trips to Clare for a few weeks.'

'Ah, indeed.'

'You are often a visitor to Gleeson's tavern, as are some others of us, of course.' Tibbs looked up at James with a chuckle; there was no use hiding things, not in this place.

'Ah, yes. The characters of the town do fill me with amusement.'

'So it's the characters that draw you, eh.'

But Tibbs did not judge Matthew for his aberrations. On the contrary, he had had his own times of melancholy. But he could not prescribe Matthew with bottles of whisky and he felt under some pressure to provide a solution to something, especially now that this native nurse had apparently brought down the fever.

'There may be something I can do to help you with the pain, of whatever kind it is.' Tibbs produced from his visiting bag a dark brown bottle with a cork stopper. 'Take this bottle. Extract from the poppy seed, if you can believe that. Damned Germans, don't know what they will come up with next. Latest thing, this. Take a good tablespoon full for sleep every night and whenever the pain becomes too much. I'm sure you must walk for the purpose of performing certain functions. If it hurts, take a swig of this. I will be back in a week with some more if you need it. Until then, stay off the foot as much as you can – you will be cooped up in here, I'm afraid. I'm sure James will find you a forked branch to help you walk.' He looked across at Grace. 'Er, yes. You are a man of letters. Read a book, write a poem.'

The doctor rose and bade good day to James and Joe. He turned to Grace and, not knowing what to say, he grunted and half nodded in her direction. 'Damnedest thing,' he said. 'Well, I'll be off then. Must drop in at the Phillips place on my way through.'

'You will stay for tea in the house, doctor? And perhaps a look at the property while you're here?'

'Tea, ah yes, don't mind if I do.'

'Something stronger if you've a mind.'

'Ha, yes. Good day to you,' he said again to Matthew.

The doctor and James closed the door and went into the house.

Grace rose from her squatting position on her cot and came over to the bed where Matthew lay waiting for her. She pulled back the covers. 'Warm here,' she said.

'Yes, warm here,' Matthew agreed, and parted the covers, opening the way for her.

*The public house at Kapunda was made of sticks, of palings to be more generous, that had been rammed into the earth and held fast with blocks of wood that had in turn been secured by rocks then covered over with earth of clay. Small windows were open to the weather and when it blew, there were light sheets that had been cut and planed specially to fit in their place. Inside, though, the bar was made of cedarwood and had been imported and set as pride of place. There was a cabinet above the head for glasses, a rail below for boots, and hooks of brass fixed in for jackets. Of hearth and fireplace there was none, but that mattered not on this warm November afternoon. The feeling that surrounded the place seemed to be: let's have a proper bar and construct the building around it later.*

*This seemed to suit the little assembly of lads who came up from the pit at the end of the day. There were mostly Cornish men for the digging of holes, with a few Welsh lads thrown in who had been brought for their knowledge of the smelting business. Cornish or Welsh, it made little differ- ence, for there was no way to be but to mix together in this little mining town on the frontier; and with just one pub with a bar about the size of their front parlours back home, they all knew each other like brothers, or even worse.*

*They had seen a few oddballs blow in, characters heading north: graziers would stop, shopkeepers making for good pickings in Clare or Watervale.*

The doctor had made his presence felt and stood the lads a round. But nothing had prepared them for the appearance of the young woman that late afternoon around four o'clock.

Amused as they were by all visitors, the lads had their ears pricked by the sounds of hooves cantering up then stopping outside. Tommy Cook would always be the one to report on the arrival and he scurried over to the window for a look.

'Oo is it, Tommy?' said the landlord.

Tommy hesitated for a moment and then was heard to say, 'I doan' rightly know.'

'How's that, Tommy? Can't ee see with own eyes then?'

'It looks like a gel but my eyes doan't tell un sure.'

'A gel? Out 'ere?' they cried as one and crowded to the window at just the time Lucy had completed the strapping of her horse to the post that held the veranda of their rickety building.

She looked up and saw five grimy faces at the aperture. 'Good evening, gentlemen.' She greeted them with a nod.

Owen Teagle's bent pipe fell from his mouth and landed on a wooden chair that was beneath the window. He stooped to pick it up and nearly overbalanced as he did, so his mates could not resist giving him the shove that sent him through and into a heap on the outside.

Amid a chorus of backslapping guffaws, Owen picked himself up and mustered his dignity to say to her, 'You're right welcome to Kapunda, miss.'

'And will you get the door for me, er…'

'Owen, miss, and, the door, certainly, of course.' He clambered to his feet and, clenching his pipe back between his teeth, he opened the door for her with a bow.

'Thank you, Owen,' she said as she passed regally through, her eyes adjusting to the light and taking in her new surrounds. 'Not so bad once you see the inside, is it then?'

'Not so bad at all, miss, if I do say so,' said Lambert the publican, a big man whose stomach and cheeks told the tale of permanent proximity to drink.

The men scurried back to their positions at the bar but somehow they all found themselves standing, not where they had been three minutes before, but in a circle around their new arrival. They all introduced themselves. There was Williams, with Blanchard and Teagle, as well as Owen and Cook. With Lambert behind the bar, they made a famous crowd.

'Can we get yer sumthin'?' said Lambert. 'A lemonade perhaps?'

'A lemonade would be delightful.'

'You're heading north, miss.'

'I am. Will you be able to provide me with accommodation for the night?'

'Yes, miss. There is a room, at the back, that travellers sometimes use. Else there is a room at Widow Worthington's that can be had.'

She took a look about her at the bright and grubby faces, all anxious to please. 'I think I find the company here to my liking,' she said and brought smiles all round.

'It would certainly be verra quiet at Worthington's, miss,' said Owen.

'I can imagine. Is the bed soft here, Mr Lambert?'

'Very much so, ma'am.'

'Then all is settled.' She reached inside her purse.

'There is no need, ma'am.'

'I will be up early, I have no doubt, and will be away with the sunrise. Best to settle now.' The girl fished in her bag for coins.

'You will be travelling further out, miss? It's not so safe, I think, on the road. I mean for a woman alone, it's, well, a difficulty. It may be best to wait on Mr Watson, the carrier. He'll be through tomorrow and will leave again the day after that.'

'Mr Watson, you say.'

'Indeed, ma'am.'

'I have heard of Watson. In fact, he seems to be dogging my steps. A broadcaster of good tidings or ill as the occasion pleases him, so I am told.'

'That would be Watson, ma'am.' Lambert sounded knowledgeable on the subject. 'He does hear many things on his travels up and down.'

'Are they always accurate?'

'How do you mean, ma'am?'

'He strikes me as somewhat rubicund.'

Blank faces were around her.

'Are his stories ever exaggerated by, well, drink, Mr Lambert?'

'Aaaahhh,' the faces around her relaxed in perfect understanding.

'Aaaarrr,' said Owen. 'Mr Watson does take a snifter with him on his journeys.'

'Speaking of which, do you have anything stronger than your excellent lemonade, sir?'

'Stronger, ma'am?'

'To drink, man.'

'A sherry, perhaps?'

'One large sherry then.'

Lambert filled a four-ounce glass to the top and they all watched as Lucy took a solid slug from it, then another, and wiped her mouth with the back of her hand.

'Now, your payment.' To access the coins inside her bag, Lucy extracted her small pistol and placed it on the bar.

The men sprang back as one, as if menaced by a prancing cobra. Looks of incredulity were arranged in varying degrees upon their faces. The only two firearms in Kapunda were in the keep of the constable and the presbyterian minister, and they were both used principally for the shooting of kangaroos for meat. Mr Lambert kept a cricket bat behind the bar in case of emergencies.

'One can never be too careful, gentlemen. I think that should be sufficient coinage, Mr Lambert.'

Where the talk of the men had been familiar and friendly, it now became immediately less so, more respectful and distant.

'Thank you, miss. But I must say, miss,' said Lambert hesitantly, almost shy in his manner, 'we allow no firearms in the bar, miss.'

'Of course, landlord. I am gratified to hear that you run such an orderly house.'

Lucy swigged off the last of her sherry and took the key to her room from

Mr Lambert. 'This way, you say? I am sure I will find it without assistance. I am, well, rather tired. Good evening, gentlemen.' She nodded to all and disappeared through the door to find her room.

In her wake, the bar was quiet as the mining men looked each other over. They had never seen or heard of such a woman before.

**6**

# The Town – November 1842

Mrs Cawthorne received very little civilised companionship; all callers before Matthew Larkin being either black or brutish, it must be said that she had come in time to develop a small but appreciable preference for the former. Cawthorne had told Matthew that in the early days she had been 'somewhat affrighted' by the frolicking dances of the native, but that her toleration of these events had now smoothed to mute assent, possibly even to some silent enjoyment. But whatever the colour or creed of those who knocked upon her door, their single uniform factor was a lack of interest in or knowledge of poetry. But on his second visit, Matthew had made reference to Mr Keats. The very word 'Keats' had floated like balm upon the air and Matthew's young and sweet but manly voice had been pressed to read aloud to Mrs Cawthorne from her own prized collection of a dozen or so volumes.

So now with Cawthorne wanting to use each moment of the day to paint or study at philosophy (when he was not walking to the river), it was his mother who became the more welcoming of the two. So Matthew and she would sit and read. The poetry took her away from 'the room', as she called it, jerking her head towards the staircase and the direction of their little school, and away from 'this place', which she said with nothing more than a dreamy glance out of the window at the invariable sky, bleached of colour, enamelled, bald.

Since his conversation of some days previous concerning Cawthorne's father, Matthew had listened for further mention of him, but there was none. This absence of reference implied that enquiries regarding the man's nature or the relationships which had existed in Durban were not welcome conversational gambits. He noticed that Cawthorne referred to his mother once having played the piano quite well and he also recalled that she had taught her son to speak French. He thought of the one or two pianos sitting unused in the better houses in town, but shrank from inviting her. However low the Cawthornes might seem to the better part of his society, they were never so low as the captain had been, and people in town remembered the captain. After the marriage and the birth of William, the captain had appeared in the lives of his wife and son only briefly and infrequently. During one of his lengthy absences from Durban, he made a brief stay of some two or three months in South Australia, where he was a frequent visitor to the wine shops and ale houses in Hindley Street, only sobering himself to attend an interview for lighthouse keeper on Kangaroo Island, at which he was unsuccessful. After that, he did gain mastery of a trading ship bound for Java, and was never seen again. Mother and son arrived but three weeks after his departure, and were forced to make their way without support. So much was the common knowledge.

So Mrs Cawthorne took solace in the printed word and that Matthew would read for her was a matter of comfort. He had a different way of accentuating certain passages that gave the poems a bright new meaning. This afternoon, with Cawthorne himself immersed in some book of Thomas Paine, he read to her some favoured lines:

> One impulse from a vernal wood
> May teach you more of man,
> Of moral evil and of good,
> Than all the sages can.
> Sweet is the lore which Nature brings;
> Our meddling intellect
> Mis-shapes the beauteous forms of things:--
> We murder to dissect.

Enough of Science and of Art;
Close up those barren leaves;
Come forth, and bring with you a heart
That watches and receives.

'A heart that receives…' Her hand touched Matthew's once, lightly, then retreated to its sleeve of worn brocade. It was an almost furtive pat that touched him more than all the boisterous backslapping of the rest of the colony put together.

'We hear that Mr Wordsworth is to become Her Majesty's Poet Laureate, mother.' Cawthorne did not look up from Paine, and seemed to be fanning up some small matter between them.

'He writes of different things now,' said Mrs Cawthorne with some apparent regret.

'Our "meddling intellect" indeed. Is it for moral evil or for good that we come here, to this place? We were told in Africa that this was a place of reason and freedom and that a man might rise through merit, were we not, mother?' He motioned to the window and the sky and to all the stone buildings that were springing up.

'A man may worship as he pleases in this place.' Matthew sought to mitigate the low temper of his friend.

'Aye, and starve as he pleases. The new order differs little from the old. Do we come to take and give, just as we please? Are we god or man?'

'I do not know, William,' Matthew replied, 'but I suspect that I am but a man, for I must do as I am bade.'

'Ha, as must we all, in truth. And what of our Kadlitpinna? A chieftain, he. But does he not do as he is bid?'

'He does not in the natives' camp.'

'So does that not make him a god on one side of the river, and a man on the other?'

'In the same way, perhaps, that you are a man in the street, and a god in your schoolroom.'

'Ha,' said Mrs Cawthorne and she smiled for the first time that

Matthew could remember. 'Zeus with his thunderbolts perhaps,' she said, thinking of the cane and yard ruler that were the tools of their godly offices.

'As are we both, Mother.'

He seemed to muse bitterly for a moment on this. He deplored the violence that he must use in order to survive.

'So it would seem. In all of us this must be true, in part, that we can bid in one place and be bidden in another,' Matthew ventured uncertainly. 'Does your Mr Paine have much wisdom on this matter, William?'

'Ha. Much wisdom, I expect, from one who would tell us that all men are equal,' he sniffed. 'Would that it were true. My Mr Plato wrote of his teacher Socrates, who would forever mock those who spent lavish amounts on tutors and the like. He thought that good character was a gift of the gods.'

At this, Mrs Cawthorne inclined her head and smiled another small smile like a zephyr breeze that came and died in a moment.

'Not that we were equal in any sense at all,' her son went on, 'but that inequality of character was bestowed from above.' Cawthorne returned to his book. 'But read on with your poesy,' he said, 'and do forgive me, I am given much to melancholy on this day.'

And so Matthew went on with the next poem which Mrs Cawthorne had already bookmarked for him. He read,

> Oh! pleasant exercise of hope and joy!
> For mighty were the auxiliars which then stood
> Upon our side, we who were strong in love!
> Bliss was it in that dawn to be alive,
> But to be young was very heaven!

'Hah,' cried Cawthorne. 'Heaven indeed, to take on the nobility, and to be Mr Wordsworth with pension sufficient to write and nothing else, and the patronage of Mr Coleridge to smooth what waves there ever had been before him.'

Mrs Cawthorne nodded patiently to Matthew to continue and never mind the interjections of her dear son, when there came a sharp rap upon the door: three knocks, hard and quick, as if they had been delivered not with a knuckle but with a cane or some other stout piece of wood.

'We were not expecting anyone,' said Mrs Cawthorne at once and wore her fearful look again.

'Do not disturb yourself, Mother,' said Cawthorne, and he rose from his reading.

From the place that Matthew occupied, he could see the corner and handle of the door as it arced open and the bright light of afternoon stabbed into the dim parlour. He saw the look on Cawthorne's face as he, fixed of expression as he generally was, betrayed an expression of wordless astonishment.

'Mr Cawthorne.' The educated voice was smooth and almost oily in its assuredness and unspoken assumption of control.

A hand was extended into Matthew's field of vision – the voice, he recognised. For a moment, Cawthorne was unable to speak, so astounded was he by the appearance of the man at his door. Then there was the shaking of hands and a clapping on Cawthorne's shoulder.

'May I come in?' said Mr George French Angas.

'Sir, I…'

'But allow me to introduce myself. I am Angas,' and he stepped through the door, directly into the parlour. He paused for a moment and sniffed the cabbage-and-mutton air, but gave no hint of revulsion.

'Yes,' said William, skirting around Angas, 'I am Cawthorne…'

'And your dear mother, I presume. Good afternoon, ma'am.' Angas inclined his head and smiled, half closing his eyes in deference as he did so. 'Do not rise on my account, I bid you,' he said as Mrs Cawthorne gripped the arms of the chair in an effort to get up and greet him. 'And young Matthew,' he inclined his head towards Matthew, 'we have met, and an unmistakable young man you were, at the tea at Woodhall's.'

'Good afternoon, Mr Angas.'

'And these,' turning to Cawthorne, as he motioned at the native items which were propped by the fireplace and against the walls, 'are your native treasures.'

'Indeed, sir,' replied Cawthorne with caution. 'I have thirty five objects described and listed and some painted so far, as well.' His speech was halting, abrupt.

Mrs Cawthorne's mouth was slightly open, caught there by the blazing impact of Angas on the room.

'If you would come into my study, sir, I will show you the best of them.'

'Your study? How charming.'

With a bow, Cawthorne motioned towards the little door that led off to his study and Angas preceded him thither. He had been in the parlour less than a minute.

'I say,' cried Angas with a lilt of surprise on entering the room, at the very smallness and decrepitude of it. His eyes then gathered in the further native artefacts which stood within, and the door was closed behind and there they remained for twenty minutes or more.

'This could not be,' said Mrs Cawthorne, grasping at Matthew's sleeve, 'the patron that William has so long been seeking?'

'I did mention to Mr Angas that William was a collector, and a painter. He did seem so very interested in all these things,' and he motioned to the collection that was left in the parlour. 'One can only hope.'

Mrs Cawthorne grabbed at Matthew's wrist with a squeeze of hope and thanks that was as fervent as it was pathetic.

When the two men emerged from Cawthorne's little study, French Angas was holding a wotli shield and two spears; tucked under his arm was a native bludgeoning club all decorated in spots burnt on with hot sticks and painted over in ochre.

He was beaming. 'It is marvellous kind of you, sir. I shall begin to paint on the moment of my return and shall send a man around post haste to help you to bring up the other things. It will be most delightful and you must stay to tea, or something stronger if you have a mind, and tell me more of the histories of these things. Good day to you, ma'am, and to you, Matthew, good day and thank you. Ah ha,' he cried in triumph as he turned and, without saying another word, strode into the street.

The coming of a proper native fight was announced without a word being spoken. Bark was stripped in sheets of three foot by four foot from the largest white gum trees by the river. The natives cut these pieces into shields and fit them with little twine handles that they fixed with resin from the yacca trees that abounded in the plains. These trees grew a club-like stump to three feet high, then sprouted enormous spikey spears of leaves from which the sticky substance could be pressed. Once each man had cut and fashioned his own shield it was daubed with a background of white and then there was added an arc of reddish ochre, which they made from the pulverisation of rocks. Once this was done and all other spears and clubs were in their proper place, then the panoply was complete and they were ready for battle.

From his tree stump at the river Larkin could see men in serious groups, bent at their work. The atmosphere in the camp was different; the children were quiet. Cawthorne did not visit them in the prelude to an occasion of such moment.

The procedure of shield-making was not unknown to the authorities of the town. Indeed, laws had been passed against it as well as against the gathering together in affray which inevitably followed the shield-making. But the blacks lived in the pursuit of thousands of years of lore, and bore witness to their ancestors and spirits, who were above the laws of the white man. Still, no disturbances were to be made to the productive peace of the colony.

On the evening before the affray, Cawthorne walked around the town with a weight of matters on his mind. That there was no such thing as ambush in the native set of mind was of the highest importance to him. To surprise an enemy and to discharge spears without warning would be a dishonour worse than death: victory in such circumstances an insult to the ancestors. A date was set and a place agreed. It became the most civilised of arrangements, more like a duel between gentlemen; and more than that for, it seemed, sometimes the outcome of the affray was set by elders before the skirmish even began, and the whole was acted out as some kind of elaborate choreography, a deadly play within the greater play of life, which was itself but a touchstone to the greater world of spirit beings and dreaming songs. But his friends could die out on the field. Or worse, be brought home wounded and become infected and expire an agonising week later.

Fools, he thought. Could they not see that in a year, or two at the most, they would be pushed away from where they were now as the settlers' need for land grew. Had they not already been banned from swimming in the river upstream, closer to Government House, and pushed away around the bend to where they lived now. Had not the first governor of the colony been prone to taking potshots with his rifle from the window of Government House at any dark-skinned body wandering back towards its traditional bathing place. How Cawthorne loved them for their simple faith, their perfect manners, for their corroborree which he had painted six months before, for their way of taking only what they needed, and leaving the rest. He despaired of them for failing to see that others were not like them and never would be – that white man had no mind to share.

'Good evening, Mother,' he said with a tired sigh when he returned. He ate his plate of stew like a crow, the beads of his eyes staring, beak darting forward to meet his fork.

Then his mother heard the sound of his boots in the small passageway and the door of the front room was closed – the sweet and musky smell of tobacco in his briar through the one-inch gap beneath the door. The springs in the old armchair groaned beneath him. After a minute the sound of boots, one step, two steps and a shuffling turn. Her poor son could not even worry properly for want of space. Where would this end, Mrs Cawthorne wondered – the restless ambitions and concerns of men. It was possible to find peace in very little, if it was sought.

The following morning, Larkin arrived early and they set off at double pace for the clearing which had been agreed between the tribes for the definitive affray. It was further from the town than the ceremonial affray had been, to the south and west past the Black Forest, where the ground levels out and clears and space was there for a deadly run. When they arrived, Cawthorne picked out a tree a discreet distance from the field. They each took boughs that were a foot thick if they were an inch, but this time they were made to wait, and grew uncomfortable with the minutes. Matthew was more nervous than before, remembering the fierce looks and the gorgonic faces that the Murray men had made. Cawthorne kept a small pipe in his mouth but did not light it.

The Kaurna blacks at length appeared and gathered in the distance to the north on their right, while presently the river men emerged from some distant camp and began to group themselves to their left. After a considerable delay, during which there was much discussion among the men of each tribe, they began quite suddenly to form themselves into single lines which faced up to each other at a distance of about a hundred yards. They then began to advance towards each other, as if at some order or signal that remained unseen to the men in the tree. All at once, they stopped and both sides began to shout and leap about as they had done two weeks before, with extraordinary antic capering: mouths gurgling with spittle, they leapt up and down and flexed their thighs and made horrid expressions, their mouths drawn back and teeth full displayed and biting, eyeballs nearly popping from their heads. Matthew sat rigid in his spot and stared, his own eyes wide with fright; Cawthorne put his pipe away and resumed his expressionless vigil.

A shout then suddenly emerged and this was the signal for battle, as spears began to be discharged from both sides at the one time. The rainbow of spears went up, forming pleasing arcs through the air so that for a moment there was a glistening dome of missiles producing an effect that was beyond reality. The idea that this opening salvo of spears had been for largely ceremonial effect was supported by the following more deadly action. Men took one step forward and threw with a round-arm style, the spears humming along much quicker, no more than the height of a human thigh at their arc. The result of all this throwing was the most extraordinary leaping about as missiles were dodged, some jumping as a spear flashed through the legs, some taking a dart on the shield while jinking left and right to allow another past, some hopping as would a kangaroo and deflecting another missile with a downwards flourish of the shield.

The sight of two hundred blacks all throwing and cavorting at once was the single most extraordinary sight that Matthew had ever witnessed and one that could have been most amusing had the lethal potential not been so great. He thought that any white man would have been dead and lying on the ground in an instant, but the amazing judgement and athletic movement of these fellows made incisions to the flesh the exception rather than the rule.

He glanced over at Cawthorne and shouted out, 'I say,' in his excitement.

But Cawthorne simply gazed ahead of himself with that extraordinary fixed and melancholic expression and gave no flicker of recognition.

And still the spears came. It was difficult for them to see all in the dust that was being stamped up, but it seemed that the women and children who had followed along behind were acting as collectors of some kind, and were passing a storehouse of spears to their men for second and third use. Then a river man took a throw fair in the inner part of the thigh not eighty yards from their tree, and another man rushed forward to break the spear off so that it could be passed through. The face of the injured man was screwed in a torment of agony. The Kaurna men began to press in and two more of their opponents fell; their spears kept coming and it looked as if a slaughter might ensue.

This was the greatest excitement that Matthew had ever felt. His body was so acutely aware of every sensation that he felt he had never been alive until that hour. Although his head was shaking to think that it was somehow because of them, because of him, that this affray had occurred, still the elegant savagery of the acts and the inexplicable elation that he felt overlaid every pious or righteous feeling to which he had ever laid claim.

And then, suddenly, without any expectation, adding to the clamour and with a great thundering of hooves, five of the police rode up together from the direction of the town, with Captain Phillips the first among them, mounted on the mightiest and most fearsome horse that had ever been seen in the colony. He took a pistol from his holster and fired it once into the air, with a look which, even among the famous cavalcade of Phillips's looks, was the most ferocious of them all. The effect was instantly galvanising on the black fellows. The throwing of spears ceased forthwith and they looked about themselves with blank expressions which turned in time to something surly or sulky in demeanour.

With helpless looks, the natives began to withdraw back into the lines in which they had been ranged some minutes before. And where they could have turned and buried a shower of spears into the newly arrived entourage and surely wiped them away with little loss to themselves, they merely looked indignant, affronted by this unwanted intrusion. They gave each other looks such as would be seen among a bunch of errant schoolboys whose prime amusement has been taken from them by the master.

The captain waved his pistol at them, and then motioned to a place before him, in signal that their weapons should be collected there. And what a piteous sight it was, the poor fellows broken-hearted on both sides as they laid down their newly cut and carefully painted and anointed wocaltee shields, their uwinda spears and knobbly ended wirri clubs, even their spear propellers, the midlah, and the seven-foot cootpee that went with them.

Matthew had twice seen the midlah used to bring down opossum on a natives' hunt down by the riverside, a more extraordinary feat even than the death of the black swan. To think of them able to fashion a spear and handle from a tree and to bring down prey at thirty yards, and to do it all but silently, without disturbance to 'roo or 'possum or even to the birds in the trees. Indeed, to live with neither door nor locksmith, to walk the earth with the seasons. And now these fine weapons were to be surrendered.

At the orders of Phillips, the poor fellows came up in twos and threes to give up their weapons. Like mendicant mothers forced to give their babies away at the foundling house door, they stepped back and away with afflicted farewell looks at their shields and spears and then directed baleful glares in the direction of the police; looks that were reproachful and contemptuous in their countermanding sorrow.

Then last of all Kadlitpinna stepped forward with his shield and hurled it on the pile with such force that it split down one side and an ochre orb was sullied. 'You bad fella.' Kadlitpinna's forehead was creased in agitation. 'When white fella fight in Adelaide,' he shouted in his agony of frustration, 'black fella stay away. When black fella fight, why white fella no stay away?' At that, he hurled his spear into the pile and stared at Phillips, as if waiting for a reply.

'Why you…' Phillips drew his pistol from its holster once again and Cawthorne started in his place, his grip tightening hard on the branch that he was holding.

The face of Phillips screwed into an agony of self-control, as if the natural laws of man had been truly perverted by Whiggish politicians in London and their man the Protector, who was but four miles away, writing reports in his quiet office. He would have the chieftain shot dead on the spot as a lesson to the rest. But Phillips only held his pistol high once more and fired into the air as a message of his authority to the natives and as a signal to his men, who then rode forward and the deadly hooves of the horses thundered over the pile of implements and there was such a crackling sound of breaking bark and wood that was raised to the heavens as you would expect from a burning house fire. They trampled back and forth for a space of time that must have been several minutes until the job of destruction was completed to Phillips's satisfaction.

As if to celebrate the end of this passage of action, the captain fired one final shot into the air from his pistol and waved it all about to the natives that they should disperse and to warn them of the consequences should they not. And so from both sides, the natives turned their backs on the depressive scene of broken shields and of the diffusion of honour and nobility of purpose, of shamed ancestors and abrogations of the mythical code, and began the disheartened trek back to their camps.

Satisfied that his purpose had been fully met, Phillips now wheeled his horse around and, having placed his revolver in the holster at his hip, with a gesture of his head he motioned to his men to return to the town with him. But as his mighty horse was gathering momentum, his head turned to survey the scene about him one last time, and in this movement he caught sight of the two figures in the trees sixty yards or so from him. He pulled up his horse quite sharply and trotted up to face the two men from not more than twenty yards and close enough to address them without raising his voice, but speak he did not. Now certain of their identity, his look returned to that furious aspect he had shown when riding up. Then he turned and, flanked by his men on every side, he rode away towards the town.

When their exit was complete, Cawthorne and Matthew clambered down from their tree and went rummaging through the mangled remains.

Cawthorne found a shield that was half intact; its one remaining orbing ochre stripe now resembled a red and orange sun descending into a sea of white. He regarded it for a moment, then tossed it back into the rubble. 'Fit for the campfire and nothing more.'

Matthew began collecting up some spearheads broken from their shafts by the horses' hooves. The third he found was of a glass-like substance so sharp that when he touched it he received a cut so fine as a sheet of paper can occasionally impart. He held it up to see the sun glinting from its sharpened edges. He wondered why such valuable stone should be allotted the task of taking life, and not treasured and kept for decades or even centuries.

'A pretty little mess to be describing in your diarium, sir.'

'How did you know I was recording my experiences in the colony?'

'A gentleman will put his evening time to good use, sir, I have little doubt. At least for a time he will record his very important life and write letters home to the people who matter, to those who are of moment… to those who feed him, I mean. This is the kind of gentleman who would create a new empire in the colony, which brings me to a poser, sir: is it a new empire in a new colony, or is it the old empire in a very old colony?'

Matthew was stuck for a moment to answer this riddle, but in good spirit Cawthorne continued, for he had not completed his thoughts.

'These habits of industry are what differ us from the native, sir. When they have enough, they have enough. When we have enough, it is only the beginning.'

Matthew began to understand something of the meaning behind his observations. 'But surely we will live side by side with them.'

'Ha!' Cawthorne ejaculated in a sardonic, yet heartily amused manner. 'Chopping firewood in exchange for flour and shaves. You may call it living.' He watched Matthew hold up his spearhead to the sunlight whence it glittered in all directions like a kaleidoscope. 'And magical spearheads.'

'I say, Cawthorne. From what substance would the natives fashion such a blade? This is surely as fine as glass.'

Cawthorne took it from his hand. He did not hold it to the light but regarded it sadly then handed it back.

'And glass it is, sir.'

'It is glass?' I held it up again. 'But how…'

'Dear Larkin, when the natives come up to town to chop up firewood for the well-to-do, they are paid in such kind as the rich can muster.'

Matthew still was at a loss.

'You have seen them smoking tobacco, like a white man does.'

He had.

'You have seen their chieftain with freshly shaven face.'

He had wondered at that as well.

'Well, the white man's glass is more prized by them than any other thing. They fashion it to the point that you see in your hand, and fix it to their spears with cotton from the looms of Birmingham and secure it with resin from the native plants. It gives them magic, or so they think. White man's magic, which brings them closer to the land of their dream.'

Matthew regarded the object once more. Into each of the wings of the spear tip had been carved three devilish barbs as you might see upon a harpoon. And just as such barbs would bring a whale back towards its assailant when pulled upon, so they would inflict agony upon the wounded man who tried to extract one from himself by pulling it back in the direction it had entered.

Matthew shuddered with the thought of such a wound. The agonied extraction; flesh pulling away from flesh, the glass barb concealing pockets of meat that would so quickly putrefy in the Antipodean heat. The idea came to him of the frontier, of the wildness that was coming within his reach. It was there, in his hand.

'They want to be near us, to take a part in our goods, perhaps to draw some kind of spirit from our strength.'

His voice was filled with disdain when he spoke of strength, for Cawthorne truly was torn between the world of the white man and that of the native. And now for Matthew the harpoon of glass in his fingers seemed to hold some special power that burnt into his flesh also and which held him in its special thrall. He knew that he was somehow a part of that world as much as of any other. The idea radiated from that glass object through Matthew's arm into his soul that from that moment onwards his life would be enacted among these people.

'Keep it, Mr Larkin,' said Cawthorne. 'You may just as well engage with their power, as they will engage with ours. You will now be the colony's second-best collector of native goods.' He spoke this last with his most powerful bitterness and irony.

Cawthorne was ready to depart and so Matthew pocketed the glass harpoon, to gaze on it again that evening and on many subsequent. And as they walked away, he wondered whether that spearhead was the finest thing he ever saw, lest that finest of things be the red ochre and white painted shield that he had glimpsed so briefly before it was trampled beneath the hooves of Captain Phillips's giant steed.

Adela Peake leaned forward with her hands on the plank of the seat in the gunboat that brought them towards shore, the better to survey the scrubby sandhill that was her first sight of South Australia. A headland arced protectively away to the north and on her right an unbroken beach extended for miles until resolving itself into a misty rocky cliff. The two points, north and south, described a kind of broad, open bay through which she and three of her fellow passengers had been rowed by the men of the *Surry*.

On shore at the back of the sandhill there was a little hut which, even at the distance of two hundred yards, she could see was made of mud and branches cut from trees.

'Her Majesty's Customs House, ma'am,' one ruddy-faced sailor grunted and winked. He had seen first impressions before.

There was no wharf or landing. Near the high-tide line where the hard sand gave way to sunbaked powdery white there was a group of men in coats and hats, some of them taking an early pipe, some more stylish with a cigarette; but there was no figure that was familiar to her – no James, no Matthew even. Her heart sank somewhat. This, then, was South Australia, the product of her months of anticipation. In the shade of H.M. Customs, she could see to her relief two or three women, dressed in fine and bright colours. She inspected herself one last nervous time and was glad now that she had chosen to wear her best. At Rio, the costumes of both the Europeans and the local women had been brilliant. But in South Australia she had considered more practical dress, to show her empathy for toil.

Her dreams were interrupted by the unexpected halt of the gunboat;

the prow had thudded into a bank of sand some distance from the beach.

'Aaaeeey,' the sailor emitted from between tobacco-stained teeth. 'That's as far as she goes, miss.'

'The boat goes no further?' Adela looked out in desperation. 'But how are we to…' She motioned her hand in the direction of Her Majesty's Customs.

'Get to shore, miss? Are ye not a swimmer then, miss?'

'Ha, ha, ar, ar,' broke out the quiet mirth from the other three sailors.

'Me name is Thomas, ma'am. It is my duty to carry you ashore.'

'Good Lord.'

'Some of the gentlemen prefer to wade themselves in, ma'am, but never the ladies. It's against all rules, you see.'

'I do see.'

And so it was that Adela Peake was brought to shore. Thomas bent at the knees as he took her in his arms, then set straight out. He was steady and strong, his breath was not so bad, but his bristly cheek was rough against Adela's face when it brushed against her as she was hefted into place. From that moment forward, Adela kept her back straight, struck a pose – parasol perched against her knee. Her intention was to arrive in what style and dignity could still be pretended.

Thomas the sailor dropped Miss Adela Peake lightly to her feet and, with a grin of slight mischief, he touched two fingers to his forehead and waded back into the sea. He asked for no tip. She watched after him for a moment but he did not turn back, and as soon as she turned around again, Adela was confronted with another.

'You are Adela, are you not?' said a bright-eyed girl of seventeen or eighteen.

'Why, yes, I am,' she said, still looking around her, unable to take her eyes from the glaring sand and the wind-ridden trees which surrounded the Customs hut in straggly profusion.

'I am Lucy,' said the girl. She was pretty and pert, thought Adela, but with eyes that rather bored into you. Then with a flourish, the girl threw her arms out to her, 'Oh, sister,' she cried as she took Adela into her firm embrace.

Adela could feel the girl's chest and collarbone hard against her own soft bosom and Lucy's head against Adela's neck was moist.

The girl's body then racked into a kind of heaving sob. 'Adela, I am sorry, but I have so anticipated your arrival.'

'Do not be sorry,' said Adela, full-heartedly accepting the sorority that had been unexpectedly thrust upon her; here, she had a guide to the labyrinth before her. 'I am certain I would have made my way to Adelaide, but I am so glad there is someone here to greet me.' She looked around to the groups of men standing at the top of the sand, but still there was not the man she sought above all others.

'I should explain. I am a very close friend of the brothers, Matthew in particular.'

'Oh, I see. And James…'

'Sends his extraordinary apologies, but the business upon which they have waited these six months is concluded on this very day.'

'Oh, I do see.' Adela's hopes of seeing her fiancé, her steady, dependable, admirable James, were dashed. Business would take precedence, even on this day. She sighed very deeply and guarded herself from heaving a sob. 'Of course, of course. It would be,' she said. 'Business.' She placed her arm around Lucy's waist with a brief hug, then withdrew it quickly. Her full embrace of Antipodean manners could wait.

'Yes,' said Lucy. 'It is indeed unfortunate. James has been a different man since the news of your coming.'

'He has?' Adela's voice arpeggiated upwards, more avidly than she had expected. She had been one hundred and nine days on ship in the superior section, with only the company of married women and their husbands, and games of quoits and cards.

'He has, and I am glad of it. Matthew is glad of it too. Look, we have brought your horse. James's man has ridden her up and will stay to wait for your packets, which he will accompany back on the dray.'

'The dray!'

'Yes, and six oxen to bear it forth.'

Adela then noticed a wizened forty-year-old man waiting humbly in the wings, who she took to be James's man. He nodded at them both and tipped his cap.

'This is Timothy, Adela,' she said and Timothy nodded again twice.

Lucy led her through a small field of coarse grass to solid but sandy land where the two horses were tethered to a small acacia tree, stunted and bent through the prevailing salt-laden winds, but its boughs were still full of golden bloom. Striving in difficulty, thought Adela, and tried to take strength from that.

Adela was followed by Timothy, who grinned and tipped his hat again as she turned trepidly around.

When they came close to the horses, Lucy went straight to hers and flipped down the stirrup. 'We colonial women have learnt to do many things that the men do,' she said with a laugh. 'I have even sewn myself a split skirt, for riding.'

Adela was about to say, 'A split skirt, but why?' when Lucy placed her foot in the stirrup and hauled herself up to sit comfortably upon her horse astride, like a man. She flicked the rein around and the horse faced Adela while Timothy waited to assist Adela to hers.

'I see you have provided a side-saddle for me, and I thank you.'

'We shall have you up like this in no time.'

Adela could only respond with a dubious look.

'Come, Miss Adela,' said Timothy, making the first words she had heard from him, ''tis a grade up from t'bullock cart, believe you me.' And he hoisted her up onto her mount, where she sat, perched on the side.

'But you don't look right yet,' said Lucy, an excited whimsy squeezing out of her.

'I don't? This is my best morning dress,' said Adela, with mock affront.

Lucy produced from her saddlebag a soft wide-brimmed hat and handed it over to Adela. 'This is better.'

'But we will look like bumpkins.'

'Hah,' cried Lucy, and threw her head back in laughter, 'but we are bumpkins. All of us. Isn't it wonderful? You will be thought a fool if you do not wear a wide hat, and that is worse.'

'Timothy will take your other.'

And indeed, Timothy reached forward and took Miss Adela's stylish short-brimmed hat from her.

They had made their way to a rough track which meandered, or so it seemed to Adela, to nowhere in particular.

'Is the town so very far?' said Adela.

'Some miles, I'm afraid. We have made some improvements in the last few months, and there will be more.'

'However does the bullock cart get through?'

'It manages. That is what must happen here, in this place. We manage. We help each other. I like it this way.'

Soon they were passing through a forest of tea trees mingled in with banksias and wattles so that a palette of reds and yellows spread out before them and the air was filled with the buzzing of bees. Small dark birds with off-white chests and tails that wagged pertly foraged in the grasses, and honeyeaters darted from one tree to the next. It was almost high summer in Adelaide but the colour was still out. Further inland, melaleuca and dryland tea tree grew thickly. There were native apricots known as pittosporum and drooping she-oak. Bottlebrush and acacia were crammed in between them and there were more banksias, hakea and yellow cassia adding to the riot of colour.

Adela stared in wonder. She had known to expect difference, had indeed been copiously warned of it. Ashore at the Cape, she had seen some cultured gardens with native plants in bloom. They had been African, yet somehow strangely more English. Here there were enormous gum trees, some thirty yards high; massive trees but through which the sun still shone, throwing a dappled kind of shade as if the sun were not something one could ever escape completely.

Kangaroos grazed peacefully to the side of the road. She had heard visitors who returned to England proclaiming their meat the equal of hare, or better. And here it ruminated quietly, as if awaiting its fate. In the distance, she caught sight of the more shy emus, which many preferred to the taste of beef.

Three men of the town approached on foot. The girls were greeted warmly and loudly; hands were shaken and cursory introductions made. The kangaroos turned their heads and bounded quietly away in search of more peaceful pastures.

Presently, Lucy called the little expedition to a halt beside a small lagoon and beneath a spreading gum tree. She slid her right leg expertly over her mount and jumped to the ground, then produced from her saddlebag two cups and made for the water, returning in a moment to proffer one to Adela. 'Milady,' she bowed, mimicking chivalry, mocking her own manliness, but at the same time celebrating it.

'It is much needed, sir, and you are very gallant.' Adela brought her horse across, and kindly took her drink.

'This is the last of the lagoons before Adelaide.'

They gazed together across the water, where black swans and ducks sat in gaggles; pelicans glided in like implacable pterodactyls to their elegant skidding arrest on the surface.

Adela watched in wonder. 'The birds do not feel the heat?' she said.

''Tis not so hot,' said Lucy, looking about as if she were seeking heat, if only to somehow defeat it with her very audacity. 'Not so hot as it will be soon. In one month or two, the temperature will reach one hundred degrees.'

'Oh, not so much as that, surely? Even in Kent, it barely reaches eighty.' Adela could see that the girl was celebrating her own brashness but now she was making things up.

'I guarantee it will. It is a test. To be equal to it is to be a colonist.'

Adela looked again at her new friend. Her confidence perhaps was something which could be shattered. It proclaimed itself too much. She thought for a moment, then, of the impossibly thin, opaque china lamp shade in her aunt Cordelia's house at Hove. It had been the admiration of all who visited. For twenty-five years, it had been admired until a silly servant girl had toppled it while dusting. It had been a lesson for her in care – that things could unravel so easily. Her cousin Tommy had come home from war and had sat in his room for two months with a bottle of whisky, coming down for dinner only and saying little. That had made Adela careful too – quiet and thoughtful. Things were broken so easily, and the boasts of men, and women too, were no more than whispers in the wind. But then, she thought further, would this girl be broken like that? Adela looked at her closer now. She looked over the lagoon as if she was just willing a test of some kind to emerge from its depths. When she hit the floor, she would bounce and right herself; she would not smash into the myriad pieces as had her aunt's precious china, as had her cousin Tommy. She would simply say, 'Now I see what that was all about. I should have stood back further from the edge.' Adela herself had learnt to be careful from the situations of others, but Lucy would suffer the blows herself.

'I see little sign of the city,' Adela said.

'The city!' Lucy laughed in a ceremonial kind of way, as if this observation had been made and greeted ruefully a hundred times. ''Tis a village, at best, and another three miles yonder.' She waved down the track, where another group of walkers were approaching and already hailing them with friendly waves. 'The road will settle now for a mile or so and we will be able to break into a trot.'

'A trot! What luxury.'

'Then we will meet the road to the south, which skirts along the Black Forest.'

'How Teutonic.'

'It is not. A forest of box trees stretches to the hills that you see beyond.'

They both stood on the skirt of higher ground that arced around the lagoon and which was the natural barrier round which the track to the city passed.

'I can see the darker shade, which would be the forest,' Adela said, 'and also the chalky track and some distant shapes of people on it.' She was excited at the prospect that was before her; the joining road somehow spoke of civilisation, of the end of her journey, of James, and of a night of rest in a bed that sat on solid ground.


Matthew Larkin and William Cawthorne walked the long road back to Adelaide. The dismal and confusing end to the affray had left them both plunged into melancholy. Their friends were alive and unharmed but their three days of barking, of fashioning shields, the chiselling of the glass harpoon, had been reduced into humiliation.

'They can make a brawl become a form of art,' Cawthorne mumbled to himself, to the wind, to Larkin.

Mathew lived over the scenes of the affray in his mind: the arc of the spears in the first round of engagements, then the thrill of the deadly, low throws of the next. Even the approach of the two tribes towards each other was something he could not get out of his mind. Their antics were akin to the dance of Willa Willa. He had indeed taken that to be some kind of theatrical art, but in the clearing that day he had seen the meeting of art and life, of art and death. But it was the law of the colony that the art could remain, but that the decision over life and death must remain the business of the white man, for it was the Laws of Civilisation that must be observed and enforced.

'But if the Colonial Office and Captain Phillips take the warrior aspect away, we will remain with the art.' Matthew still felt that the virtuosity of native accomplishments could be kept and even promoted in a partnership between settler and native, and that his move to the north with James could somehow create a model for other settlers to follow.

But Cawthorne had seen the disintegration of native arts before, in Africa, and he had walked next to men like Phillips. 'If it remains as art alone, it dishonours the ancestors and the dreaming spirits, for it has no meaning. There is no nobility. And the native Kaurna death is not like the Christian one.'

The men remained silent for another two hundred yards or so, their heads bowed down as they walked until Cawthorne said, suddenly, from nowhere. 'But Kadlitpinna lives.'

'Yes, yes,' said Matthew, 'Kadlitpinna lives.' Was this one thought enough to engage with the idea that the death of the culture was rightful?

'If he had fallen, then I believe I would have mourned him as much or more than any person on earth. In my years in this place, he has become not only my friend, but I do admire him completely as a man. He has a greatness and gentleness of spirit that in my own travails I cannot muster. So many times, I have wished that I could be more like…'

But as they approached the joining with the Bay road, one hundred yards distant, there was beheld a hallooing and waving of hats. Two riders were there – females.

'God in heaven, what is this?' Cawthorne muttered.

'Why, I say,' cried Matthew. 'It is Lucy Bray and another!'

'What! The governor's child?'

'The one.'

Cawthorne seemed to shrink in size at this announcement and he slowed his pace to allow Matthew the front position as the two girls walked their horses up.

'We waved and waved and you saw us not. Your heads were so bent in concentration, or conversation, or whatever it was. I said to Adela that it must be Matthew because no man in the colony steps in quite the way that my Matthew does. And so it was. I was right! It was you after…'

'Adela!' said Matthew in astonishment, for once interrupting Lucy.

'Yes,' cried Lucy, 'look who I have brought you! Your brother's wife-to-be. The semaphore came in this morning very early and I came to you and you had gone. Whatever took you to disappear so early in the morning on the sabbath, Matthew? And to stay away so long?'

'Adela,' said Matthew, still unable to find appropriate words, so stark a change it was from talking with Cawthorne about life and death and Kadlitpinna to this, the social world of the colonist. For the moment, he felt alien to this world, to his world, and it was a conscious effort to drag himself, through avenues of broken glass or so it seemed, to converse in the way he had been trained and at which he had become so adept. He had seen Adela only twice before – at his brother's wedding and at a ball near Regent Street; he had been up at Oxford and supposedly monkishly engaged for much of the wooing. On the occasions he had met her, Adela had been perfect, charming without pressing herself, speaking mostly when addressed. He remembered now, she had said to him, 'So you are meant for orders, Mr Larkin?' As if at one glance she had seen that it could never be. And that look, the way she had pursed her lips, had somehow helped to give him strength to confront the admiral. Now here he was, as far from orders as he could be.

Finally, Matthew found words which were both appropriate to the moment and which expressed his own feelings of bewilderment. 'You are indeed a vision of wonder.' And he bowed.

Adela inclined her head.

'Ah, Matthew, why is it you never say things like that to me?'

'Because to say it would be to repeat the thoughts of too many men. It is too obvious and all the world can see it.' Matthew had returned quickly enough to best form.

The girls dismounted and Matthew shook hands with his sister-in-law-to-be. She was fuller of figure and bosom than Lucy, and her hair fell like an ooze of honey from her sun hat. For a woman who had spent a hundred days at sea, she was in the bloom of health; there was colour in her cheeks from the wind and the spray, and barely a day of sickness, he guessed. The throat of her morning dress was open and there was a small pendant there.

Adela saw Matthew looking at her hat. 'Lucy has prepared me well for the Antipodean sun, sir.'

'Aye, too well, perhaps,' said Matthew, drawing a look of displeasure from Lucy. 'I'm sure you are well adjusted to the elements after three months at sea. But this is my friend, Mr Cawthorne,' said Matthew, remembering his manners.

Cawthorne merely nodded and at the mention of his name he took an involuntary half-step backwards; he made no move to shake hands with Adela.

'Lucy, you have not met Mr Cawthorne,' said Matthew.

'Miss Bray,' Cawthorne managed and nodded again.

'Mr Cawthorne – the famous friend of the natives,' said Lucy, not meaning offence.

Still, Cawthorne coloured and he looked at the ground.

'I must conduct Adela to her place straight away, for we are starving for lunch. Adela has had an extraordinary morning. She was carried ashore by a sailor, fully five hundred yards.'

'It is the usual way, ma'am.' It was Cawthorne who spoke. Something in the manner of Adela gave him confidence – whether it was placidity or serenity he could not say. Lucy Bray was more complicated and difficult to fathom.

'But what an introduction to our ways, here in the colony,' Matthew beamed and looked around him, as a host would when attempting to revive the flagging humour of his party, smacking himself good-naturedly on each side of his stomach as he did so.

'Yes, it is all very different, so far.' Adela motioned around her at the abundant nature which surrounded them.

Matthew gave Adela a hoist onto her mount and Lucy leapt upon hers.

'We shall see you at luncheon then, Matthew,' said Lucy. 'Shall we see you as well, Mr Cawthorne?'

'Unlikely, ma'am,' was Cawthorne's reply.


'Lucy Bray will be looking for you at the ball this Saturday night.'

'She has found me every day to remind me, James. Thompson raises his eyebrows across the room and ensures that I see him do it, and his comments on the efficacy of my work become more pointed.'

'You are leaving and he is staying. You can expect no less.'

'I wish we were in the saddle and away tomorrow.'

'It will be soon enough, but you must do honour to Lucy on Saturday night. She might seem youthful to you but engagements can endure for many years. She will grow.'

'She is indeed a very fine woman, but we are not engaged, James.'

'Nonetheless, we must maintain the position of respect we have with the governor. We have him to thank for your position at Government House.'

'Of course, and he has earned himself favour with the admiral for doing so. Another posting awaits him after this, no doubt.'

'Ah, but will she go with him, or will she stay? You will not find a woman who suits you one hundred miles north of here.'

Matthew's logical mind agreed; what a wife she would make for a man on the land. The way she rode, tied knots; she won the respect of the servants by mucking in. Besides Cawthorne, she was the only true friend he had in the colony and she would be nearly twenty by the time their place was in order. But would he stay, in the north, after that time?

'Indeed, James. I shall do everything in my power to keep the Larkin ship on course.'

But what was more interesting to Matthew now was the realignment of temper in the colony since the appearance of Mr French Angas, whose enthusiasm for the artefacts of the native, and for their appearance and personal regalia, had acted as a check on the disdain of the burghers of the town. Cawthorne had been barely visible during his three or more years in the colony, never invited to tea. His abruptly forthright manner would have been considered worrisome if it were considered at all. But in the two weeks after the visit of Angas, he was addressed twice in the street, once by Justice Heffcott, whose own passing interest in native artefacts was shared, but who would still not otherwise have openly acknowledged the person of William. Others had touched their hats as Cawthorne passed. Mrs Woodhall stopped him once to enquire after his dear mother!

When recognised, Cawthorne would dip his head two inches; his back straightened slightly and his features took on a kind of noble fixity;

that stare-into-the-distance attitude, as he had displayed when painting Kadlitpinna – the visionary look that one sees on statuary in the great squares of London. William had the taste of social elevation, the desire for which Matthew had never been able to understand until he saw the effect of its absence on William. A crumb from the nine-course banquet of social recognition it might be, but a taste it was none the less.

Privately, William was perturbed. He returned doggedly to his easel, but his attempts to paint were now clogged in shame, for how could he ever match the glories of the French Angas canvas? French, who was trained in London and in Paris, with unlimited leisure and funds, had gone out with the governor himself to be shown the waterfalls of Stoneyfell that he might sketch and return to begin another fine painting. Every week, every day, every hour, Cawthorne fell further behind in his quest for a published folio. And his hopes for a patron: were they increased by his new fame, or dashed by the Angas primacy?

One day, while entering the Cawthorne parlour, Matthew noticed a smear of blue paint on the uncovered floorboards, smudged as if someone had tried to wipe away what could only be ground further in to the coarse grain of the timbers. There too were tiny streaks emitting from the central blob of paint, suggesting that the stain had come from a brush flung down in frustration. Matthew imagined the artist returning to his canvas, regretting the precipitate act as unworthy of him, respecting once more the piety that nothing is ever gained without struggle.

On the day that French Angas came for his collection, Cawthorne had been wounded. He fretted about the house for three days; he was sterner than usual with his 'young scholars'. His anxiety reached a point where he could not sit still. Then, on the fourth afternoon, without notice, there was the sound of a carriage outside, and moments later a knock at the door and French Angas's man was there saying that his master wished to be accompanied on a tour of the town and that he was desirous of Mr Cawthorne's company in the matter.

It was an honour beyond dreams. No doubt, Angas wished to talk to Cawthorne and to absorb his arcane enlightenment. It was clear; he would be used. But might not Angas also put a proposition to him? On some things, they could work in partnership. Before long, Angas would move to another place, New Zealand probably, and Cawthorne could be his Adelaide man *in absentia*. These thoughts went through Cawthorne's mind before he had picked up his hat. He was out of the door in half a minute.

To be seen out riding with French Angas! To be rubbing shoulders with the cream, he thought, then chided himself on the mixing of two metaphors!

It turned out that the purpose of the great man's visit was this: he had heard much of Kadlitpinna, or Captain Jack, as the colonists called him, and also of King John, who was the other chieftain much known in the town. One day some months before this, the two of them had been engaged to give an exhibition of spear throwing on the occasion of the festivities associated with the young Queen's birthday. For this purpose, they both had been provided with bright red shirts and faun moleskin trousers, and footwear as was deemed appropriate, as it was by then against the law for natives to appear unclad. The display was to be attended by both men and women, as well as the children of the colony. A target was set up and the two men went at it. However, the display of throwing was much below the expectations of all concerned. Many spears fell short of their target and those that achieved the distance were inaccurate by wide margins. Murmurs of disappointment gained momentum through the crowd and some began to turn away, until Kadlitpinna let out a great howl of anguish such as would stop any man in his tracks.

The departing crowd turned and were treated to the sight of Kadlitpinna in the act of ripping off his shirt, dislodging buttons as he did. He then divested himself similarly of his footwear and trousers, grasped his three spears, which had been returned to him by the markers, and proceeded to hurl them at distance into the centre of the target, raising howls of varying delight, amazement and disapprobation from all those gathered about. He then jumped up and down on his former habiliments, raising dust all about and shouting, 'White fella clothe no good, white fella clothe no good.'

Children gazed upon the sight in rapt awe; women did their best to turn them away from the scene, and the men's faces were garbed in looks that ranged from open amusement and approval at the character shown by the man, to disdain growing from the impropriety of his presentation. But, whatever the reaction, Kadlitpinna's fame had risen to the sky.

French Angas had heard the stories and so it was Kadlitpinna that he now wanted more than any other thing. How to make the acquaintance of the great native chieftain and to gain his confidence without Cawthorne to smooth the way? Without Cawthorne, whom Kadlitpinna counted a dear friend and wished to initiate into his tribe! How else would the great man get his man other than to grant a moment of fame to the starved Cawthorne?

And so it happened that Kadlitpinna came with Willa Willa one bright morning to the house of Cawthorne and there was fully dressed as a warrior: he was oiled, painted and decorated, regaled in the full panoply of arms, as he would be in readiness for the most monumental affray. In this state, covered only by a shield and his loincloth tied with string – and with a wooden peg stuck through his nose – he paraded, followed by Cawthorne, Larkin and Willa Willa, through Hindley Street, up Rundle Street to Gawler Place and then down Grenfell Street as far as the Angas house. Not one person failed to stop and hold them in their gaze until they had passed from it. A number followed them to further investigate the cause of the fuss, and so a little entourage of twelve or fifteen people came with them right through to the Angas doorway. Cawthorne was straight-backed and dignified, one hand held on to the left-side lapel of his jacket to furnish him with extra dignity, the other was in his pocket to give him a countering insouciance.

At the Angas house, there was a scene which called almost for speeches to be made, and indeed Cawthorne rose to the moment and formally presented his man to Angas, with the awkward deference that is sometimes seen when a father presents his daughter as a bride to her new master. So it was with Cawthorne as he handed Kadlitpinna over to Angas.

But it was not Angas or Kadlitpinna who was the centre of this piece; almost all eyes were on Cawthorne, for by now the stories of his collections, his affection for the native, and his portraits of them, had won him some respect among sections of the town. And the handing over of his fondest man to Angas did touch those who were present, sensing as they did the loss this occasioned in Cawthorne and appreciating the dignity with which the consignment was made.

He was mostly silent as he and Matthew walked back to his little house. The distant look was upon him. When they arrived, Matthew bade good afternoon to Mrs Cawthorne and left him with her, as if handing on a child who was left for caring. Cawthorne went to his room and sat deep in thought for a very long time, alone in his study chair, his face buried in a handkerchief.

Until the day of the crushing of the second affray, Cawthorne's sour auguries on the future of the Kaurna people had seemed to Matthew to be a projection of his own private despair, and Matthew's optimism had turned them to vapour that fizzed and disappeared into the air around him. But Matthew's buoyancy had been bruised that day, such that he could no longer speak of the state of the Aborigines of the plain. His visits to the tree stool by the river found them hunched and dispirited, going about their business still, but, with their self-determination stripped and dignity affronted, they were simply waiting on what the newcomers would decide for them next.

The more dismay that Matthew felt, the more he could see that Adelaide was not the place to influence the future for the good, and the more his dreams of the north fuelled his optimism. James's heart was close to his own and once they set up their own run, they would have power to decide how to live in greater harmony with the Aborigines. He could do his duty by the family and work for a greater benefit in the world as well.

James and Adela married in early December, just three weeks after Adela's arrival. The service was held at the Trinity Church just two hundred yards down from Cawthorne's house. Adela wore her best dress of fine silk in cobalt blue, with four columns of brocade running down the front to the hem, which was so neat to the ground that her shoes could barely be seen. A lace pelerine covered her shoulders and her outfit was topped by a white bonnet into which Lucy and Mary had only that morning sewn native flowers of yellow and cornflower blue. James was in his short top hat with a jacket of sky blue that complemented Adela's dress, gathered close at the waist over loose linen trousers. All present agreed that Adela was a very beautiful bride – her golden hair touching the shoulders of her dark blue gown was irresistible – and that James Larkin had fitted himself tight into an outfit which showed that he must have been something of a Beau Brummell when he was twenty.

Matthew was best man and Lucy attended to Adela. William Cawthorne and his mother were in attendance, and were treated with respect by the best levels of society. William was growing accustomed to receiving nods of acquaintanceship from those he barely knew. The governor himself had given the bride away. The contiguous arrangement of attendants, with Matthew on one side and Lucy Bray on the other, was seen by many to foreshadow nuptial arrangements of the younger brother. Lucy was now eighteen years of age and a child no longer, in her view at the very least.

The brothers were in the process of preparing for their voyage to the north. On the morning of their departure, James and Adela had been together in marriage for eleven days.

*The bar cleared early. The conversation was self-conscious that night. Games of darts were muted and no one thought to set up skittles; the young lady was in the house, resting.*

*She slept at eight o'clock and rose again at four – the dreamless sleep of the righteous. It was the last such sleep that Lucy had for many years. By dawn, she was washed and dressed. Her horse had dined on the best oats* and hay, was watered and waiting, sniffing the air for her. She trotted through the waking street, night buckets tossed in yards, chickens waking and scratching, roosters singing raucous proclamations above it all. The road to the north was clear. There were tracks to east and west but neither bore the ruts of the wheels of the legendary Watson.

The road made for the gently arcing petered folds of foothills, and there it bore her across a stream and then she climbed a small hill and looked back — the mist above a flattened valley and a chimney here and there that added to the haze. She walked along past brilliant gold acacia forests where bees were happy and productive.

She could hear them humming as they went about their work.

# 7

## The Town – November and December 1843

William Cawthorne stepped up through Grenfell Street to the monthly meeting of the Colonial Education Committee. When he walked out of his house, which was not often, he covered the ground at a pace and rarely glanced left or right, as a deterrent to unwelcome chance meetings and awkward small talk.

But that morning, a new bank building on the corner of Gawler Place was skirted by Lucy Bray returning north to Government House at the very moment Cawthorne was charging east to his meeting. Cawthorne glanced right to see Lucy at the moment she looked up to his eyes.

'Why, Mr Cawthorne. Good morning to you.'

Lucy Bray was the very type of person Cawthorne should be cultivating, but who he had difficulty in talking to – pretty, youthful, of the superior class, a wielder of influence.

'Why, uh,' Cawthorne stammered for a moment. 'I, uh, well…good morning to you.'

'We met one day on the track from the Bay. I am delighted to see you again.' She looked at him earnestly, as if her eyes were seeking help.

'Ah, yes indeed. I…but…I am gratified that you remember me.'

Cawthorne was not surprised that Lucy remembered him but was indeed gratified that she was delighted. He had already learnt that Lucy was not the kind to say she was delighted in that manner without meaning it. His mother kept him in view of town gossip and he had learnt that Lucy Bray was not one for falsities; she would let her mind be known when she wanted it known. He had also been advised that Lucy had struggled through the winter without Matthew. She had kept up her round of engagements, of course. But she was now deep into her second year in the colony and, while she made herself out to be as bright as she ever was, sometimes she betrayed an air of weariness. What had once been novel and stimulated her energies now required the kind of effort that sapped them. Rumours came off the ships that her uncle would move on during the next year and there was already speculation that Lucy would not leave with him. She could not go to the Lingalee unwed and her options would then be to marry someone else or return to England.

'I expect your life is the lesser for the absence of Matthew, as is mine.' Lucy went straight to the subject that was common to their hearts, and didn't mind revealing what was in hers.

Cawthorne admired her forthrightness and the deliberate avoidance of conversational craft. Indeed, he took it as a kind of compliment that she would talk so directly to him.

'There is certainly not another man like him in this colony.'

'For me, it was a privilege to have such a friend, Miss Lucy, if only for a few months. We have shared…' Cawthorne was doubtful how to pursue this unanticipated conversation. What aspects of his sudden intense friendship with Mattthew should he place in Lucy's domain? He was accustomed to excluding his interest in native culture from street corner conversations, but with this girl he was not sure. She was almost a kindred spirit. 'We have shared many things.' Cawthorne pulled back carefully from disclosure. 'He was very good to my mother.'

'There is a golden heart within.'

'He read to her poetry, which she did appreciate so much. I believe her heart did rather melt at the sound of his voice.'

'Huh,' laughed Lucy. 'He always spoke most enthusiastically of you, and of your learning. And of your regard for the culture of the native.' Cawthorne nodded in acknowledgement. 'I would sometimes that I were a man, that I might more actively pursue such things, such interests. I fear I was not born for cups of tea and chatter, Mr Cawthorne.'

'That much I can indeed observe, Miss Lucy,' said Cawthorne, beginning to thaw.

His mother had told him the story of the opening of the new port some weeks before. Lucy had been closely attended by Mr Stewart on the day. When a group of native children came too close to a presentation Lucy was to make, Stewart had taken the initiative to wave them menacingly away with his silver-handled cane. Lucy Bray had scolded him openly, then bade the children come closer to see.

Then when the news of Matthew's injury was received, it was reported that Lucy had had to be dragged from her horse by the governor himself, no other man would dare try it. Miss Lucy's impulse was for riding alone one hundred miles north to nurse Matthew through his convalescence. Such a venture would be madness and the governor had of course acted properly, but Cawthorne had been struck by the spirit of the girl. There was not one other colonist he could think of who would risk so much for what she believed in, except perhaps for Matthew himself.

'However, I do have duties here...' Lucy was proceeding with some gambit of conversation.

'Indeed.'

'...which keep me most enthralled, I am sure.'

Was the girl alluding sarcastically to her official life? Was she openly admitting her weariness? If so, Cawthorne had almost been drawn into a confidence – a very private thought.

'I understand that stone for the house at Lingalee has been procured and that work is proceeding apace.' Lucy kept a watch on Cawthorne's face as she spoke. She was working to some point of interest to her, and would gauge his reaction. 'A neighbour named Jenks has loaned them two men for a week, to lay stone and to show them the arts of their trade.'

'Ah, that would be most beneficial. I have heard of Jenks – a famous empire man. I'm sure his assistance will be a boon to progress.' Cawthorne's face was like the sphinx; she read nothing.

'Yes, they have their own rooms now. Privacy! After all these months, ha ha.' Lucy tripped self-consciously on. 'And they even have their housekeeper. A native girl, called Grace or some such thing.' Lucy's eyes betrayed her anxiety. 'Have you heard of her?'

Cawthorne had indeed received news from Matthew of Grace. Her qualities of calmness and sense had been extolled.

'Just a name,' he said. 'I understand she does cook and clean.'

'Oh, I see. I am sure they will be needing someone to do that. With the house and the fields and flock, and men to manage, they can't be washing sheets and cooking stew, I'm sure.'

'Indeed, it must be a strenuous life.' Cawthorne had not known what to say. The education committee was waiting. They were on a street corner. He was unprepared for any such interview.

'Well, I must be attending to my errands. Good morning, Mr Cawthorne. I very much hope we shall meet again soon.'

'It would be a great pleasure.'

Cawthorne bade her good day, and walked on up to his meeting. He had not known what to say. Indeed, he had no hard information to give, but Matthew had mentioned Plato's Form of Beauty in a letter. Damn! He wished he had never mentioned Plato to Matthew. He was anguished now, for Lucy. She had grown somehow, not in size, but in stature. An edge had gone from her eagerness, but still there was the intensity, perhaps she was one whose soul would never be at rest. Eighteen years old, he smiled to himself; at that age everything in the world is so very important. Was it a trait that was innate to her, he pondered as he walked on, or was it simply the strongly held conviction that there was no one else in the world who was right for her?


'Ah, Mr Cawthorne, only two minutes early today.'

Messrs Edmonds and Gouger joked as Cawthorne handed his hat to the maid and stepped from the hallway into a high-ceilinged and freshly painted room. Three other men sat at a long mahogany table, and with Cawthorne they exceeded the quorum of five.

'Gentlemen, good morning. I was…' he hesitated to relate the reason for his 'lateness', so unaccustomed was he to such occurrences. 'I was delayed by an unexpected encounter in the street.' He finished his sentence on a self-deprecating note of surprise which he expected his colleagues would understand. He did not share the identity of the person he met. It might have enhanced his standing had he done so, but he was still confused by the importance and the nature of the conversation he had shared. He needed to go home and think about it over a pipe.

'Ah, very good,' said Gouger. 'It is a reliable man indeed who paces himself to be ten minutes early in case the unexpected happens and when it does he is still in by five.'

'Or two,' Edmonds chimed in merrily.

'Or two.' Cawthorne gave some finality to the discussion.

The business of the day was attended to. Chief among the items for discussion was the matter of expenses for the next year; chalk and blackboards were difficult to obtain. As for the precious commodity of paper, students would have to write neatly in lines, then turn the book upside down at the end and start again to write between the old ones.

'When the Caledonian School is completed, the crowding in other places no doubt will ease,' said Gouger.

'Do we know yet who will be headmaster?' Cawthorne was interested to know.

'It seems that distinction has fallen to me,' said Edmonds. 'It will be my honour to conclude my days as an educator by establishing a school which will rival the best in the colony.'

'Indeed, sir! Congratulations. A most worthy choice, I must say.'

'It is uncertain how many enrolments there will be in the first instance. It may be many, it may be few. But it will be sure to grow.'

'Of course, sir.'

'I may have to take a mixed class myself. Versatility will be of the utmost importance.'

The last sentence was stressed in tone; Cawthorne noted the importance of it and the other men seemed to also. No man was as broad as Cawthorne, who had taught himself the philosophers, was as proficient in mathematics as he was in grammar and who could manage a conversation in French as well as teach the history of the Roman Republic. The men of the committee were not without respect for what Cawthorne could do.

'We also need someone who is proficient in the use of the stick, sir. There will be no easing of discipline in this school. Our lads may not be as reliable as those at Trinity, not at first, but that is the point. We will need to whip them into shape.'

'Well, I, sir…' Then Cawthorne realised he had not been asked his view, nor had it been put clearly that he might be considered for such a post. But a suggestion had been made, veiled perhaps, but made.

'Your own school, Mr Cawthorne. I understand your mother has a hand in running it.'

'Oh yes, sir. In the rudiments of grammar and arithmetic, she is well able in particular.'

'So, if it happened that you were absent from your school for a time at some other position, would it be fair to say that your own school would remain open?'

Cawthorne thought of his poor mother, with chalk, blackboard and yardstick, alone in a crammed roomful of louts – the horror of her days.

'Of course, sir.'

'That is good. If it ever were to come to that, we would not want any of our schoolrooms to close, and it would appear that our colony is growing faster in general population than it is in its population of suitable masters.'

The conversation shifted into a discussion of the style of tutelage to be employed at the new school and considerations of its staffing drifted away into the ether of possibilities.

At the conclusion, Cawthorne bade his farewells in the usual manner and stepped back into the street. His progress was measured and thoughtful – Lucy Bray, then this. Nothing had been said outright, but no doubt he would be considered; it would take weeks to decide and, as ever, he must wait, and wait, for the forces of destiny to work on him.

Lucy Bray stood upon the carriage of Mr Williams the undertaker and lifted her lorgnettes towards four upheavals of dust which proceeded steadily across the back of the extensive grassy paddock which, for the day, had been deemed the race course at Thebarton. The Ladies' Purse was in progress and Lucy was to present the ribbon to the winning owner and rider in approximately nine minutes time. Plodding along the back of the course were two farm nags, another horse had come with stock overlanded from New South Wales, and there was a fourth, a little known stallion brought by a Mr Morphett in a ship from Tasmania – that was the field for the Ladies' Purse.

All the best costumery was out in force and beside Lucy was Mr Stewart, in a black velvet waistcoat and hat of stiff felt and soft leather riding boots. In his few months in the colony, he had expressed strong interest in the formation of a jockey club and had been invited by Messrs Morphett and Fisher to join them as inaugural members. With the bold figure of Lucy Bray by his side, the picture was complete. He had danced with her at the Midwinter Ball and had ridden with her to Klemzig to see her friends. He was impressed with the easy way she was with people, even the Germans. He wanted all that to be wrapped up and delivered with his name on the paper, but he felt in moments of reflection that he had to try with her, where he did not with others, that she had set some benchmark higher for him. There was some figure in mythology who was always straining for water that was just out of reach. That was how he felt.

Despite the low quality of the equine component of the day, the meeting was a sensation. Vehicles of every description had been in pressing demand throughout the morning. Every barouche and bullock dray had been hauled into service from city and country to ferry the crowd of more than a thousand to the course. It seemed strange to Lucy that gentlemen who thought nothing of walking the eight miles from Adelaide to Glenelg to visit or do some business, and then would walk the return journey in the afternoon, could not on this day take the mile and a half stroll out to the plains at Thebarton. Lucy assessed these logically inexplicable aspects of human nature as part of her study of the general human comedy – the symbolism of traps and carriages. She herself had been perfectly happy to walk out but had been precluded from doing so. Mr Stewart had been adamant that to travel in Mr Williams's hearse was the very thing, and he had been very strongly supported by the governor. But now that they had arrived, she was glad of the hearse to stand on; it had even been worth withstanding all the cheery enquiries on their way out as to whether there was a passenger 'inside'.

Lucy looked across at Mr Stewart, whose features were set in concentration, his neat moustache clipped back in the restrained manner of the younger men of the day. He'd had a pound on Morphett's Vandemonian horse, called Cossack, with Mr Chambers, whose farm horse Black Jack was said to be the fittest it had ever been and trained up to run on this day. The hotelier Mr Farquarson had been allowed to open a book for the day but the crowd around his stand was full of labouring knaves investing pennies so Stewart had sought side bets as the dignified way to involve himself in the day's entertainments.

As Cossack bore the lash of his rider and passed the post in first place, Lucy wondered what Matthew would have made of the races: the excitement of the crowd, the refreshments, the ride upon a hearse and the cheerful greetings of the other folk walking out, the jokes about death. The high life juxtaposed with the crushing mediocrity of the nags. 'Dromedarial,' he would have said of the racing, and Lucy smiled to herself at the thought. He would have respected the effort, and taken harmless amusement from the incompetence.

'Well,' said Mr Stewart, 'quite a sound contest in the event. Three lengths the winner, I'd give it. I knew Morphett would not bring a horse on the ship from Tasmania simply for the fun of it.'

'But some thought he had not sufficient time to recuperate from the ordeal at sea.'

'Hmmph,' was all Stewart would say, in modesty.

'But of course, you were right.'

'Hmmph,' said Mr Stewart again, not wanting to criticise any of the horses. A word out of place could get around in this small community and then one could find oneself offside with an important chap one had no idea was a part-owner; best to be polite even when one thought oneself in the restricted company of disinterested parties, and even ladies. 'How did you enjoy the race, my dear?'

'Dromedarial.' The word was out of her mouth without thinking.

'Oh, I say, how do you mean?'

'I mean they ran like camels. Did they not? Dromedaries.'

'Ah, yes, I do recall now having heard the word before. There was an uncle who strayed to Egypt on his return from the Khyber. Rode part of the way on the hump of a camel.' Mr Stewart attempted to switch the conversation. 'People seem to think the typical camel is bi-humpal, but apparently those are extremely rare.'

'Bihumpal! Oh, Mr Stewart, your conversation is so diverting.' Lucy fluttered her fan affectedly, as if to flush away the wit of Mr Stewart. The object of her sally smiled to himself, saying nothing.

'I still think they ran like camels,' she said, putting an end to the subject. 'I believe we should make our way to the presentation yard.'

'Of course, Lucy,' said Mr Stewart, with a tight smile and an incline of the head. He offered his arm and escorted her away.

Other ladies and gentlemen climbed down from the rows of vehicles drawn up by the winning post and made their way to the tarpaulins and tents which sat under a clump of gums and served as the hospitality rooms. Around about, children chased each other and were in turn chased by their dogs and were tolerated on account of the paucity of attractions for them.

When barrels were emptied inside the tents, they were rolled outside and stood together upright with a plank of wood between to serve as impromptu observation posts for customers. As the day wore on, there was much rolling about and falling from the planks and catching and setting to rights, but no serious injuries were reported. The atmosphere was high and festive.

Lucy caught sight of Mary and waved her over. 'Come and watch me give the sash to Mrs Morphett, Mary.'

'Oh, how could I miss it, miss,' said Mary. 'Good afternoon, Mr Stewart, I'm sure,' and she curtsied very briefly as she spoke. 'I'll go and get me friends. They won't want to miss it for quids, they won't.' So Mary hung on to her hat as she bustled off to rouse her friends from outside the hospitality tarpaulin.

'Ooh gawd, was that the Ladies' Purse already,' Lucy heard from one of them and she smiled to herself.

'Hmmph,' Mr Stewart sniffed in a different way to that he had a minute or two before.

'Aren't they marvellous?' said Lucy.

'I expect so.'

'And now, to present the sash to the winning owner, I call on Miss Lucy Bray.'

As Lucy stepped forward, a cheer went up around the rather large crowd which had gathered for the ceremony. She had wondered that so many had been drawn out into the hot sun, out of the tents, away from the wagons and the trees. But in that moment, she saw something that she had not seen before. She saw faces around that were beaming, not just with drink or the sun or the good fellowship of the day. All were pointed in her direction, at the orphan girl who had come to the colony with her uncle the governor. She had met them all, at the many receptions that her uncle was obliged to run, at the Winter Ball, in the street and at the innumerable afternoon teas to which she was invited. They had all responded to her in the way that she would expect them to respond to the governor's niece. But now she saw, there was more than that. As she stepped forward, someone cried for three cheers and so three cheers were given in the fervid English fashion. Lucy knew that when her uncle stepped out to present the cup for the main race of the day, there would be respect and a strong round of hand-clapping ap-plause. She could see that she had carried the day. But more than that, she had carried the year. She had diverted attention from her uncle; she had made him human, or at least more than he could ever have been without her.

As she stepped forward with the sash, she began to feel a measure of her worth that she had lost sight of in the months since Matthew's departure for the north. She had won the race day crowd and she was closely attended by the most sought-after bachelor in the colony. As she embraced Mrs Morphett, she convulsed with a tiny sob. As she placed the sash around Mrs Morphett's shoulder, she composed herself, as her training dictated; but it had been noticed, and charmed them all the more. Behind them, Mr Morphett stood to bask also in the well-being of the crowd and as he did so he nodded, as one gentleman to another, to Mr Stewart, standing behind Lucy. Mr Stewart nodded back to his new friend and turned his face back full into the sun.

Adela folded up the letter Lucy had received from James and handed it back to her. More than a year in the colony and even she, who had been raised by her mother to be a creature of comforts, was beginning to adopt some colonial ways. She was pitching in with the work of the house, went out walking alone to the furthest reaches of the town. She was developing her own mind on colonial political issues and had begun to speak that mind at social gatherings, then even at public meetings. Her view was that the colony could not be a happy place until the natives were compensated somewhat for the lands they had lost, that there should be a space set aside for them to come together and use as they would. The idea had been countered by a long-term colonist who pointed out there were different tribes and some could not understand each other's speech, but the conversation had been polite and her view was respected. After six months, she began to flow into the space that was around her in the town, but ahead of her was the next phase of her life in the north. She retained a kind of awe for bush women.

But now this letter. She could see that James had written with carefully chosen words. They had not been dashed off with items of news as some of his letters to her had been. This was a constructed work; it was even written more neatly, as if it was an official missive. It could even have been a second draft with corrections and some things omitted.

'How terrible that Matthew is wounded again,' said Adela. 'And fever. But he is through the worst of it, or so it seems. So, that much is excellent.'

'I would like to know more than what seems, Adela. If Matthew is so well as James says, then why doesn't he write to me himself? He is not out in the fields and has only just begun to ride again, but I have had no word from him in six weeks. And there is no invitation to visit.'

'Would I not want to visit also,' said Adela, with a shake of her head. 'But it is not yet safe. The affray that James has described is proof enough. A spear dipped in poison. It is most horrific. The surrounding area must be made safe.'

'Phillips has a wife, and this Jenks.'

'But they have houses established.'

'You will be there in a few weeks.' There was an implication that if Adela could go in a few weeks, certainly Lucy could go now, for Lucy was forever the more fit person to make such a journey and survive the conditions that would be found at its end.

Her words hung on the air for a moment. Adela looked down into her soft hands and fingers, which she tried hard to keep still.

'Read it again. Is there a word about this native nurse of his? Look, here is his previous letter in which he tells of this woman who has come to their hut – Grace. The doctor from Clare cannot be there every day. If he has been in fever, who is with him each day? Surely not James. The shepherds? And why does he not write for himself, this hero who is now so well?' Lucy held the letter out to her.

'I will not read it again, not with you boring your eyes into me.' Adela's voice rose, and she checked herself. The speed of Lucy's mind had wrong-footed her; the connections she had made and her explanations for the absences in James's letter had come too fast for her. She had sensed a kind of wrongness about it, but Lucy had been stewing it all night. 'It is not for us to…'

'Oh, it is not for us! How tired I am of hearing that. They bring us here to the other side of the world and tell us we must be colonial women and then say it is not for us to contend with men!'

'The road to Clare is still not fit for carriages.'

'Foo to carriages. I shall ride.'

'Lucy, you cannot. Besides, you have a duty here. You are the governor's consort, in fact. You do play that role. To leave the town without permission would be scandalous. For the governor to be unable to govern his own household would be to render him laughable in the eyes of many. And you know there are still many people in this colony who would not hesitate to spread such a story, exaggerating it as they went.'

'What would I care for scandal? And uncle is considered to be the next governor in New Zealand. We will not remain here forever.' She turned and threw herself at Adela's knees. 'What of me then? Must I go with him, to New Zealand? Begin it all again? Adela, I am done with pots of tea and charming conversation. I must know about Matthew.'

'But there is Mr Stewart.'

'Mr Stewart. Yes, Mr Stewart,' said Lucy, looking up, as if only now remembering him with surprise, as if her thoughts had not crossed Mr Stewart that day, or that week. 'Of course, Mr Stewart.' She stood and threw her arms around herself and her feet began to move in the steps of a dance, mimicking romance, skipping lightly in ballroom sallies.

Adela thought her a little mad.

'Mr Stewart is the perfect husband for you. He is charming and handsome and has a property near the town,' Lucy recited the too-familiar words. 'It is the third time I have been told that in a week,' Lucy turned on Adela, 'by people who know me not.' The rebuke in this last was half intended, and half meant as a joke, for Lucy knew that Adela knew her better, but still had to scotch her from mentioning Mr Stewart again. 'I have no need of a carriage, Adela. I can ride.'

Adela laughed out loud. 'My dear, you cannot. It is two days on horseback, three more likely.'

Lucy looked up, resolve in her face.

'Come here,' and Adela drew Lucy to her bosom and stroked and kissed her hair. 'We will talk of this again tomorrow.'

'Yes,' said Lucy, with a sigh, 'tomorrow.'

As Adela held her close, Lucy felt like a baby that had never had a mother and here, now, with her head on Adela's chest and with her arms around her shoulders, she felt how she must have felt as a child, with a mother who not only scolded her when she was silly but comforted her when she was sad for good reason.

'What will become of us, Adela? In this place.'

'We must wait. The men are making the land safe. They are taking great risks for us.'

'For you. Only that much is certain.' Lucy sat up now, and brushed a tear away.

'You are tired,' said Adela, and Lucy nodded, pushing her hair into place.

'I did not sleep.'

'It must be so hard.'

'I shall go and lie down.'

'I well send for Timothy to take you.'

'No, please, I will walk. It may clear my head.'

It was ten o'clock and the day was warming. Lucy stood by the window: outside, lorikeets in the trees went happily about in pairs; white cockatoos in the higher branches nuzzled each other, then set off together, frighted by two boys who passed, talking loudly. Tomorrow night, there was a reception. Her presence was very much required.


It was a chance conversation that did it in the end.

Mary was in Hindley Street and her basket was filled with vegetables when a cart pulled up with a bundle of wheat from Clare, or so someone idly said. Mary turned to face the street and there the name of Watson the carrier was stencilled on the side of the rig and a man, Mary presumed the man himself, was standing in his seat and stretching.

'You have come from Clare?'

'Aye, I have, and tough goings it is. With all the rattlings and bouncings, it is a treat to return and behold a lady such as yourself, ma'am.'

Though rough of appearance, the man spoke well, with only a faint trace of dialect. His coat was shabby, but he was a carrier after all, Mary thought, and why would one wear one's best on the road. His beard was that of a week at least, but again that was little more than the time it would take to get up to Clare and back again with a day in between for rest.

'Oh, ho, go on with you, Mr Watson. A lady indeed!'

'You are a vision of loveliness, ma'am,' said Watson, removing his hat and placing it back on his head with a smack. 'Especially, might I say, to a man engaged in such a lonesome profession as myself.' He deliberately pronounced the word 'my' before 'self' in conscious avoidance of the 'me' self into which he may have occasionally lapsed.

'Have you news?'

'There is always news of one sort or another. News of great things, empires fallen. News of small things, a chicken pilfered from the master's yard, a heart is broken. Small things, miss. What manner of news are you interested in, miss?'

'Of the Larkins of Lingalee. Eleven miles past the town. Do they thrive?'

'Oh, ho ho.' Watson rocked back on his seat, as if the very jackpot of news had been struck in one hit. 'I do 'ear that the young Master Larkin has gone and made a name for hisself again. Oh ho, so he has, so he has,' said Watson.

Listening closely now, Mary could hear the dropped 'h' and the slurred 'm' as Mr Watson's concentration dissolved.

'You've been drinking, sir.'

Watson removed his hat and placed it on his head again. ''Tis a lonely drive, miss, with no company. Still, I never has one until we pass Kapunda. There's a wee town springing up and a nice little store that I do frequent when I'm about that way and they allus has a quart of something warm for me in store.'

'Something warm indeed,' said Mary. 'You'll be needin' nothing warm on a day like this is what I'm sayin'.'

Still, Mary was teasing, not scolding, and the carrier could tell it. He wondered if the woman might be interested.

'But what of young Master Larkin? We hear very little but we know he has made a hero of himself of some sort.'

'Well,' said Watson, taking off his hat to her yet again, dipping his head respectfully then replacing his hat again, 'I don't know about no hero, but he has a way of making a name of hisself and that is straight.' Watson thought about what he would say next, what artful play he could make of events to suit his audience, but the sun was indeed warm, he thought about how much of his bottle he might have consumed on the road, and his head was too fuddled for artifice.

'Well, out with it, man.' Mary still looked upon him with an amused gleam about her.

'Well, Master Larkin is famous thereabouts and there are some neighbours what is none too pleased with 'im.'

Mary was waiting, impatient to hear more.

'He was received of a wound to the arm, you see.'

'Yes, we know about that.'

'Some native concoction of a poisonous nature, it would seem.'

'Yes, yes.'

'And it would only be cured by his native lady.'

'Native lady?'

'The doctor from Clare had not the faintest clue. If it were left to him and him alone, the boy would of bin dead before the night were out. But his native woman cured him in the old way, with a poultice.' Here, Watson winked at Mary and drew forward and looked about him as if he were to impart a secret that was for her ears only, and which would make a bond between them that would stand the ages. 'And there's more…' He looked left and right as if to ascertain that no one but her was listening. 'The native lady and he have become very friendly.' And here Watson winked at Mary, as if the salacious implications in his gossip might induce the two of them towards following the suit of the young master and his paramour.

'Are you certain, Mr Watson.'

'As certain as I can be, Miss. Was talked of in the tavern as far down as Kapunda, miss. Now who would make up such a thing?'

Mary stood on her spot, wondering how to take the news, what credit to give it.

'It is a lonely business, miss, and there's no doubt there, living away on a station. As is drivin' these horses from one end of the world to the other, too.'

Mary thought about Watson's words for a moment, then looked up at him. He was not a bad man. 'Yes, Mr Watson, I fear there are many lonely occupations in this world. My mistress is the dearest girl who ever drew breath,' and she looked to the ground and spoke in a lower voice, 'though difficult at times.' Looking up and addressing him properly again, she said to him something that made Watson's heart skip. 'You are going to Clare again?'

'Oh, yes, miss. I will rest a day and be on my way again. A weekly service is guaranteed, or near enough.' He took his hat off and replaced it yet again, with a wink this time.

'You will enquire again, after the Larkins.'

'I will, miss.'

'Rumours spread like fire. What you heard in the tavern at Kapunda can hardly be the Lord's gospel truth, with men in drink and little on their minds.'

'No, miss. I daresay.'

'I will be here next week.'

'I can call, miss, at some appointed time.' Mr Watson removed his hat again.

'That won't be necessary, Mr Watson. I will find you.'

He replaced it.

Mary turned and her neat but mannish steps took her away towards her home. Watson saw the agitation in her gait and his heart went out to her. What would happen to Mary when her Lucy was married or went with her uncle to his next appointment, as he must some time do?

He thought that he would keep the gossip to himself; no need to spread it about. No reason to dilute the need for his information services. He would be there next week, sure as eggs. He might even shave and wash at Kapunda. Womenfolk notice these things, he thought, as he cried 'Gee up' and wheeled his horses into stable.

*The road began to bend and rise into a formation of small hills called the Hummocks. The track went around the right side of one of the hills and there was a view that stretched to infinity inland over paddocks patched into gum tree forests like lost chequerboard squares.*

*The track was pitched so sharply around huge gum trees that there was a view of only a few yards and without warning a horse and rider stepped from between the trees and into the way. A cold shiver of recognition went through her. The man was large, his chest like a barrel of beer; on his face there was a red beard, closer-cropped than she had seen before. It seemed to her that the beard could have been shaved clean two weeks before for a visit to the town, and was in the process of growing back to its previous glories.*

*'Mr Moran,' said Lucy, in the most even tone she could manage.*

*'Why, Miss Lucy.' Moran swept the hat from his head in an exaggeration of deference. 'How charmin' it is to see you again. Why, I was just lookin' out from me little hidey-hole on the hill, many of which abound in these parts, miss, it must be said. And I'm thinkin', what sort of a woman would be mad enough to be ridin' out here all alone? I keep lookin' behind her for the entourage that may be followin', but not a speck of dust for a mile. And so I come down here to make me acquaintance and I have the answer straight away. How could I doubt that it would be any other than me grand little friend, Miss Lucy.'*

*After holding his hat on his heart throughout his speech Moran placed it on his head again. The two horses sniffed at each other over the distance of three yards that separated them.*

*'You were expecting me, weren't you?'*

*'News travels. We may hide ourselves away but what proper villain would not keep a good eye on the road?'*

'You will need all the hidey-holes you can find, Mr Moran, what with all the new people making paddocks and building huts.' She looked out to the oblongs of pasture on a board of blue-grey foliage.

'There will be pickins enough for a while yet, Miss Lucy.'

'And then?'

Moran scratched his beard.

'And what of your assistant? The man whose name I never did catch.'

'Ah,' said Moran, his eyes moistening. 'Gone to heaven, miss, to be sure.'

'And what does that tell you?'

Moran looked away, to the patches of green below. 'Are you totin' your wee pistol today, ma'am?'

'It's close enough to hand.'

'No doubt, but the element of surprise on this occasion has been switched to me.'

'I see you have found another.'

'Aye, ma'am.' He wiggled the pistol in his hand.

'By the side of the road, where someone left it?'

'Exactly, ma'am.'

'Very careless.'

'Exceedingly, ma'am. But which of us has not made profit from the misfortunes of others, now?' He gazed back over the patches of green and the wisps of smoke from settlers' huts. 'At some time or another. I'm sure you understand.'

'Quite.'

'Which of the natives hereabouts is not less wealthy now, in terms of food and land and freedom, than he was five years ago? That is, if he is still living.'

'You have taken nothing from them yourself, Mr Moran?'

'I? Nay, ma'am.' He turned serious for a moment. 'Why should I take anything from those poor devils? The worst I can say for meself is that from time to time a jumbuck may have disappeared from the fields of our good Mr Jones and that blame for such a deed has been referred to the native, and it does me heart a sadness to say that reprisals may have been taken out upon them as a result, but that would not be stealing from them, would it now, just an adroit manipulation of the situation, if I may say that.'

'I see you have some education, Mr Moran. You express yourself so…'

'Enough about me,' his voice rose for the first time. 'And don't be makin' any sharp moves, Miss Lucy. If it comes to a case of it's you or me, I will not hesitate to shoot you dead. And your body will be just as warm alive as dead, for a time. And just as pretty too, although, I might say, not as wild as ye might have been with the breath in ye.'

The shiver that had passed through Lucy on recognising Moran now was eclipsed tenfold. The moment she had asked about his person, he had turned suggestions of brutality on her. She sat as prim in her saddle as she could manage, holding tightly the reins of her horse.

'All right, so where are you going?' Moran spoke roughly, impatiently.

'To the Lingalee, north of Clare.'

'Ah, ha, ha, ha,' Moran broke into feigned laughter as he had done that day with the Germans, to make a point. 'To see…your…lover!'

Lucy flinched but spoke not.

'How could a man of heart and sentiment stand in the way of such an enterprise? The raw emotion of the lass. I congratulate the man, whoever it may be, who takes ye first.' Then he spoke quietly, almost gently, as a brother. 'Miss Lucy, I do respect a woman of spirit. I promise you will be safe in your journey as far as Clare. From there, I cannot say.'

'You can vouch me safe?'

'I can.' Moran reined his horse to the side of the path against a callistemon tree, which dropped a shower of weeping red flowers in a veil over his coat. 'No one will harm ye on the way, but I won't speak for the harm that may be occasioned when ye arrive.'

Lucy passed and flicked her reins once and she wondered at the peculiar remarks of Mad Moran as her horse cantered to the next bend. She would not gallop, would not run; she would not show her fear. At the turn, she stopped to look back for one last glance of the mysterious Moran, alone on his bush track. But there was only a lilt of breeze and red flowers falling, on a sidetrack a puff of dust and the clop of disappearing hooves as a horse beat its way back to a lonely hilltop hidey-hole.

# 8

## The North – January 1844

There was fire in the hills; the natives were burning back forest to make grasslands once more.

James and Matthew Larkin stood on the porch of the homestead at Lingalee and watched the smoke curl into the sky and fade away to the north and east.

'Where have they come from?' said James, more to himself than to his brother.

'We have driven them away but they return.'

'They went beyond the ranges. There is land there.'

'The land is poor, brother, and you know it. And the natives out there do not want them. I'm sure there have been fights just as there were in Adelaide when the river men came. Burning is a signal of permanent return for the few of them that are left.'

James stepped out to the veranda of their homestead. His boot heels rang on the hard wood. His hands clenched the railing.

'This is the only mark on the earth they make. There is no temple, no pyramid, no boundary stone – just these fields like parks.'

Since his sickness and since Grace had come up from the hut to the house, Matthew went out seldom and had become less inclined to argumentation. The business of running the property had fallen to James alone and his occasional visitors asked about his brother only enough to satisfy obligatory social niceties. But James's concern was that, with the poppy seed medicine, shadows had begun to form under Matthew's eyes and with them his conversation had become less vivid.

'Burning fields could sway the Protector and the governor to award them land of their own if enough talk were to travel south and make its way to their ears.' James turned on Matthew. 'We teach them language so that they may know our wishes, so they may do our work for us. But if they learn too well, they may find some way to talk to the Protector too.'

Every settler in the valley was looking at the hills that morning with the thought that the natives had come too close – rescinded the retreat that might have saved them. They thought of Winnaraburra provoking in them the feeling of shame to be living as they did now.

Matthew could see the dancing in his mind at that moment, as he had seen Willa Willa dance in Cawthorne's room. Was it a year ago, or two? It was last summer that they had come, or autumn, so they had been in the north for most of a year. Matthew passed his hand over his brow and rubbed his temples as if to force crystal thoughts and memories through the fog of his mind. It was Cawthorne who had taken him to the affrays, who had taught him the love of the native and their ways, who had told him about Plato's ideals. And now he had Grace who fitted the Form of Beauty, who was his own healing Scheherazade. And it was all against the wish of Winnaraburra, who was the one Matthew wished more than anyone to appease and to join with.

Smoke drifted into a haze that stained the sky into a colour that was no longer blue. In Matthew's mind, Winnaraburra set the fires to cloud his view. It was aimed at him. When the smoke appeared, he saw again the skull of the native at the river, half blown away – his dream of Phillips shaking grey ooze from the head like sauce from a bottle. He saw the headless torso of the girl in the hills up from Jenks's place, her black fuzz laughing at him. The world made sport of him, he thought, for reasons that he could not countenance or abide. What he did with Grace was natural; it was the wants of the world that were mad. And now that he saw the smoke in the hills, he knew that he must tell the truth of it all and do it very soon or something irrevocable would happen to make the telling of it impossible.

And in that moment, Matthew saw that Winnaraburra saw the world in the same way as he – that it had gone mad. But Winnaraburra's course was to rectify it all by continuing the reasoning and practices of thousands of years. His people had been driven into the far plains with its mallee scrub and low trees and where little rain would fall, where lizards were choice takings, where there was paltry cover for the spearing of the big red kangaroo. The only water that sprang from these hills came in trickling runs, and seeped away into the red earth if not soon captured into wooden vessels; and which did not form into ponds for fish. They had been squeezed between the white man's claim and the country of their neighbours. But surely the resisters would know by now what reckoning awaited them on the white man's side of the mountain?

And now, fire in the hills.

The markings of the white man's civilisation had been put in place. There were shepherds' huts and men and stock to be seen as signposts of possession. The next great undertaking had been to fence the property; to make an obstruction that even the native could understand. But Matthew knew in his heart that they would not shy at fences. So Matthew Larkin came to believe that the only solution was that, before fifty years had passed, a mingling of peoples should come to pass and that there would be some new race. What did the Spaniard make of the Mexican Indian? Why, a mestizo race which had the benefits of the both and which retained the native myths and Christian virtues together.

In his youth, he had read the story of the conquest of the Aztecs. There was no stopping the greed of the conquerors, but in time there had come the foundation of a great new people. This colony of South Australia was to be a paradise of dissent and freedom and would write new rules for the rest of time. We must forge a new race, he thought, or else extinction would come and nothing else. The native girls would make good wives and Englishmen good husbands to them. Those who would come to them must come and those who would be driven into the earth must regrettably be so driven.

He and Grace would form a new dynasty, an example to the colony.

He ran inside to tell Grace of his visions and became excited and Grace put him into the bed and she removed her calico and lay next to him and he placed his head upon her and kissed her breasts and her nipples and moaned until he was erect and then he was inside her with her arms around him and then, only then, he would sleep. He would sleep and he would dream and then his dreams would inform his waking moments until Matthew Larkin could little distinguish the waking from the sleeping, the day from the night time; all he had was Grace and, like the men in Plato's cave who looked at reflected light but did not see the world, he had what he thought and had been told was love.

In time, Grace was allowed into the Larkin kitchen and, as they had brought some chickens across from Jenks's, Matthew taught her how to cook eggs the way he liked them – in the skillet with some butter, under the lowest flame and the lid on top to cook the yolk until it wobbled and didn't run. And then, a month later, even bacon, from the new piggery at Watervale. With his damper, eggs and bacon, Matthew felt, for a brief few mornings, a taste of the good life. He had visions of Jenks in his mansion house, his wife and child around him.

Grace's smile of enquiry as she took the plate from him.

'Hah,' he laughed, 'a damned fine breakfast.' He drew her to him, then lifted her shirt and ran his hand along her growing stomach.

Her hand went around the back of his head, holding his face to her breast. For the first time, he anticipated the months ahead with eagerness, rather than with dread.

Matthew began to go down to the hut to see Grace's sister and her little ones. The boys played games, pretending coyness about Matthew and their auntie, when they really felt none. It was part of their natural repartee of teasing – irony played out as some literal thing. The subtle forms of their jokes were understood perfectly by them, if not sometimes by Matthew. But still he was delighted, feigning surprise at their fey games, pretending to be upset, recovering all too quickly and making them laugh again.

But they were not to come up to the house. It was the line drawn by James. People could arrive on horse at any moment and while it was not unseemly to have a native servant employed in washing clothes or sheets, toting wood, building fires, or even cooking eggs, half a tribe was not within the bounds of even the most loosened form of propriety. James knew that their household was already the most relaxed in the valley, but still he had managed to keep on the good side of Jenks and the others. But of the neighbours it was the prowling unease of Phillips that was the most difficult to appease, with his Biblical condemnation of the younger Larkin and his unholy miscegenatory deeds.

Grace had washed the breakfast dishes with hot water and scraped them with a flat stick she had found in the bush up from their hut. She was standing bare-footed on a stool and balancing plates in their places on a new sideboard when James's man brought in a letter for Matthew.

'Letter for you,' said Grace, when she returned from the kitchen.

When Matthew read a letter. he was often jolly with her for hours afterwards.

It was Cawthorne's hand which had addressed the letter and Matthew tore it open and fell eagerly upon the contents. In the first few months away from Adelaide, Cawthorne's letters had been a welcome relief from blighted days of toil and boredom. Matthew looked forward to news of Cawthorne's extraordinary little school and of the deeds to which his mother would lift herself to exercise control over it. In person, Cawthorne's tale-telling was dry, the half-raising of an eyebrow his only concession to physicality; indeed, in another life, he could have been the sober man in a comic pairing. Still, stories of the knavery of the butcher's son and the tripping efforts of Mrs Cawthorne to catch and flog the miscreant were even more amusing when committed to paper. They were written with a matter-of-fact detachment and a flintish economy that brought the actions more vividly to life, for the leaving of details to the reader's imagination.

Matthew shared his appreciation with Grace and explained to her what he could. But, much as he loved her for her gentleness of spirit, she was years from being able to appreciate the subtleties of the Cawthorne prose. He must wait for the end of the day to tell James, who would smile and make some wry comment, and that was the limit of Matthew's fellowship in the Lingalee. He wished often for Lucy, who would understand the nuance, and who would strike up some repartee upon the matter and make him laugh: Lucy who was in Adelaide, who was not here.

Matthew remembered Cawthorne's last letter and how the boys had discovered that his middle name was Anderson and that this gave him the initials W.A.C. This was then made into a new nickname Wacs, or rather, Mr Whacks, on account of the vigour and regularity with which the yardstick was applied to them. On the first Saturday after inventing his name, the boys had run out into the street with a chorus of 'Goodbye, Mr Whacks,' confident that in the choral nature of their singing he would never tell which voice belonged to which particular scalliwag, and that their cheekiness would therefore remain undetected and not punished. By the time he rushed to the front door, all he could see was heels and bottoms rounding the corner in haste. He had a fair idea, of course, who were the responsible lads. On the Monday, he merely narrowed his eyes at them, to show them he was no fool, while he patted his yardstick with his right hand into his left, to show what would happen were there a recurrence, and from then onwards the name was repeated in strict privacy only.

However, regardless of the tact with which Cawthorne might manage such an incident, it seemed to Matthew that he was trapped in time, engaged in a never-ending struggle against odds that were too great for him to overcome. When they first met, they had both seemed in a kind of holding pen, each engaged in labours with which they were unsatisfied, waiting for the greater purpose to reveal itself: Cawthorne with his dreams of artistic significance, Matthew with his foreboding sense of adventure.

Now that Matthew's life had changed so much, he opened his letter from Cawthorne with more than his usual fill of tenderness towards the man. It was the longest letter he had ever received from him, but as he read, his mood began to turn to disquiet.

Dear Matthew

All is well, as ever, in the Land of Civilisation. The weather warms, of course, and as it has done so, Mother's cough has melted away and that is good. But from where I write in my little study, the heat is infernal. Mother sends her love of course and we both do miss you, but I fear the lack of your melodious voice and what she calls your 'sensitive' readings of the poets has made your absence even more piquant for her.

Of callers, we have few. Kadlitpinna and Willa Willa come but rarely now. The constables have driven the whole mob of them away, further around the bend, for they fear the natives are bathing in the water and turning it brown on that account. There were reports that native girls were bathing closer to the King William bridge than is allowed and the opinion was that they would continue to do so until their camp was moved yet further away. I vigorously opposed the motion at the town meeting, but to no avail. Our native friends were most displeased with this treatment and, as they cowered away in fear of the rifles, they served the constables with whatever rhetoric they could muster in English and then some in their own tongue as well – the men and women both. I am sure you remember my forebodings in this matter. It has been sadly inevitable.

I have written to you in instants past of the building of the Caledonian School situate on the South Terrace of the town, which seeks to answer the Collegiate School in its accommodation of the gentler scions of Adelaide and also the sons of pastoralists and graziers hither and yon. Although my estimation is that the new school will lag behind the Collegiate in gentility, it is still a place of great interest to me. To be a master there would bring me eighty pounds per year, without consideration of bonuses that will apply if enrolments are enhanced. I was encouraged to apply for such a position and have now attended an interview.

During the course of my discussion with the school board, the matter was raised of my, or rather our, association with the natives and of the nature of that association and of its potential for continuation. I was somewhat disconcerted at the question, as the gentlemen who interviewed me are all known to me personally as members of the Colonial Education Committee and have long been aware of my friendship with Kadlitpinna and the other natives, as I now understand is the entire town.

However, as the conversation continued, it seemed to be more accented by the topic of our own friendship, rather than that of you or me with the natives on the plains here, and of the extent of our current fraternity. It would seem that news of your situation in the north of our colony has come to the attention of the governors of the Caledonian School. It is of some concern to them that a master of their school would be seen to be in close friendship with someone who is living in a situation of consort with a native woman. It is seen as highly undesirable for a new school that a master may be in a position to attract the ridicule of his charges.

It would seem that a resolution of this situation is required with some urgency. Talk of the native question still runs through the town; rumours of conflict and affray in the regions abound. What is the appropriate solution to the problem? I am sure you can imagine the discussions at tea and dinner. You will have experienced them more than I have. I talk on street corners; you talk in parlours. I saw your friend, Miss Lucy, in the street some weeks past. She recognised me and did bid me good morning. I was gratified to receive her greeting. I must make my way in the world; your way is made. It is an absolute requirement that I support my mother, and a family which will come soon. For yes, Matthew, I am to be married in the autumn.

You must cease this association of yours forthwith. No good can come of it. Some of the denunciation of your situation has been quite passionate here in Adelaide, and reports are that similar views are held in the north. Our own discussions in months past have revealed to me that your attraction to the native races is in many ways intemperate. Your letters to me indicate that your enthusiasms are running away into madness. This behaviour may be tolerated were it to be seen in an ignorant shepherd, but in your situation there is an example to be set, and in any case moderation is an absolute requirement in the frontier setting.

I am engaged with the Caledonian School from the beginning of next term, which is but three weeks away. It will be a step up in the ladder of society for me. There will be the headmaster and I and no other in the school for some while; we will be instigating the Monitoring and Simultaneous System, a mixture of the Lancastrian and Glasgow plans of instruction, enabling a master to control large numbers of boys at one time. I will be teaching across ages and disciplines. It seems the versatility I have gained over long hours at books and in my own schoolroom will finally pay me out. Mother will continue our school as much as she can, so the household will be much improved. I have become very interested in real estate and mother and I have inspected properties with a view to the expansion in our prospects. At last, something.

Matthew, I urge you to consider your position, for your own sake, for the sake of Miss Lucy too, who will be broken when she hears of your situation, which as yet I understand she has not. For all of our sakes, try to find some moderation in you.

Your lifelong friend

William


At the mention of the removal of Kadlitpinna and his friends, Matthew sat up in bed and was filled with alarm. When the Caledonian School was mentioned and his own situation involved, Matthew cried out, which brought the alarmed Grace to her feet. His hands began to tremble at the mention of his infamy having spread to the town. The thought of Lucy in the street, at her shopping, hearing of him – the idea of Cawthorne, married. It was all so preposterous and confusing that Matthew could not consider these problems all at once. He screwed up the paper and threw it across the room and Grace came to his side.

'A "step up in the ladder of society," he says. What do I care for his ladders? That town is so far away now it could be England. In fact, it is England, or worse.'

Grace tried to hold him close, but her own hands were agitated. She knew nothing of ladders and England.

'Cawthorne!' Matthew went on in disgust. 'He has no sooner a nod

from the burghers than he has reproved me for my own great under-
takings. Ha! And the parlour room gossips! Cawthorne does not mention that it was he who took me to the affrays! Who made me know
the ways of corroboree and to love the black man like a brother! But
no, Cawthorne would never take one to his bed. He too was excited by
the native girls, but he would stop short of truth. He would not proceed
to the Form of Beauty.'

He looked at Grace in the eyes and saw the beauty there, then lowered his voice and spoke quickly, as if having to convince himself of the
truth of what he said. 'He would but tinker – a collector he of artefacts,
a lender of sticks to Angas, his forelock bent before any who would hint
of patronage, or who simply had the means withal and threw him a
glance in the street some morning. Now he writes to me of moderation.'

His voice rose again in theatrical soliloquy. 'Oh, Cawthorne, you
crush me with anguish. For all your books and learning, all your philosophy, was it to achieve true understanding that you learnt, as I
thought you did? Or was it because that knowledge would be taught
onwards by you in some school on the South Terrace to the third sons
of the third sons of lesser English gentlemen, and that by so doing you
would get your step up the ladder?'

He motioned to the letter on the floor, in the corner, and Grace
scurried over, her face wreathed in worry, and brought it back to
Matthew, who opened it out once more and scanned its three pages.

'What do you really know of life, Cawthorne?' he said, as if the
letter was the man himself. 'Or of death? Have you stared it in the face?
Have you pulled the trigger and heard the crack of breaking skull bone
crash in your head, mixing with the boom of the cannon in your hand?
What have you done to break this country, Cawthorne? And this school
of yours, will it take my little boy, the one that lies now inside my Grace
and will be born in six months? Will my boy be good enough for your
school? Here,' and he waved the letter again in front of him and screwed
it up again, 'here you tell me not. He will not be good enough for you.'

But Grace had left him for a moment and came in to him now with towel and cold water, for Matthew's anguish had turned to heat in his face and tears in his eyes. Her training had been to soothe and suppress Matthew when he became excited and this was the worst she had seen. She made him lie down, and settled him onto a pillow, and pressed herself to him, and held his hand to her belly, and told him to hush in the way that she had learnt, with her finger to her lips and a long sibilance lisping between them. And then she took off her shirt and came in with him. She propped him on his pillow and proferred to him his bottle of poppy seed medicine, of which he took a goodly swig. It made him well and calm again. She pressed her head onto his shoulder and he closed his eyes and began to calm, and his thoughts began to return to her as they touched each other and he dreamt of the future once more.

And so Matthew drifted into sleep, and woke in the late afternoon to prepare himself for dinner. No need to dress; a wash and a clean shirt only. When he woke, life was well again for a few moments, he felt the joy of Grace's body beside him, but when he opened his eyes and saw the troubled look in hers, he remembered all that Cawthorne had written: of schools and ladders, of expectations and duties. And as he dressed, he thought of the betrayal of unspoken bonds, and then of the curious problem of the natives in the hills.

The next morning, Matthew heard two horses come up from the direction of the Phillips place. Grace hurried out of the kitchen as Phillips marched in with his son George behind him.

The instinctive side of Matthew's spirit would have him remain in his room with Grace. But the urgent arrival of Phillips the morning after the fire and smoke of the day before would mean decisions were to be made and he had to show his capability. To achieve his visions, Matthew had to stand his ground with this Phillips.

Before he could decide, however, the door was opened and James was there.

'I thought you should hear this. The natives: they have come through the hills again.'

Matthew looked up from his book and did not speak for a few moments. 'Of course, there have been fires.'

'More than fire today, brother.'

Matthew sat up straighter at the urgency of his tone.

'Eleven sheep disappeared and native tracks gone with them, shepherded away.'

'Phillips awaits us to spring to horse?'

'The more urgent the punishment, the more clear will be the reason for it. The sooner these people learn…' James stopped for the sake of Grace in her chair, pretending to be sewing a button onto a shirt of Matthew's. 'Come,' he said, and led the way back to the kitchen.

Matthew took a hat from the stand inside the door and followed James into the passage, leaving Grace where she was.

'It will take years for them to learn our ways, James.' Matthew grabbed at his brother's elbow. 'They think that all in God's world is there to be shared. On top of that, they have developed a taste for mutton.'

'They will never learn.' James turned to face Matthew.

'There are two ways to follow, brother. There is a choice.'

'I know your views.'

'Wipe them out so there is no other solution, or blend with them, to make a new race. The latter will take time and patience, but it will make us all stronger. We have much to learn from them.'

James pursed his lips and drew in breath. 'I know your views,' he repeated, with an edge this time. 'But I must say my own views now begin to run full stream with those of Phillips.'

'You mean you have no views – no patience, no time. Your will can now be imposed upon. James, I am too wounded now to leave this valley, and if I am to stay, I must have Grace.'

'I understand your position, but I begin to prefer the complete solution.'

'We don't have to be the same as the others, James.'

James stopped in the passageway, short of the kitchen door, beyond which was Phillips taking tea and talking with Joe. 'There are those who will learn,' said James, and Matthew took him to be referring to Grace and the others of her family who had taken residence in the hut, 'and those who will not.'

James took off his hat and brushed it in an agitated manner, cuffed it with his right hand as if smacking a daydream from it. 'Those who will not must go.' He looked at Matthew with meaning. 'When they are gone, perhaps you can have your Grace.'

James had thought it through. There could be no action today with only one brother. This could be the final act and Matthew must take part to retain his stature in the valley.

'Brother, there are those who I fear would not allow me even that,' and he tossed his glance in the direction of the kitchen door.

'Matthew,' James whispered now, Phillips only yards away, on the other side of the door. 'We must acquit ourselves today. Our neighbours are our survival. We must be for all of it or none. We cannot pick and choose our moments.'

Matthew's gaze left his brother's face. He saw the skirting boards which had been knocked in to their passageway the week before; he had had to walk the property with Grace to escape the workmen's din. He saw those boards as something virginal pure – hard timber from the forest, sawn to fit the Larkin hallway. From nature, they would be stained and glossed next week to dovetail with the homestead vision.

James's advice was inevitable.

Matthew looked around to the ceiling, as if taking in the work for the first time. 'It is dark in here, brother. We should let in some light.'

'We will.'

'If the hotheads go, the cooler ones can stay. I will accept that much. And I will keep Grace.' Matthew sought his brother's gaze again.

'You will keep Grace. But are you well enough to ride?' his brother went on.

'Why should I not be?'

'Your poppy seed medicine, your morphine. It takes away the pain.'

'So it does.'

'Your wound is good as healed, yet you take it just as you did in the first.'

'And what of it?' Matthew looked away again.

'Is your mind awake?' he pointed to his own head, 'or asleep?'

The sockets around Matthew's eyes were darkened and his eyes were tracked with fine red lines as if he had been rubbing them, but he had not. This was the first time in three weeks that James had looked on his brother so closely. He chided himself silently now for being so concerned with his property; he had left his brother's well-being to Grace, and to Dr Tibbs.

'I will acquit myself,' Matthew raised his voice, almost impatient.

James held up a hand to silence him; Phillips was the other side of the door and there was no time for further argument or discussion.

They entered the kitchen, where Phillips sat, a cup of tea in his adroit hands.

'Young Matthew,' he nodded, in a voice which indicated something other than full confidence. 'You are well enough to ride and shoot?' Phillips's eyes narrowed into Matthew and bore through him.

'I have recovered well enough. I will do my piece.'

Phillips looked with disdain to James, then back to Matthew. 'You look unwell. You have you been in the care of Tibbs?'

'He pronounces me fit.'

'And what other "medicine" might you have received?' Phillips received no answer from either brother and so he sat back in his chair and looked from Matthew to James and back to Matthew again – summing up, surmising, planning. Then he went on with extra meaning. 'If you come out today, it will be the end of you.'

'Matthew is well enough to ride, Phillips, there is no doubt.'

Phillips grunted, 'Have it your own way.'

'The tactics are different now,' said Jones, brought down by Phillips to join the final shoot. There was steel in his voice, a sense of aggravation and exasperation over his thwarted entitlement. 'They steal the sheep and drive them off to different corners of the hills.'

Once more, the constable from Clare was required to give consent to the undertaking with a word or a nod or at least a grunt.

'Yes,' the constable took up the thread, 'all have joined in the game and as a consequence all are deemed fair quarry.' That was clear: all were guilty and could be shot on sight.

'Mr Jenks sends his apologies,' the constable went on. 'His son has only last evening fallen from stones on their river bank and his attendance at home is required.' Any reference to Jenks's boy stiffened the resolve of the men. All the more reason, it seemed, to purify the valley and to protect their women and children from the ever present menace that hung over them all.

'They have sentries now, lookouts,' said Phillips, 'and abandon their campfire without defending it. We must decide whether to pursue them severally or to group together against ambush.'

'Their weaponry being so puny, we can take ten of them with three men,' said Jones.

'But it is unlikely there will be gangs of ten, they are already decimated. So groups of three will dominate them without trouble.' Phillips was putting forward what seemed a plan of his and none were of a mood to go against him.

'I say we stay in groups of three then.' The constable made his pronouncement.

'Matthew and I know these hills the best,' said James, 'and so does Phillips.'

'I must confess I am out of my ground,' said the constable. 'I will need the best guide.'

'That is James,' said Phillips. 'George will stay with me. So that leaves Jones to go with James and the constable. Matthew will come with me. Is that well with you, Matthew?'

'Certainly, Phillips. None other.'

Matthew wondered how life would be for George with a father like

Phillips: his older brother dead, the expectation on his shoulders. The lad was sitting in his saddle straight, his hands gripping tightly on the reins. His horse protested and backed away and was in danger of wheeling away into the mounts of others until Phillips placed a calm hand on the reins and George nodded as if to say, Of course, of course. Matthew could see that to divide the expedition to two parties of three would reduce the cover that would come from experienced men in an emergency. He could almost see George think these thoughts: in a group of three, we could be surprised and my ability with the handgun will be tested, as will the nerve that I must show; I am among men now and this could be the day that I am wounded, or worse.

But of course George had to go on to whatever fate lay before him. Was this to be his own day of fate, Matthew wondered, or had that already come? Was the test made the day they ventured to the Murray with Phillips to face the natives there? If so, what a day it had been, with him shooting two, but being struck himself. It was his life, he thought, in capsule: two steps to the fore, and then one step back; glorying in my deed and paying for my hubris before the passage of five seconds.

Matthew sidled up beside George as they walked their horses away. 'You will be fine,' said Matthew, happy to be speaking as a veteran.

But when George looked at him, it was not the look of a nervous youth which greeted him; the boy's mouth screwed up and his words were spat. 'I am not concerned about the way I will perform,' he said, without looking at Matthew. 'I have been waiting for this day.'

George had revealed the private vision of his birth and permanence as a man. Matthew's eyelids closed and blinked open again; his own certainties were evaporating now, like mist on the creek at sunup. It occurred to him then that his life might have been its most perfect on the day of the black swan, with all before him and his own vision of sharing seemingly within his grasp. He had thought the natives' lives unspoiled. He had seen the metal axe-head in their camp but had not perceived its irony. The pipes and baccy, the personal adornments, and the glass;

yes, the glass harpoon he had collected that day with Cawthorne. How long ago was that – six months, a year, two?

He felt for the glass harpoon in his pocket. Had he left it behind in their rush to be away? He took the bottle of poppy seed medicine from his jacket and drew the cork from it with his teeth. As he swigged, he heard one word from George beside him.

'Father!'

Phillips turned and saw. The look he gave was steady, unflinching, without expression. He drew a very deep breath and turned back to the track before him.

Matthew could see the river before him now on the day of the swan – the slow and steady flow of October, its bounty of bird life. The one native man shepherding away the cygnets and the mother to live and grow, the stealthy pair silently emerging from the river, and the flash of spears above the glittering stream about to turn to crimson pools, the spear handles sunk into the stream and their flashing heads pointing to the sun. Were they glass that day, those spearheads? For there to be a balance in this world, for there to be meaning, it must lie in the hybrid object.

He remembered Kadlitpinna, or Captain Jack, his nobility and his humour – his friends the white men whom he trusted and loved. Willa Willa, whose antic dances made such amusement for them that day in Cawthorne's parlour. And Mrs Cawthorne, left now to run her horrendous school alone. And Cawthorne, become respectable, minding the scions of the landed classes. Matthew thought with wonder that if he had been ten years younger, then Cawthorne might have been his master now. He thought with fear of how little we do understand of this world, of how much is random and violent, and of the precarious position of those who question their birthright as part of a natural gang.

The hunting party passed by the charcoaled fields of the hill fires that had burned for the last two days. They slowed their horses to a walk in a mark of respect of which they were not even conscious. It may have been the thousands of years of land-burning practice that hushed them, or simply the belligerent effort it had taken by the natives to achieve such an outcome. The men knew full well too the profit to be gained from the grassland that would spring there, come the sweet April rains.

A network of creeks ran down from the hills through a kind of plateau or tableland that then fell away by degrees to the valley floor where the creeks collected into streams that ran past the homesteads of Jenks and Jones and Phillips and the Larkins. But up higher were pockets where shepherds would take the flocks for superior grazing and drive them back again at night. The loss of these spots to the Aborigines was unthinkable, but the stains of smoke that streaked their sky troubled them also, the affront that they were to the settlers' ideals of permanence and primacy.

''Tis an extraordinary sight, you have to say,' said Jones, sniffing the air on which the blistered burnt smell still hung.

'It seems precarious, yet it is not,' James replied. 'To destroy so much and be so confident of its renewal.'

'It is done in the plains as well, on even grander scale.' Matthew could not resist an airing of his experience.

Phillips returned the discourse to the practical, to the now. 'I say we look at the ridge above,' he said, speaking of his team of three. 'If you go ahead,' he said, looking at James and pointing at the track down the valley, 'we shall see you' – he pointed to an outcrop of rock five hundred yards along the high path – 'up there.'

'Right.'

'If there is engagement, we shall each hear it soon enough, and we will be close.'

With that, Phillips picked his way up the slope and was followed by Matthew and George, while James led the other two down the rough track that wound up to the farther end of the field.

The Phillips trio was silent on the ride, each in his own thoughts, each listening for movements in the bush. Matthew felt the same vulnerability as George over the splitting of the groups. Away from James, he was exposed and more required to rely on himself. Phillips was the best man, there was no doubt about that, George the least experienced, and he, Matthew, had seen two engagements.

Phillips had chosen him.

They walked their horses along a native track, from which branches had been pulled away to make easier pace. To their left as they climbed, there appeared acre by acre the view of the valley: there were patches in pasture and some in sheep. In the distance, Matthew could see a wisp of smoke against the sky and a hint of whitewashed chimney against the dull greenery of the gums that segued grey then blue in the distant mist. The sight resembled more now the patchwork of the English countryside than it had even two months previously.

He had stopped his horse to look and George edged past him and Matthew was awoken from his brief dream. With neither of them watching, he drew his bottle of medicine from the saddlebag and drained it to the last. He tossed the bottle over the escarpment and heard it swish through some leaves and then thud into the ground below. He was good now; he was exultant.

'Come,' he heard the voice of Phillips hurrying him and felt no resentment in complying.

His senses now were tuned to the sounds in the bush like never before. Every falling callistemon leaf or acacia blossom was a part of his world, every caress of a zephyr breeze in its canopy was his to know. He heard the giggle of a kookaburra resounding from the trees above them, and its mate answering a hundred yards further on.

Then a shot. Two, three, more. Whinnying horses – the ruckus of full engagement from the direction of James's group. Phillips spurred his horse, but warily, for they were still on a track and progress was such that horses could never be made to a gallop.

Heaving to view ahead of them lay a clearing of a quarter acre or more. Phillips pulled up his horse, looking about for the best way out to follow the ridge of the escarpment further away towards James's group. Then there was a terrible yelling and hullooing as six or so native figures appeared from the side of the clearing that was away from the escarpment. A spear came from that direction, then another and another. One came at Matthew but missed him by a yard; another was for George and he ducked. Phillips was the first to fire and he downed a native at his first shot. George fired into bushes and drew blood straight away. Matthew drew his pistol and fired at what he knew not, so overcome was he by the sudden onset of violence, so jarred by the shattering of his idyll, so full of poppy seed medicine that he was unable to distinguish between the euphoria of illusion and the realities of engagement. The sound of shot was all around, reverberating in his head, crashing about inside him and without. He fired again and the bullet grazed the flesh of George Phillips's left shoulder and passed through the hide of his jacket and a small gush of blood besmirched its ripped fabric.

George stared down in shock at his shoulder; his features went pale as he felt the spanking tang of his wound and smelt the sweet and acrid odour of his own blood. He then placed his right hand there over the wound even though it still held his revolver. Phillips fired again as the natives retreated, then drew his mount alongside and quickly inspected the wound before turning on Matthew. His son's wound was superficial but Phillips's mouth and eyes were set in a look of such fury at the thought of what could have been. Then George summoned up the pluck to fire off another shot at the backside of a fleeing native.

In that moment, it was all too foolish; the ambitions of men seemed so ridiculous and transient to his mind that Matthew sent his head back in one derisive and maniacal shout of triumphant laughter for the idiocy of men.

Phillips wheeled his horse about and Matthew's derision did nothing to dispel the rage in his face: one son gone and the other fired upon by a deranged, native-loving fool. He pulled his horse up almost level with Matthew and drew his revolver one last time and in his fury fired it into the chest of Matthew Larkin.

The force of the shot drove Matthew backwards, off his horse. His hands flung the reins skywards and he fell flat on his back, his head cracking against the dry earth and the sweat of his brow mingling with the blood and dust. He stared up at the wide blue sky that he had long equated with freedom and with purpose in the world. Now it was obscured by the clouds of dust that had been kicked up all around by horse and man.

The shot had passed clean through him, two inches below his heart. Blood came from his wound, not in a stream but in surges as it was pumped by his confused but still weakly beating heart. A patch seeped across his chest. The material on the back of his vest was quickly soaked and the pool which spread on both sides crept outwards like the inexorable march of empire. He tried once to raise himself but there was no strength in his arms. The dust began to settle on his face and mingle with the sweat and to make a bloody porridge of the crater in his chest.

As his vision began to dull, he felt himself to be leaving his body; he was a lorikeet, like the red and yellow and green and purple wonders he had seen on the day he proceeded with Cawthorne to the native affray. What beauties they were. But now he saw as they saw, hovering above his own affray: men and horses, spears and shot, gaping wounds all staining the earth they were meant to win. It was the solution, the only way. Matthew Larkin tried to laugh, so hysterical did the whole procedure now seem to him. But the effort only made him twist in his place and that was the end. His eyes turned to glass and when the other men dismounted and addressed their attentions to him, there was a sardonic twisted grimace of a grin upon his face, as if triumphant to be leaving now and that it was all those who remained who were the fools, not he.

Steel wool clumps of cloud hung over the village of Clare as Lucy rode in. A blacksmith and farrier, a general provisions store, a saddler, and a chandler for those who would not make their own candles out of mutton fat; scattered around were crude bark dwellings and three or four made of stones that had been heaved from paddocks and creek beds and placed un-mortared into walls.

Narrow-eyed stares. Let them look, thought Lucy. They probably peer at any stranger who rides into town.

The wife of Mr Gleeson the publican came out, drying a soup pan with a scruffy towel as she did. So too did the Lutheran missionary, who had come with his wife six weeks before, seeking natives to en-lighten, and had disappeared into the bush for three days, then returned with half a dozen fine prospects and set up church at the end of the main street.

Lucy sat her horse outside the general store, where a gentleman of about fifty years rose slowly from the bench outside, withdrawing a bowler hat from his head as he did so and placing it over his heart as he inclined his head.

'Good afternoon, miss,' he said. 'I am Colqhoun and this,' he said with some little pride, 'is my store.' He motioned with his bowler to the crude painted sign upon the porch overhang, which did indeed pro-claim the insoluble fact of Colqhoun and his store. He turned back to her with a smile of warmth. 'May I be of service to you, ma'am? You have come far? From Auburn perhaps?'

'I have come from Kapunda today.'

Mr Colqhoun removed a pipe from his mouth. 'Good lord. You must come down immediately. We have an excellent pie…'

'I must proceed directly, Mr Colqhoun. It is mid-afternoon and there is no time for stopping.'

'Proceed?' he motioned his pipe to the north as if to say surely not.

'I must make it to the Lingalee tonight.'

'The Lingalee! But Miss –' he hesitated.

'I beg your pardon, Mr Colqhoun. I am Miss Bray, Lucy Bray.'

At the mention of this name Mr Colqhoun bowed again, more deeply than he had done before. 'You are the niece of the governor, miss?'

Lucy nodded her assent to his question. 'I am simply Miss Bray, and require no favours greater than would be extended to any fellow colonist.'

Colqhoun inclined his head in appreciation of these sentiments. 'But you must go no further north without an armed escort, ma'am.'

'I am armed.'

'Oh, oh, I see. But the natives have been very restive of late. There may have been an affray…or two.'

'Affray?'

'Armed conflict, miss. The natives are very slow to learn the principles of private property, if I might say so. They have acquired a taste for mutton, but as yet only few of them will take up employment of a regular nature in order to acquire their share.'

'Few?'

'Very few, ma'am. And now, if I might entreat you to take your rest for a moment, there is plenty of time for us to make it to the Lingalee tonight, and you with a slice of pie inside you.'

'Us?'

'I will take you myself, miss, for having met you these last three minutes, I would not allow the duty to be undertaken by any other man.'

'Ha.' Lucy laughed for first time in three days, and climbed down from her horse.

The road out from Clare was easy but Lucy's thoughts were cluttered. The ranges sat grey blue on the plain to the east like vain toy things that had no proper business with the world out here. Lucy's fancy would have Zeus fly down on invisible wings from his Antipodean Olympus, seeking amusement, before turning himself into…into what, she wondered: perhaps the local missionary returning from the hills with the remnants of the native tribe and with salvation first and last on the agenda. But she could not see Zeus extracting amusement from the life of the mission, not without a concubine or two, or three. The game of marriage and love: Matthew ahead of her, so close now and that closeness won by such struggle on her part that her apprehension began to turn oddly to a form of indifference. It was as if the journey itself had been her destination and now that it was over she had altered to such an extent that whatever it was that lay before her mattered little. She was struck silent by her epiphany of feeling. Where her bow had been highly taut, her string was now loosened; she had arrived and that was enough. Matthew and James and their life in the bush, the frontier – power and love, morality and murder. What was it all to her? She had come so far, alone, and had seen so much in two days. She had once stopped Moran with an extraordinary shot – a lucky shot perhaps. But now he had backed away from her; not only that, but he had made her safe. She had won him. But she also observed that she had pushed her luck as far as it could go, and it would go no further. Patient Adela, waiting for the men to clear the country; perhaps she was the wiser and more suitable colonist after all.

If there was any unaccustomed muteness on Lucy's part, that was more than made up for by Mr Colqhoun, who was one of nature's conversationalists. Taking Lucy for the reserved type, he spoke at length of mundane matters: the hills, the birds which flew, the lizards that sought insects in the undergrowth, the characters of the town. But he was a calculating chatterer, and every few minutes – once he felt he had drawn his object into confidence – there would be a question buried in his charming parley, something to draw the unwary out.

'Aren't they the most devilish things in the whole world, Miss Bray, the lizards of the undergrowth. You see this one, now, he'll be sitting there waiting, still as a rock and with the patience of Job. Sitting there in that place all day it might be, just awaitin'. Awaitin' for what, you might ask. Well, we could wait awhile and see, that's if we didn't have such an important task before us, now. Why, he's waitin' for a fly or any other such flying bug to come along and then out with his devil of a blue tongue and the fly is no more. I wouldn't be surprised if that was a bifurcated devil of a tongue that slipped out and if it wasn't so fast in its action you might be able to see. Now isn't that somethin'?'

'It certainly is, Mr Colquoun.'

'Ah, but our friend with the blue tongue is not so different from all of us now is he, miss. We must help ourselves and sometimes it's not such a good idea to give ourselves away in our planning is it, now. The element of surprise! Heh, heh,' he paused. 'This would be a surprise visit of your own that you're making, I suspect.'

'I wrote a letter.'

Mr Colquoun was silent.

'But to wait for the weekly dray…and then it takes four days to reach here.'

'Ah, yes, the wheels of transportation turn slowly for us out in these parts, miss. So it is.'

Lucy relapsed into silence.

'So you took it upon yourself…'

'I did.'

'You are a very bold young woman, if I might be allowed to say so, miss, and I'm taking my hat off to you.' And indeed he took his hat off and saluted her with it. 'It is women like yourself that will make this land, Miss Bray, and I am hoping your visit turns out.'

'Why should it not?'

Now it was Colquoun's turn to be quiet, to pick his words even more carefully than ever. 'Well, miss. It may be that the party that was being visited may find it convenient to be putting their house in order, miss, before welcoming their much treasured guests.'

The silences between the two were now growing.

Lucy stopped her horse and turned to face the man. 'You mean they may want to clean their sheets, Mr Colquoun?'

'Well, miss…' Now Colquoun had been turned by Lucy's unexpected blend of directness and metaphor. He did not know in which style to make his reply.

Lucy exulted in her victory. 'I am well prepared to see whatever is there, Mr Colquoun.' Lucy bore her eyes into his. 'I have come…' and here she herself faltered, not knowing what she had really come for, just knowing that coming to this place was a thing which had simply had to be done, given the way she had seen the world two days before.

Mr Colquoun took his hat off once more, and dipped it slightly to her, before settling it back upon his head. 'Very well, miss,' he said, his disingenuous cheek turned finally to sympathy that is born out of respect, or at least of having been unexpectedly bested, 'let us proceed.'

They trotted their horses now, for walking somehow seemed improper, and anyway the homestead was near.

'The road goes away to the right here, to the property of Phillips, the neighbour.'

'I have heard of him.'

The road swung around by a stand of ten or more acacia, still heavy with the bloom that was beginning to settle into a golden carpet all around. They walked around and in the road there was a gate and then, just as it had been described in letters by Matthew, the stone house halfway up the hill, protected, secure; before that, the hut that would have served them for a home in the early days. Outside it, she could see three native girls huddled together, talking.

Mr Colquoun dismounted and began to untie the gate, when Lucy's gaze drifted up to the famous flagpole and there flew not the Union Jack as had been promised, but a sheet of black or deepest navy, no doubt the darkest thing that could be found. She gasped, and drew a look from Mr Colquoun, who stopped his task and followed her line of sight.

'Oh, my goodness,' he said, and took his hat off once more and placed it solemnly over his heart. 'Now that was one thing I was not expecting. We've had no word.'

And Lucy knew, in heart, for whom the black flag flew; never James – too careful, always working within his abilities.

'I shall proceed from here alone, Mr Colquoun. Thank you so very much for your assistance.'

'But I must see you safely to the house, miss.'

'I will go alone from here, Mr Colquoun.'

'Then I'll bid you good day, miss.' Colqhoun had already measured the determination of the girl, so he simply tipped his hat to her once more and turned his horse and walked back through the gates. Lucy's eyes followed him as he turned, not back to Clare, but to the left, up the incline and into the low part of the ranges in the direction of the Phillips house.

Lucy tied the gate up as it had been and walked the few yards to the hut and sat her horse. The three girls all wore blankets or shawls against the chills of early evening and, as Lucy drew closer, they stood in silent greeting, by way of their natural deference to a newcomer.

One girl stepped forward and, as she did, her shawl slipped away, deliberately perhaps, and Lucy saw her stomach; little swollen, but enough. She saw too the girl's hand move as if to comfort the child within or to draw attention to her state. The native girl drew her shawl back around her and hunched her body. The two girls' eyes locked for several seconds.

'You are Grace?'

Grace nodded and bowed and mouthed her assent in a whisper, 'Yes, ma'am.'

Lucy saw the sincerity and the bereft, empty sadness in the girl standing bent before her.

'Very well.' She looked at the house, the fine stone, the woodwork that surrounded the windows and doors, the fresh varnish, the flagpole and its simple black ensign.

She turned back to the native girl. 'I am Lucy,' she said, and nodded good afternoon to the girl, who looked up, straightening and returning the gaze of the woman on the horse.

Lucy flicked her rein gently at her horse's neck and walked up to the house, into the gathering night.

**9**

# The Town – March 1844

The office of the headmaster of the Caledonian School guarded a short corridor which also provided access to four pristine classrooms. On this morning, little sound emerged from the one room which was in use, though a cough or scrape of chair from time to time would resonate down the hallway and out the double doors of the entrance portal to vanish into the thin warm air outside. There was the low drone of a teaching voice; the scrape of chalk on blackboard.

Lucy Bray sat erect, with her knees close together, at a wooden pew outside the headmaster's room, and opposite another door bearing a gold-lettered sign – 'Office.' She had knocked on this door and received no reply but for the echoing of her own knuckles; so hollow was the sound that it proclaimed the absence of even furniture within. So she waited, with perfect patience, her eyes focusing on a speck on the white-washed wall opposite her, balancing on her knee the bag of hard black leather which she often carried with her about the town. Almost square in shape, with a handle that flopped it open at the top, it was a curio – practical and unusual.

She had come that morning because she finally felt ready to do so; to talk with this man who many had thought a little queer, with his abrupt, pithy speech and his rare enthusiasms. But he was a man who also possessed the quality of persistence, a commodity of the first importance to colonists whose crops would sometimes fail and who had to think and adapt – above all, to persist – who had had to share rooms and tents with Germans, Irish and Chinamen.

243

Of course, Lucy had been the subject of talk, but who in the colony had not been the subject of talk at some time? After a setback, it was what you did next that mattered. All of South Australia knew the circumstances of her visit to the north and what had waited for her there. Word had even gone to the Germans at Klemzig. Some did not care for her choice of beau, but every person respected her solo ride and her need to know. The more adventurous type of society dames even gazed upon Lucy with a kind of longing, as if their own youth had passed by without such a galvanising event, and that they were all the lesser for that. People she knew little now raised their hats to her in the street, or winked and nodded in one motion; and she knew they knew, this girl had ridden as far as the Lingalee without escort, and had returned the same way too, by herself, had stopped along the way and drank a pint of bitter at the Cornishman to the amusement of the mining lads who gathered there. She was thirsty from her trip was the way she had explained it.

Presently, she heard a door open at the end of the corridor and an almost orderly procession of lads made for the double door portal, then yelling and laughter from outside as the lunch time games began. Soon came the ringing sound of sensible hard-heeled boots. She kept her head erect and her face stayed in profile to the man who approached until he was just a few steps away, then she stood and turned to him and smiled in greeting.

Cawthorne's step quickened as he recognised his visitor and he grasped her proffered hand in a shake that was mild but warm. 'The famous Miss Lucy,' he said, with as much of a grin as he would ever muster.

She inclined her head and softly closed her eyes for two seconds in acknowledgement of the compliment. 'The very singular Mr Cawthorne,' she replied.

He opened his office door and bowed her inside. It was an austere room, but she expected nothing else. There was no rug or carpet upon the boards; the place smelled faintly of varnish and there was an even more distant antiseptic tang in the air. The walls were washed all white and there were two plain windows giving out upon a field where boys were beginning to assemble in teams. There were two new wooden chairs, polished, no padding or cushion, and Lucy took one of them. The only worn item in the room was a huge-armed mahogany chair that waited behind the headmaster's desk, its notches and cuts dark with age. It gave the room a gravitas, an anomalous witness to the Spartan undertaking that was the Caledonian School. Behind this desk Cawthorne seated himself with conscious, dignified satisfaction.

'It is good to see you, Mr Cawthorne. One does not see enough of you in society.'

Cawthorne inclined his head in appreciation of this remark. 'My life has always been one of work and study, Miss Bray. And now,' he motioned around him, 'no less.'

'I trust your new position is to your satisfaction, sir.'

Cawthorne nodded. 'I was fortunate to be considered on the passing of poor Edmonds. It is a joy to teach Latin, the classics, as opposed to the rudiments of sentence structure and of arithmetical calculation as was my lot at my own little venture.'

'It must ease the burden on your good mother.'

'My mother runs the old school still. She attends to the lower orders as well as she can.'

'I have come to bring you something,' Lucy went on. 'An item that I believe Matthew kept with him at all times. It has puzzled me these few weeks, but I expect it may be less mysterious to you.'

She extracted from her bag a swatch of shirt material she had taken from Matthew's bedside chair and unwound it to reveal the glass harpoon. She held it out to Cawthorne and he pushed back the chair and came around to take it from her.

He took a step toward the window and held it to the light. 'I remember. He was so terribly taken with it: the white man's glass and the native harpoon barbs – the marriage of artistries.'

'You were together when he found it.'

'Yes, it was a different time – a long time ago, or so it seems to me now, although it must be less than two years.' He turned towards her and held the harpoon out to her. 'I think it should remain with you. I have some similar pieces, in my collection.'

'Yes, but this one…'

'Yes, it is his. I fear I shall be unable to gaze upon even those ones I have now with the same…how shall I say, the same detachment, as I once did.' He went back to stand by the window, his back to Lucy for a moment. He drew a handkerchief from his pocket and held it to his mouth. 'Matthew was taken by its…savagery. Ironic savagery, I suppose – so beautiful, yet so damaging. It perhaps evoked the streak of harm that lies within us all, self-harm even. Perhaps it should be you who keeps it, Miss Lucy, even if only as a kind of…warning, perhaps.'

'I have no need of warnings, Mr Cawthorne. Six months ago, I might have benefited from such a portent, but then I might not have heeded it. I have seen enough of life in the colony now to know what works and what does not, but I will keep it always.'

They were both silent for a moment as Lucy fumbled with the clasp of her bag.

'I am attracted by calculated risks, Mr Cawthorne,' she went on, 'but I am not overtaken by excitements as dear Matthew was.'

Cawthorne turned to Lucy again, interested in the statement of self that she had made. 'Calculated risks.' He paused for thought. 'The colonies are made for calculated risks, Miss Lucy.'

'But not so much for the other.'

'Some may take risks, Miss Lucy, and some,' he glanced around the room and its schoolmasterly trappings, 'some may not. The life of the frontier has called to me, more than you might think. Perhaps there is some vestige in me of what my father felt for the sea, but which I have buried deep. The wilderness calls, but I may not follow its clarion.'

There was a silence in the room as Cawthorne contemplated his fate, and as Lucy saw into the life he had been given: his ever-present mother, his absent father, the call of the wild, burdensome reality.

'Matthew…' he faltered. 'Matthew…' Cawthorne was unable to put words to his thoughts.

'You may speak plainly, Mr Cawthorne. God knows there is not one person in this colony I can talk with besides Mary, and now you also, if you will allow it.'

'There has been some talk.'

'About Grace.'

'Yes,' Cawthorne turned to face her, 'about Grace.'

'The rumours are true, Mr Cawthorne. I saw. It was perfectly clear.'

'You believe the father to be Matthew?'

'Judging from the crestfallen bearing of the girl during the time I was there, I have no doubt of it. We buried Matthew. She stood on the outside of the circle with two of her relatives. The talk was all around that the natives had got a gun and had shot him.'

'You think not?'

'It was the cleanest wound, through the centre of the chest, fired from close range. It was no native potshot, and who would give them guns? When the last spades of earth had fallen on the grave, we turned round and the native girls were gone – vanished. I sought her out at their hut later that day, but their disappearance was complete, and per-manent, I have no doubt.'

Lucy stopped for a moment, the both of them staring at the floor, thinking of the implications of a Larkin born in the bush, of further affrays and shooting parties.

'The girl is no fool,' said Cawthorne.

'They were all relieved to find them gone. I could see it in their faces – every one of them. They'd been saved a hard decision. I felt only heavy in my heart: not for Matthew, not for me, but for her, Grace. I am changed, Mr Cawthorne. Some weeks have passed now and I feel it still, the gravity of life. And one's insignificance in it too, I expect. I see her often in my mind, that girl, Grace.'

They both sat quietly for a few moments. The cries of lads and games were in the distance. Somewhere behind Lucy, a clock ticked.

'I am to marry, Miss Lucy.'

'What excellent news, Mr Cawthorne.'

'Yes, she is a good and quiet girl. The day is fixed – quite soon. She will love my mother, and will read poetry to her, as Matthew did.'

'Yes, the poetry,' said Lucy, her eyes for a moment filling with tears. 'Always the poesy.' Lucy took a handkerchief from her black bag and dabbed at her eyes.

Cawthorne did not move to assist her; the girl did not need his help to compose herself, he could see that. 'But what of you, Miss Lucy? What lies before you in the colony?'

'My uncle lies sick, a fever. I must nurse him to health. I must return there now. He was out to Inman Valley last week, where the weather can turn very cold and very wet. They lost their way and spent a night in the open, huddled beneath a tree.'

'The perils of the wild. But what then? The governor will be well in a week.'

'The question is unanswered. My uncle's tenure will not last the year. He may return to England, or to sea. Talk persists that he may go on to Wellington, to be the governor of New Zealand.'

'New Zealand is not the place for you?'

'Nor the sea,' she joked, and Cawthorne smiled and nodded in appreciation of it.

The story of the bravery of this girl had made him reassess, not just her, but many things. 'You could surely marry.'

'I received three callers in the first month of my return.'

'Good God. Do they have no shame?'

'I think not.'

'Mr Stewart?'

Lucy looked down at her bag with a frown, as if this question had been more difficult. 'I think not,' she said quietly, without looking up.

Cawthorne dwelt no further on the subject of marriage. 'Surely there are many things a girl of your accomplishments can do in a young colony thirsty for knowledge and for refinement.'

'Ha,' she exclaimed, with a trace of bitterness, 'I can speak French and play the piano.'

'Yes, and write in the most splendid manner. And learn. A teacher needs above all things to be a learner. The colony needs your abilities.' He saw her hesitate as she thought of it.

'Spinster Bray's School for Girls of Gentility.' Lucy had not lost all of her mordant irony.

'Ha,' Cawthorne threw his head back and laughed; this girl would never be anything but a tonic. 'I can employ you here, at the Caledonian School.'

'Here! But there are only boys.'

'The boys will dissolve beneath your gaze. I guarantee they will be in your thrall.'

'You would employ me, Mr Cawthorne?'

'I shall scan the statutes. But there is no law against it, that is my further guarantee.'

'Probably no one thought to write one.'

Lucy stood, overcome. She had until that morning felt that Cawthorne was distant to her, somehow disapproving. But she had learnt too that Cawthorne's distance had been his defence against the world: to avoid repudiation, do not invite yourself in. She tucked her black bag under her arm, flustered for a moment. 'Good day, Mr Cawthorne.'

Lucy extended her hand and Cawthorne shook it again, firmly and formally, as if in his mind at least some deal had been done.

'I shall return to my uncle now, and I will consider your proposal very carefully. In fact, I think I find the idea a little thrilling.' She let out a forced little gasping laugh, meant to cover over the sudden thickness in her throat.

'There is no rush, Miss Lucy. This term has six weeks more to run but we could begin presently. There are new enrolments every week. We shall split the A class. I will take them in Plato and mathematics, and you will teach them French and English composition.'

'Thank you, Mr Cawthorne,' she said, turning to him as she stepped into the corridor. 'Thank you.'

'Would that you had been born a man, Miss Lucy. What a fearful colonist you would have made.'

'Ha,' Lucy threw her head back and laughed; the first time she had in weeks, perhaps in two months, since Mr Colqhoun had offered his services as guide and escort, free of charge. 'Fortunate that I am born a woman, Mr Cawthorne, and need not be. I have seen enough.'

'Then come and see me on Monday next, here, at ten o'clock? We shall have an idea of enrolments then and can make some plans.'

'Thank you, headmaster, I do believe I shall.'

'Ha!' It was Cawthorne's turn to exclaim in his characteristic manner, but the coil of bitterness that had attended his exclamations in the old days had all but drained away. Now he was exultant.

He closed the door and leant with his back against it, listening to Lucy's quick step on the boards, echoing down the new passage. He drew his pipe from the top drawer of his desk; he stuffed it with tobacco and struck a match. As the flame glowed within the briar, William Cawthorne turned back to the window of the headmaster's study, watching his boys at play.

# Acknowledgements

The story of this novel goes back more than ten years to the time I read and reviewed the wonderful book *Ochre and Rust* by Philip Jones of the South Australian Museum. The stories of artefacts from frontier contact and first-hand reports of affrays between Aboriginal groups which were collected in that volume, not to mention the account of interactions between William Anderson Cawthorne and George French Angas, inspired me to take up the pen. In fact, for three weeks after reading it, all I could think was 'Someone should write a novel about this stuff' before the penny dropped that the someone could easily be me.

Entwined with the stories of Cawthorne and Angas is that of Kadlitpinna, the famous Kaurna chief, whose portrait stands in the Aboriginal Cultures Gallery of the South Australian Museum. Angas's portrait of the great man drove me on with further determination to complete this work. All other characters are my own invention.

I wrote five drafts of this novel between 2012 and 2015 while I was working at a teaching job. Then came a hiatus of four years in which time I completed a doctorate in creative writing and wrote the novel *Places You Never Dreamed Of*. When I returned to *The Glass Harpoon* in 2018, I changed the time frame structure and wrote the whole novel again, toning down the early Victorian language just a little. I am greatly indebted to Pip Lewin for reading drafts throughout this period of gestation and for commenting on characterisation, plot and pacing. Denise Keenan read two later drafts and made suggestions, pointing out among other things that I absolutely had to have a wedding scene. Mark Badger also read an early draft and provided insights on plot and character. I am so grateful for the support of all these people.

I would also like to pay tribute to three important volumes which support assertions I have made throughout this novel about aboriginal land clearing practices. Rupert Gerritsen's *Australia and the Origins of Agriculture*, *The Biggest Estate on Earth: How Aborigines Made Australia* by Bill Gammage, and Bruce Pascoe's *Dark Emu* have all helped to increase the sense of normativity about the idea that Aboriginal people in Australia deliberately burnt forest areas in order to create grasslands as an aid to hunting. If my own novel contributes in any way to community acceptance of this idea, I will be very happy.

## Uncle Lewis Yerloburka O'Brien AO

This novel has been written with the consent and active cooperation of Uncle Lewis Yerloburka O'Brien AO, elder of the Kaurna Aboriginal people and Adjunct Research Fellow at the David Unaipon College, University of South Australia. Uncle Lewis has been enthusiastic in his support for this novel and has personally enlightened me on the following specific matters, which have been included in the story:
– the very high number of conjugations in the Kaurna language
– the way Kaurna women were educated with the men
– the term Kumangka: women walk with men in all things
– that Kaurna hosted conferences of visiting groups from all over Southern Australia
– the agitation that existed between Kaurna people and those from the Murray River
– the use of smoke signals for communication.

Lewis has also confirmed for me the existence of strong oral history supporting the idea that systematic shootings of Kaurna people occurred in northern regions of South Australia in the 1840s and 1850s.

My great thanks go to Uncle Lewis for his support and to former Labor Member of the South Australian House of Assembly, the Hon. Stephanie Key, for bringing Lewis and me together in this undertaking. This novel simply would not have been possible without them.